This book is dedicated to Bronte, Frainey and Darcey Spurge.

I've been very lucky to have three wonderful great-nieces!

MIRIAM

The Cousins of Pemberley: Book 3

LINDA O'BYRNE

First published in 2022 by SpellBound Books

ALSO BY LINDA O'BYRNE

The Cousins Of Pemberley series in order:

Cassandra

Catherine

THE COUSINS OF PEMBERLEY

Pemberley:

Above Stairs:
Elizabeth and Fitzwilliam Darcy: children, Anne, Jane, Bennetta, Fitzwilliam and Henry.

Visitors:
Edmund Avery - artist, Fletcher - valet

Below Stairs:
Miss Reynolds - housekeeper, Mr Charlton - tutor, Grace Frost - lady's maid, James - footman, Archie - head groom, Sally Finch - maid, Tabitha - maid.

Clifton Park:
Jane and Charles Bingley: children, Beth, George, Sophia and Alethea.
A frequent visitor: Mrs Caroline Tremaine, Mr Bingley's sister.

Wyvern Lodge:
Dr Richard Courtney and Cassandra - daughter of Lydia Allerton, née Bennet.
Susannah Courtney, Richard's sister.

Courtney Castle, Northumberland:
Sir Robert Courtney and Catherine - daughter of Mr Collins and the former Charlotte Lucas. Also Matilda, Sir Robert's daughter by his first marriage.

Cape Town, South Africa:
Mary Malliot, née Bennet and her daughter Miriam.

Longbourn, Hertfordshire:
Mrs Bennet, Mr Collins, his wife, the former Kitty Bennet and their daughter, Harriet.

Deerwood Park, Dorset
Colonel Fitzwilliam - Mr Darcy's cousin.

CHAPTER 1

AFRICA, 1833-34

It is a truth universally acknowledged, that a young lady who has grown up knowing she is the plain, unloved misfit of her family, will not be a happy woman when she is older. Mary Malliot, once Mary Bennet, should have been such a woman.

The third daughter of five, she had been lonely all her childhood. Jane and Elizabeth, her older sisters, were already firm friends by the time she was born and did not want her to join in their games or gossip with her at night from their beds. And when Kitty and Lydia had arrived, they too became a partnership of silliness and mad-cap behaviour that she couldn't, and wouldn't join.

And so Mary had turned to her serious books, her music and the bitterness in her heart when even her beloved father laughed at her. She had adored her papa, but knew she wasn't beautiful like Jane, or witty like Elizabeth. All his love was given to his favourites and she was not wise enough to realise that the flaw in his character that led to his dismissive behaviour where she was concerned, was not her fault.

Perhaps it had been no surprise that she had married an older man, who gave her the attention she craved. She had met the missionary, The Reverend Matthias Malliot, on one of her rare visits to Pemberley, to admire Elizabeth's newly born twin daughters.

The Reverend Malliot, a tall, thin gentleman well into his fifties, had looked beneath her plain, awkward surface and to the astonishment of her whole family, most of all her mother, had seen - well, whatever he had seen, he had married Mary very quickly and within months they were out in Africa, preaching to the native population. Their family had increased by one baby they had called Miriam, born early during a storm on the outward bound vessel.

In Africa, Mary had found a life she enjoyed, where she was valued and important to her husband, who was a very vague gentleman who often forgot to eat unless she reminded him.

She had lost touch a little with her family in England - letters took months to travel between continents and sometimes failed to arrive when ships foundered in a storm or became wrecked. Jane did, however, write regularly, Elizabeth less so, Mrs Bennet occasionally, Kitty and Lydia only on her birthday.

The one exception was when Kitty wrote a long letter in glowing terms to say she was finally getting married, to William Collins, their distant cousin who had recently been widowed. And then, when the sad news reached Africa of Mr Bennet's passing, amongst Kitty's grief was the hardly disguised triumph that the Collins family had moved from Kent to Hertfordshire and she was now mistress of Longbourn, her childhood home.

Mary had, of course, sent news of Miriam's birth and had been pleased to receive a large parcel of presents for the child, none of which were actually suitable for the climate and their humble lifestyle. For several years the Malliots lived and preached at the Reverend's mission station where they were indulged and cheerfully ignored by the local population, except for the children, who were curious about Miriam's bright red hair.

By the age of ten, the soles of her feet were just as hard as theirs as they ran and played together and the little girls of the local community taught her how to cook over an open fire, weave a basket and sing their strange, plaintiff chants. With masculine disdain, the little boys showed her how to throw a spear. None of which activities were known to her parents who were unaware that she regularly gave her nurse the slip to explore on her own.

Miriam flourished; stubborn, hot-tempered, and having inherited several of her father's characteristics, she was always on the side of the downtrodden; any child she thought was ill-treated or bullied. Then, when Miriam was eleven, Mary had suddenly realised that her little girl was little no longer and turning into a young lady.

With great regret, the Malliots had said goodbye to their mission and returned to Cape Town where the Reverend was granted a living in a small run-down church and Mary spent her time playing the ancient harmonium for his services and administering charity to people in need.

The dilapidated little house that went with the church was hot and dusty and Mary battled continually with the insects that infested the rooms and a roof that leaked whenever rain fell. She could never quite overcome her dislike of the smells from the street outside, however, and the constant noise from the people in this overcrowded part of town.

Miriam hated Cape Town, she missed the wide open spaces, the freedom of her life before. Because there was no money for a governess, she was sent to a school run by two elderly ladies who had both been widowed by one of the fevers that struck that part of Africa at regular intervals.

They taught sewing, geography and the history of England to young ladies - it was accepted that as long as you understood how many shillings were in a guinea, arithmetic and other mathematical subjects could safely be left to boys.

Miriam attended some classes but regularly spent the hours when she should have been studying, roaming the town. She was a familiar sight wandering around the harbour, watching the boats unload, gazing out at the horizon, wondering what lay beyond. She knew the school's owners would never report her to her mother; they needed the fees she paid them too much.

She had not the slightest interest in sewing or embroidery and her piano playing was of the very basic kind. Often Mary wished there was some nice, quiet hobby she could discover that would interest her daughter, other than rescuing lost puppies and bringing home abandoned kittens and once even a baby piglet she had found wandering the streets! Mary had to admit that Miriam had inherited her father's desire to help every lame dog she came across which was all very commendable but it made for a difficult home life.

Then the Reverend's fortunes changed, and although the Malliots' style of living didn't alter, enough money had somehow become available for him to open up his own small school for the poorest children in the neighbourhood. Miriam had been told all her life that she was there to serve the deserving poor. By the time she reached thirteen and realised that their family was living just above poverty level, she wondered why they weren't the deserving poor, too!

But the Reverend Malliot gave away every penny he had to whomever asked. Together with his wife, they taught the lessons of the Scriptures, the basics of reading and writing, their pupils learnt to recite the kings and queens of Great Britain and the books of the Old and New Testaments in chronological order. A new harmonium was purchased and Mary delighted in playing all the tunes that her family had detested all those years before, secure in the knowledge that there was no one to criticise her.

And so, under the shadow of Table Mountain, Longbourn, Meryton and Pemberley, the soft green of England, faded into the distance, only remembered when letters arrived, folded and salt stained, to tell - happily - of various births and - sadly - of Mr Bennet's death and a small bequest to his granddaughter - and the shocking news that Lydia's daughter, Cassandra, was shamefully illegitimate, although that did not seem to have stopped her marrying some young doctor.

The last letter from her mother, received only days ago, told Mary of another wedding, her distant cousin Catherine Collins to a Sir Robert Courtney. Even at this great distance, Mary could read the irritation in every crossed line that slashed blackly across the paper. None of Mrs Bennet's daughters had a title, even the wealthy Elizabeth remained plain Mrs Darcy.

Mary was pleased to hear about Catherine's great success in the marriage market; she had liked the girl's mother, Charlotte Lucas, when they were growing up as neighbours, and envied her marriage to Mr Collins whom she would have been only too pleased to have married herself - if he had ever looked in her direction.

Charlotte had never been sarcastic or impatient with her when they'd met and, although she had been Elizabeth's special friend, she had always had a kind word for Mary. It was delightful that her daughter had married so well, outdoing the Darcy and Bingley girls in society, if not in wealth.

Now black edged envelopes were on their way to England, informing Mary's relations that the Reverend Malliot had passed away from a fever, leaving his wife with no money. After Mary had sold the school and settled his affairs in Africa, she intended to return to England to devote her time to what good works she could continue to achieve and trusted that between them, her older sisters, who had great fortunes at their disposal, could find her a small house in a pleasant neighbourhood for her use.

Friends of hers were travelling home on the next ship to dock in Cape Town and they had agreed to chaperone Miriam who could spend the time in England making a house comfortable for her mother's arrival.

The African sun glared down outside and Mary dabbed at the perspiration that gathered on her temples and dampened the bodice of her thinnest dress.

"So Miriam, my dear, you will return to England at once. I have booked you a passage on a fast ship, the *Sea Sprite*, so you will be comfortable. Dear Reverend Poole and his good lady have agreed to take care of you on the journey, you will have their daughter, sweet Delphine, for a companion and your Aunt Jane will send someone to meet you when you arrive in England."

"Go to England? What will I do in England? My home is here in Africa." Miriam Malliot, just turned eighteen, tall, slim, with dark brown eyes and a mane of red hair, fiercely braided to protect it from becoming tangled or attracting flying insects, stared at her mother in consternation. "I won't go! And I loathe Delphine Poole. She is the silliest girl ever."

Mary sighed and rubbed her forehead where another headache was forming. She hadn't found motherhood an agreeable state. To be fair Miriam had been very little bother as a child, as long as she got her own way, but the young woman standing before her was a constant thorn in Mary's side.

She could see nothing of herself in Miriam; no liking for quiet contemplation of great thoughts, sensible books or music. The red hair, hot temper and stubborn disposition must have been inherited from somewhere in the past of dear Matthew's family, but the dark eyes and passionate tones could have been those of Elizabeth Darcy and her complete disdain of proper behaviour reminded Mary only too well of her younger sisters.

She admitted to herself now that, absorbed as she had been in all the good works that needed doing in this vast continent, she had left her daughter too much to her own devices and to a succession of nurses who had had no sense of discipline at all.

Miriam had grown up for the first eleven years of her life doing exactly what she wanted, when she wanted. It was a legacy that was hard to eradicate and Mary worried that her headstrong insistence on getting her own way could lead her into trouble. At the back of her mind lurked the dreadful tale of Lydia and George Wickham and their elopement all those years ago.

"There is no life here in Africa for a young, unattached woman. You know that you are already drawing the attention of certain young men whom your dear papa and I would not approve. And as a widow I cannot protect you, especially as you have no mind to keep from behaviour that causes gossip. Why, only yesterday, when you went to the haberdashery to buy black ribbons, you were seen talking to two young Dutch officers from the militia! Your reputation will soon be in tatters if you stay here.

"Now, let's have no more arguments - I have to oversee your dear papa's grave and sort out all his papers and business affairs. The Reverend Ogden is interested in purchasing the school: such a kind, dedicated teacher. I think our little pupils will be in good hands. But I cannot have the worry of caring for you at the same time. It is much more sensible for you to go to England straight away."

Miriam sighed: she knew from the stubborn expression on her mama's face that nothing would change her mind. And it was good news that the Reverend Ogden might purchase the school. She knew her parents had sunk all their capital into the building, although they relied on the charity of others to run it.

Surely the Reverend would be able to repay some of that money to her mother? He had been kindness itself since her papa's passing. She turned her mind to other problems. "But where shall I live?"

"I have written to your Aunt Jane, requesting that you stay with her until I arrive in England. She was always the kindest and most considerate of my sisters and your Uncle Bingley is a very agreeable man. Their oldest daughter, Elizabeth, whom they call Beth, is only a couple of years older than you and I am sure you will get on splendidly. Jane has often written that she is a quiet, good-natured girl."

"So I am not to journey to Longbourn to my grandmother or travel to the great house of Pemberley and stay with the Darcys?"

Mary frowned: she wanted to have her own house and life back in England. She could still recall the way she had been treated when she was growing up, the feeling of being disliked, overlooked, laughed at. She had a feeling that if they once moved in with her mama and Kitty, they would be there forever. Kitty, whose letter boasting that she was now stepmother to a Lady Courtney, would play the queen of the house and Mary feared she would end up having to obey her orders, perhaps taking care of her small daughter.

"I believe we will be better suited going to the Bingleys when we first arrive. And their home is only twenty or so miles from Pemberley. I do not care for Mr Darcy - a proud man with an arrogant manner - I always felt he held me in contempt because of my views on literature and music which were different from his own. And Lizzie was never the kindest of sisters as I have often told you.

"Well, well, I'm sure his wealth has helped her cope with him. And with all the great estates that both Bingley and Darcy own, they must have some small house that would suit us. Perhaps in a village close by to a church. I am quite used to hardship. I do not require luxury but you can spend your time making it as comfortable as possible. I am sure my sisters will help with furniture and fittings."

Miriam was annoyed and bewildered. She could not remember a time when her mother had not spoken of the harsh treatment she had received from her sisters, how her father's love had been turned into scorn and sarcasm by the other four girls.

"But Mama, you have always said how much you disliked our relations in England. How can you bear to send me to them and ask for their help? I loathe the Darcys for how they treated you. What sort of people can they be? They must be without compassion for their fellow beings. Papa loved Africa, he wouldn't want me to leave. He wanted me to take care of you. And the thought of being shut up in a ship with Delphine Poole is unbearable. She is such a silly, insipid girl."

Mary sighed: she felt a little uncomfortable, wondering now if she hadn't rather paid her family a disservice. She had only spoken the truth as she saw it, but then she'd never thought Miriam would ever meet the Darcys and Bingleys, except through letters.

"Nonsense, Delphine is a delightful young lady. She is only just sixteen, admittedly, but the Pooles have brought her out into the world early and so she will be amiable company. And forget about me - your father wanted what was best for you. As for the Darcys, they are my family and yours and hopefully time has softened their behaviour. I have learnt to turn the other cheek and you must do the same.

"Unfortunately, there are no connections on the Malliot side that I can call on. My family owe you their support until I can settle our affairs. Obviously you will find their ways obnoxious - you have been brought up to a life of service and denial, but there is no need for you to engage in any activities you know will offend me or your papa's memory. Don't forget you will have your grandfather's bequest to draw on now you have turned eighteen. That will be of a great help to us. Now, run along and finish addressing those thank you letters for the condolences we have received."

Miriam hesitated, longing to say more, feeling all her pent-up grief at the loss of her father swelling up inside her. But she was reluctant to upset her mother, whose grey hair and a face aged before her time by the relentless sun aroused all of Miriam's protective qualities.

How she missed her papa! He had been such a kind man, sometimes peering at her over the tops of his spectacles as if he was certain they had met but wasn't exactly sure who she was! Saying goodbye to him had been the hardest thing she had ever had to do in her life. He had clung to her hand, his face as white as the pillow he lay on and begged her to take care of her mama.

"You are such a strong young lady, Miriam," he had whispered. "You face every problem with courage and fortitude. Mary will need your strength. Promise me you will always be there to take care of her." And she had promised.

She accepted that Grandfather Bennet's bequest was going to be useful. Thank goodness she was now eighteen. She smiled a little as she remembered the odd wording that papa had read out to her.... "a sum so that none of my granddaughters need to marry the first fool who asks them."

Miriam wished she had had the opportunity to meet him: she was sure she would have liked him. Her mama had loved him dearly and cried for days when news of his demise reached Africa. Miriam had been unable to ease her grief and had listened, once again, as her mother had declared that her sisters, especially Elizabeth, had stolen all of Mr Bennet's affections.

And now she was to meet that very Elizabeth, to leave Africa - on one hand she hated the thought but then to travel by ship, to cross the oceans! She had always longed to do that and had often lingered on her way back from shopping or her weekly French language lesson to gaze at the ships in the harbour and dream that one day she would be carried away across the waves. She knew she had been born onboard a great sailing vessel and felt sure that was the reason for her desire to travel and explore.

Once she had reached the age of sixteen, she had realised that she should no longer wander around the harbour as she had done when she was eleven, even though she always felt perfectly safe. Her ability to talk to the local people in their own language and the fact that she was the daughter of their much admired Reverend, endeared her to them.

She wondered what her English relations were really like. Her mother had never said a great deal about Grandmama Bennet, just that she enjoyed ill health and often took to her bed for days at a time. Aunt Jane sounded kind; she always sent good wishes on her birthday but her daughter might not be as pleasant as people thought. And as for the Darcys!

Miriam felt a renewed surge of resentment and dislike against her Aunt Elizabeth. From what her mother had said over the years, she had been the sister whose sharp words had hurt the most, who had taken all of their father's attention, leaving none for Mary.

Well, she would have to meet her, no doubt, but Miriam decided she would take care not to listen to her aunt or let her have any say in her future. In fact she was quite determined that no one would ever tell her what to do again now that papa had gone.

There were two other aunts as well: Kitty, who had written the first letter to her sister in a year, only to boast that her step-daughter was now Lady Courtney! And Lydia whom her parents had only spoken about in hushed tones. Miriam was curious about Aunt Lydia and determined to find out all she could when she got to England.

And cousins! For the first time Miriam sat considering all the cousins she had never met. She pictured them all as tall and fair-haired with blue eyes, picking flowers in huge gardens, drinking tea in elegant rooms, their hands white as alabaster. She stared down at her own, square and tanned, scratched from where she had been trying to mend a broken window shutter.

Would they laugh at her? At her speech, her manner of dress? It would surely be very different from theirs; she was well aware from perusing the fashion magazines that sometimes appeared in the shops that her clothing was old-fashioned.

Let them laugh: she wouldn't care. She decided she would hate them all. When she had lived at the mission, she had experienced being close to wild animals. She had learnt to be wary of their devious behaviour. For some reason she had the feeling that her cousins might need to be treated in such a way.

Their life would be so strange; here in Africa she walked by herself to the store or even down to the harbour. As the daughter of the much loved Reverend, she was completely safe in even the most insalubrious of districts. But Miriam had the strongest feeling that her life as an eighteen year old girl in England would be vastly different.

Tossing back her long red plait, she set to work addressing the envelopes as requested, sighing as she dropped a large blot of ink on the desk top. Obviously there were no condolence letters from England, news of her father's passing wouldn't even have reached them yet.

She felt tears burn her eyes but resolutely continued to work. She had loved her papa, admired his studious nature, his dedication to the poor and was determined to keep the vow she had made him on his death bed. If a part of her wished that he had thought as much about his own family's future as he did others, then she pushed that aside. She was going to England; she had her grandfather Bennet's bequest in her name to draw on, she was young, strong and determined. Life was sad now but the future looked exciting.

CHAPTER 2

The three-masted sailing ship, *Sea Sprite,* laden with silk, tea and spices, was heading for the English Channel, running before the wind. The voyage up the west coast of Africa from Cape Town had been fast and even the gale they had encountered in the Bay of Biscay had not prevented them from making very good time.

Now they were sailing towards the English Channel and it was growing dark. The skies were full of rain clouds and the temperature had dropped violently as they left the tropics behind and headed for the colder northern waters.

There were only a few passengers on board - traders from Hong Kong coming home with their wives and fortunes, travelling first class, eager to buy land and settle back in England, several government officials who kept their thoughts and ideas to themselves and a clerical gentleman and his family who had boarded at Cape Town, whose cabins were the cheapest, two decks below the fresh air with no portholes.

Tall and thin, with a face burnt brown by the African sun, the Reverend Poole had brought on board his wife, his sixteen year old daughter and another young girl whom most people took to be another daughter, until she was introduced as a Miss Miriam Malliot who was travelling under their protection until they reached England.

Miriam appreciated that it was kind of them to take care of her but she was desperate to be free of their kindly attentions. Mrs Poole was a short, stout woman whose abiding passions in life were her husband's career in the church - she was determined that one day he would become a bishop - and finding a wealthy husband for her daughter.

She knew it was her Christian duty to guard Miriam on this journey until she could hand her over to her relations, but she found the girl difficult and uncooperative. She had hoped that Miriam would be company for Delphine, but whenever she wanted her, she was missing - out on the deck or wandering all over the vessel, asking questions, getting in the sailors' way as they went about their duties.

Miriam found Mrs Poole's guardianship just as irksome; she couldn't remember a time in her life when she had had to obey so many rules and regulations. Her parents, absorbed with their missionary work, had paid her little attention whilst she was a child. Those bright days of freedom had lessened slightly when she attended the school for young ladies where she was not allowed to run but only walk, and singing was confined to hymns and psalms. She had been punished when she had been heard singing one of the African songs her little friends had taught her.

She had found her patience sorely tried by Delphine, who was small and pretty with big blue eyes and fair curls. She had a trick of looking up at gentlemen through her lashes and her lips would tremble as if she wanted to give some compliment, but never did.

Miriam had tried to encourage her to accompany her on deck, explaining that the fresh air would do wonders for the vapours caused by the motion of the ship, but Delphine just squealed when the vessel rolled and felt faint. To her disgust, Miriam had also come to realise that the other girl was always inclined to be indisposed when one of the officers was nearby, relying on him to support her languishing form, to help carry her below, or bring her a sustaining drink.

But now, with the weather worsening, Delphine refused to leave their cabin and so Miriam stood alone, as far for'ard as she could get on deck, glorying in the rise and fall of the vessel, the wind tearing her long red hair into a flying battle flag, the pins and bonnet long gone overboard in the wind.

"Miss Malliot! - what are you doing on deck? Would you please be so kind as to go below. We are running into bad weather. I have asked you before - several times."

Miriam glanced round. It was the First Officer Nicholas Sullivan; tall, bronzed by the weather, broad shouldered, his fair hair clubbed back in a short plait that was thicker than hers. His bright grey eyes always seemed to have a disapproving expression when he was talking to her.

Ever since she had come on board, he had found occasion to chide her about her behaviour. He did not approve of her talking to the crew, or wandering around the decks, or refusing to take shelter when they hit a squall.

Once she had taken several steps up the rigging to get a better view of a family of dolphins keeping the ship company. Mr Sullivan had shouted at her quite loudly to get down immediately, even though she knew she was as sure footed as most of his sailors.

It was quite obvious to Miriam that he wished she would emulate Delphine's behaviour and act with more modesty and decorum. He did not understand, and showed no tendency so to do, that she enjoyed the rough weather, that the wind and spray invigorated her and raised her from the depression of her circumstances.

But, on the other hand, when the weather had been fair, Mr Sullivan had been constantly at her side to point out the shoals of flying fish that surrounded the vessel and when they crossed the equator, he had allowed her to be greeted by one of the sailors, dressed as Neptune, in an uproarious ceremony for those who had not crossed the equator before. The Pooles had retired to their cabins; they did not care for such rough events, which the Reverend also thought were surely un-Christian, probably Pagan.

There was, however, something about the First Officer that irritated Miriam, although she would have been surprised to discover that she irritated him in return. The stubborn streak they both had running through their characters resulted, inevitably, in a clash of wills.

"I am quite safe, Sir. I believe I have told you that I was born on board such a vessel as this. I think I have the sea in my blood. Look, I have a good hold of this rope and I wish to remain on deck so as to see the first glimpse of the light from The Lizard lighthouse. One of the sailors told me that you can see its beam miles away at night."

"That is not a rope, it is called a stay, Miss Malliot," he replied shortly and shot out a hand as a sudden stronger gust sent the vessel diving forward into the waves, Miriam's grasp loosened and she was flung towards him. He gently pushed her back onto her feet and she pulled herself away from him, angry with herself at being so feeble.

"You see, the deck of a ship in a rough sea is no place for a woman. The Captain will have me dismissed if I lose you overboard and I don't expect your family would be pleased, either."

"It is good to know that my death in the deeps is not your primary concern, Sir," she replied, her dark brown eyes flashing in her tanned face.

Nicholas Sullivan swore silently to himself. This girl had irritated him since the moment he had first set eyes on her boarding in Cape Town. Before the Captain had retired to his great cabin with several bottles of rum, he had told him to keep her under control as she refused to obey the rules.

Miss Poole, her travelling companion, was a comely, well-behaved girl, delicate and feminine, just the way he thought all members of the fair sex should be. She wore pretty bonnets and gloves and her skin was as pale as any English girl, even though she had lived for years in Africa.

But this girl, with her wild red hair and tanned face, behaved like no other young lady he had ever known and sometimes he was hard pressed to remember she was a passenger and that he had to act towards her accordingly. There had been times when they had conversed on deck however when he'd realised how much he was enjoying her company.

A wave crashed across the prow and he wiped the spray from his eyes. "I apologize, Miss Malliot, if my manners are too sailor-like and abrupt, but I am truly concerned for your well-being. And I am sure you would not like me to lose my job."

Miriam fought against her inclination to continue the argument, but night had fallen, the seas were growing rougher and rougher and she could tell that First Officer Sullivan was becoming genuinely anxious, not just trying to exert his authority. With a nod of her head, she took the arm he was offering and let him escort her down to her cabin.

He hesitated as the foul smell of ill people rushed to meet them and he saw the girl grow paler than she had been on deck. "Miss Malliot, if you promise to stay in your cabin, as soon as we sight the beam from the lighthouse, if it is not too rough, I will have you sent for and accompanied onto deck." He bowed to her at the door and left, wondering why he was bothering to help this irritating girl.

Miriam sat on the narrow bunk, listening to Mrs Poole and Delphine groan from across the tiny cabin. They had been sick almost constantly since they reached the Bay of Biscay and in the dark, enclosed space, the smell was unbearable.

She was just about to forget her promise to Mr Sullivan and find sanctuary outside, when a sailor knocked at the door and, with a grin, helped her to climb the companionway up and up to the top deck where the freezing fresh air filled her lungs like nectar.

It was fully night now, but there was a sprinkling of stars, different from the ones she was used to seeing at home. There was a low crescent moon which did not shine enough light to help her see clearly, but the wind was still blowing hard and she was glad that she had rebraided her hair so that not a wisp escaped .

As she reached the top of the companionway, a hand closed around her elbow, she felt herself almost lifted up the last step and Mr Sullivan was there, dismissing the sailor and reaching out to steady her as the ship plunged and reared in the swelling waves.

"The motion does not bother you, Miss Malliot?"

"No, Sir, not at all. I find it invigorating. Thank you for giving me permission to come on deck. It is all so wild and exciting. It must be a wonderful life, to sail the seas for days on end."

Mr Sullivan frowned, wondering what she would say if he told her that with a Captain who liked his drink too much, trying to guide this heavily laden vessel through wild seas was not an easy task. "I fear you are somewhat of a romantic, Miss Malliot. The life of a sailor is very hard and always full of danger."

"But think of all the wonderful things you see! The exotic places you visit."

"Harbours are very similar all over the world. There is no time for the exotic when you are trying to get a cargo stowed on board in the middle of a storm!"

Miriam bit her lip and turned to face the darkness of the sea. She had never considered herself a romantic, as someone who did not see the world as it truly was but only a storybook version. Of course she realised that a sailor's life was difficult and dangerous; even now she could see several high up in the rigging, attending to the sails, their shouts to each other heard above the wind. She'd only meant that even if it was dangerous, there was still the opportunity to see things that shore-bound people never would.

Nicholas Sullivan cursed under his breath. He hadn't meant to sound so critical. Indeed, he privately admitted to himself that he often came on deck early, just to watch the sun rise because it was such a beautiful sight.

He loved this life and was waiting, impatiently, for the day, hopefully not too long in the future, when he would be master of this ship. It was what he had dreamed of his whole life. He had gone to sea when just a boy and worked his way up to First Officer. The next step was nearly within his reach and he would be free to make his own rules and regulations, one of which, he suddenly decided would be not to carry women passengers at all!

Suddenly a flash of light, no more than a pinprick pierced the blackness and from the crow's nest, high above their heads, came the joyful shout that heralded the first sight of land ahead.

"The Lizard lighthouse, Miss Malliot," Nicholas said, pointing through the rigging.

Miriam gasped. They had sailed such a long way and it seemed miraculous to her that they could have found the entrance to the English Channel and the light that meant their journey would be over in a few days time.

Suddenly, all her questions and worries about her future came flooding back. During these weeks on board, her future had seemed suspended, unimportant. Now she could no longer pretend that a different life did not await her. A strange country, unknown relatives, a way of life that would no doubt seem very alien to her. She shivered; more from apprehension than cold but Nicholas Sullivan frowned down at her.

"I trust you have a thicker cloak than that one for your arrival in England, Miss Malliot. It is winter here in the northern hemisphere. The temperature seems chilly at the moment but it is late January and there will be biting easterly winds and snow, no doubt. Your African attire will certainly not suffice."

"It is not always hot in Cape Town, Sir. I can assure you that I have plenty of suitable clothing in my trunk. Or do you wish to inspect the thickness of my stockings and petticoats? Do you always concern yourself with your passengers' form of dress? It seems a sad waste of time for a First Officer!" She tossed her head, her temper quick to rise at what seemed like unwarranted interference.

Nicholas touched his forehead in a quick salute. "My apologies, madam. I meant no disrespect."

Miriam swayed as a bigger wave caught the *Sea Sprite* and tossed it to one side. She didn't exclaim as Mr Sullivan's hand once again reached out to steady her. She was already regretting her flash of temper, knowing it was a grievous fault of her character, one she had tried hard all her life to overcome. She thought she had it well under control but this sailor seemed to release all that was unruly and hot-headed in her.

"I was at fault, Sir," she said bravely. "I spoke without thinking, a sad flaw in my character. I am certain that your observations were based on concern about my well-being."

There was silence for a few moments as they both watched the distant light flash off and on, leading them onwards to their final destination.

"Are you to make your home with the Poole family, Miss Malliot?" Nicholas asked. He admired Miss Delphine Poole's big blue eyes and wondered how the two girls would get on under the same roof. Miss Malliot seemed to have a temper to go with her red hair and Miss Delphine was all calm serenity and quiet good manners.

"Indeed no! The Pooles are waiting to hear where the Reverend's next living is to be and are staying with relations in Canterbury until it is announced. I am to reside with my Aunt and Uncle Bingley who have a house in London, in Grosvenor Street."

"They will be meeting you at Gravesend when you disembark?"

Miriam nodded. She wasn't sure about her Aunt Jane because her mama had told her that she was still in poor health following the arrival of a daughter late in life.

"My Uncle Bingley will be there, or if he is detained in any way - because he is a gentleman of consequence - he will send a servant with a carriage."

Biting her lip, she wiped the spray from her face with the end of her shawl. She hadn't meant to sound boastful. She had no idea how much money a First Officer made every year, but she didn't think it would be the type of wealth that would lead to houses in Grosvenor Street and comfortable carriages.

"Sir - " she started to explain that she herself had only ridden in a carriage once or twice in Cape Town and that she was not a girl who held possessions and wealth in high regard, but Mr Sullivan had turned away to issue orders to one of the sailors and when he returned to her side, the moment had passed.

"I must request that you go below now you have seen the light from The Lizard," he said, his tone more formal than before. "The men will be working on the sails very soon and it will be all bustle and noise. By first light we should be inside the Channel. My regards to Mrs Poole and Miss Delphine and I trust they will soon recover when we reach calmer waters. It will be good to see them on deck once again."

Miriam dropped a short curtsey. Obviously he would prefer to show the sights to Delphine. She was the milksop type of girl he would like, although she was quite certain that Mrs Poole had visions of a much grander match than Mr Nicholas Sullivan for her only daughter!

CHAPTER 3

When you have three daughters of marriageable age, your thoughts turn regularly to finding suitable young gentlemen for them to meet and hopefully join in wedded bliss. Mrs Elizabeth Darcy of Pemberley in Derbyshire was no exception to the rule.

A few months ago she had hosted the wedding of her distant cousin and god-daughter, Catherine Collins, to Sir Robert Courtney and waved them a fond goodbye as they left for Courtney Castle and the run-down Northumberland estate they both loved so passionately.

Although she had enjoyed arranging the wedding, Elizabeth felt that she would be far happier if it was one of her own daughters who was the centre of all the attention.

Of course she was not as driven in this quest as her own mother had been. No, there was no financial reason for Anne, Jane or Bennetta to marry. They could live at Pemberley in comfort, pursuing their own hobbies and undertaking good works if they chose so to do. No one was going to cast them out.

Elizabeth knew the wording of her husband's will and the three girls were protected, even if their younger brother eventually married a woman who disliked them and wished them gone when Fitzwilliam inherited the estate. And if they did marry they would take with them a substantial settlement to be held in their own name. They would always be very wealthy women.

But, that was one of the reasons why Elizabeth had to be extra vigilant in assessing the worth of any admirers who arrived on the scene. Rich young women were not that common and, although she was fairly sanguine about Anne and Jane's sense, she was quite convinced that Bennetta would cheerfully elope with the young man who brought the fish from the market to Pemberley if he caught her fancy!

To be fair, during breakfast on this bitter late January morning, Elizabeth would have been quite happy if all three eloped with the breadman, butcher or gamekeeper!

The breakfast room at Pemberley was situated on the east of the building, a handsome room with a high, ornate ceiling, restful landscape paintings in fine frames and windows that reached down to the floor, catching the morning sun until well after ten o'clock. During the rest of the year it was a pleasant place to start the day but from November on, Elizabeth would have given much to have taken the early meal in a room on the other side of the house.

Admittedly a fire roared in the grate but the wind was from the east and every time the door opened for another footman bringing hot dishes, or a maid to add logs to the fire, cold air from the passageway blew in and a gust of smoke seeped from the chimney.

The freezing draughts seemed to be making everyone argumentative and tetchy.

Not for the first time, Elizabeth felt a pang of remorse at all the times she had silently mocked her mother for the way she had worried constantly about whether her daughters would marry or not. Mrs Bennet had fallen ill a week after Catherine Collins' marriage and her family had feared for her life.

Elizabeth had chided her husband when he told her that it was due to angst caused by the Lucas' grand-daughter becoming Lady Courtney when none of her own grandchildren had yet to marry into a title. Everyone had feared for Mrs Bennet but, for all her fainting and nervous disposition, she had rallied and was, apparently, now driving to distraction the Collins family whom she lived with at Longbourn.

Elizabeth was honest enough with herself to admit that her mother irritated her. But sometimes, like this morning, she felt a fellow kinship with the poor woman who had had five arguing daughters to contend with. At least she herself only had three. Although to be fair, she had to admit, only two were really difficult.

This was Jane's first morning out of bed for a week: she was just recovering from the bad cold that was running unchecked through the Pemberley household. Sitting quietly at the table, wrapped in a thick woolen shawl, a faraway expression on her face, she sipped her hot chocolate and didn't seem to be listening as Anne and Bennetta argued with their father.

Elizabeth worried constantly about two people - her sister and the girl who bore her name, her daughter Jane. Giving birth to the twins had been so easy, it had therefore been an even greater shock to discover that the second twin was tiny and not expected to live.

She could well remember all the nights when she and Fitzwilliam had sat, watching the small creature wrapped in sheep's wool, praying that she would survive and join her healthy, bouncing sister in the nursery.

And she had lived, but was never strong, always the first to fall ill with childhood complaints and now Elizabeth was beginning to wonder if she had protected her too much as she grew up, always checking that she had dry feet, that she never left the house without a shawl, had the chair closest to the fire, away from any draughts.

"But Papa, there is nothing wrong with having perhaps just one or two waltzes played at a ball." Anne, haughty, blonde and beautiful, tapped the table with her finger to emphasize her point. She had recently been staying in London with Mrs Caroline Tremaine, formerly Bingley, the sister of Mr Darcy's good friend, Charles Bingley.

At thirty-seven, Caroline had married Frederick Tremaine, a very rich, although much older gentleman, whose main hobbies were hunting and fishing. His first wife had died, his children had left home and he wanted a pleasant woman to run his various houses. They had no children of their own and although Caroline professed to love her Bingley nieces and nephews, she had little in common with them. But, for some strange reason, she and Miss Anne Darcy got on very well together.

Elizabeth thought it was probably because they were both single-minded women who set out to get what they wanted from life at all costs. As much as she loved her first born, she had no illusions about what she considered certain defects in her character, ones that she was constantly trying to rectify, without much apparent success.

Caroline had recently invited Anne and Jane down to London to stay and celebrate their birthday and Christmas with dinners, theatre outings, dances and social gatherings.

At first Elizabeth had been pleased with the arrangement, because she wanted Jane to come out from her twin's shadow and the protection of the family circle and shine in society of her own accord.

When the Christmas celebrations were over, she had arranged for her to travel to the county of Dorset to stay with Mr Darcy's cousin and her godfather, Colonel Fitzwilliam, at Deerwood Park, his country home. Jane had professed to have enjoyed her visit, but had returned in time to catch a violent cold.

A frequent visitor to Pemberley, Colonel Fitzwilliam had always been very fond of Jane, watching her over the years growing up in the shadow of her domineering twin sister, then worrying as she was eclipsed by the ebullience of young Bennetta.

Twenty and more years ago, he had fallen in love with Elizabeth Bennet, although he had, he hoped, never given her any cause to know this. He had realised a long time ago that he was not a man who felt passion in the way his cousin, Darcy, did. He had never married and his health, due to a wound he had suffered whilst abroad with his regiment, caused him, as the years passed, to lead the quiet life of a semi-invalid.

Jane had grown to return his affection over the years, looking forward to his visits to Pemberley when they would walk together in the gardens, talking of books and music and art. She loved Deerwood, his rambling old house, built in the reign of the great Queen Elizabeth and so very different from the new houses such as Pemberley and Clifton with their high ceilings and many great windows.

Anne had returned from London, flush with being a success: she had been feted everywhere, her blonde beauty admired and she was now full of plans for the great house. She informed her mother that she was very old-fashioned and afraid of change. Never a day went by when she did not come up with schemes to buy new furniture, new drapes, new everything.

She insisted on moving out of the room she had shared with her twin and having a bedroom and drawing-room of her own on the far side of the house, away from "the children" as she called her sisters and brothers, more in keeping with what she saw as her status as Miss Darcy of Pemberley.

Her latest plan was for a ball to be held to celebrate her and Jane's nineteenth birthday which had fallen the day before Christmas whilst they were away in London.

Anne's enthusiasm infected her younger sister, Bennetta, and although they didn't usually agree, this time they were in perfect accord and came up with more and more outlandish ideas every day. It was one of these - the inclusion of waltz dances in the repertoire - that was causing the row over breakfast this cold morning.

"Papa, it is the very latest fashion, everyone in London is waltzing. You make it sound as if it is immodest, that only people with loose morals would dance facing each other. Yes, the gentleman's hand is touching the lady's waist, but he doesn't hold her particularly closely. It is all quite proper."

Mr Darcy gestured to his empty coffee cup and a footman leant over to refill it. Elizabeth sighed: her husband never had more than one cup with his breakfast. Two cups of such a strong liquid would not make his demeanour any more sanguine.

She also suspected he was about to succumb to the cold that was infecting the household and she had learnt to her cost that this particular gentleman did not react well to coughing and sneezing, especially one who would no doubt refuse to stay in bed and be cossetted.

Indeed he had already informed her, in the privacy of their room that morning, that he never took a cold or a chill and the girls' passion for fires in every room was weakening their constitutions. He refused to let either of the boys have fires in their bedrooms.

"Papa, are you reluctant because you don't know how to waltz yourself? I can teach you; it isn't at all difficult."

Bennetta, turning a concerned gaze in her father's direction, was throwing all caution to the wind and Henry, the youngest of the Darcy children and the most light-hearted, burst into giggles at the thought of his parents dancing face to face.

"Henry, Fitzwilliam, if you have both finished, I believe your tutor is waiting for you upstairs," Elizabeth said swiftly seeing the frown on her husband's face growing deeper. "And don't forget you children are to attend in the studio at eleven. Mr Avery is keen to continue his portrait of you all. He couldn't proceed when Jane was absent."

Her eldest boy looked up from where he was concealing a book on his lap under cover of the table-cloth and gazed round, the dark eyes so like her own showing that he was miles away in his thoughts.

"You are right, Mama. We mustn't keep Mr Charlton waiting. I do believe it is Latin this morning! But I fear it is an enormous waste of time having our portraits painted."

Henry nodded his agreement and pocketed a large piece of cheese in case he fell prey to hunger when sitting in one position for the artist. Elizabeth noticed but didn't comment; she knew she was lax with her youngest but he was such a cheerful, happy boy that it was hard to be as strict as she should be. He was growing like a weed and seemed to need food at every hour of the day.

"You should be grateful an artist such as Mr Avery is prepared to transmit your silly face onto canvas for all our ancestors to look at," Anne snapped.

"Mama, must I sit for my portrait this morning? I do not look my best."

Elizabeth sighed: looking at Jane's red nose and pale complexion, she was forced to agree. "I expect Mr Avery can manage with just Anne, Bennetta and the boys. But do try to attend tomorrow. It is so....."

The arrival of a footman with a salver interrupted her. "A letter delivered by the Bingley footman, Madam."

"Goodness, what can Jane possibly be writing about so early." Anxiously, she reached for the missive. Since the birth of her daughter, Alethea, who had arrived long after the rest of the Bingley family, Jane had not been strong. She had never fully recovered from the difficult birth and led a very quiet life, hardly venturing from home.

Elizabeth slit open the envelope and pulled out a letter and another envelope, frowning at the black edges. It was obvious it was written in Mary's hand so it could only mean one thing.

"Bad news, my dear?" Mr Darcy had also seen the black trimmed envelope.

"Jane writes that she received this missive from Africa yesterday but as Charles is away and she does not feel strong enough herself to cope, she has sent it to me. Mary's husband has died - a fever, she writes. Really, her hand is so bad, I can hardly make it out. And I fear this letter has been badly delayed."

"The Reverend was very old, though, wasn't he?" Bennetta said callously and reddened at the frown her mother sent in her direction.

"He was a very kind man and Mary and Miriam will surely miss him."

"What will they do now he has gone?" Anne asked. "Will they stay out there in the wilds? What an odd life they do lead. And what type of girl must our cousin be? She will have no manners or knowledge of the civilised world. A little savage."

"Cape Town is not exactly the wilds of Africa, it is a thriving port. But if you will let me finish....oh my goodness. Listen, ...*I am sure that between you and Elizabeth and your great estates, you will be able to provide some small house where Miriam and I can live. I find her a difficult girl; she is too headstrong and opinionated and I fear that she has been making some very undesirable acquaintances. I have to stay for a few more weeks here in Cape Town to finalize all Mr Malliot's affairs, but I wish for Miriam to travel to England immediately.*

"I have booked her on the sailing ship Sea Sprite. She will be under the protection of a Reverend Poole and his wife. I am sure dear Bingley will discover when the vessel is due and arrange for her to be met. The first port of call when it reaches England is Gravesend."

"That will be no problem," Mr Darcy said. "Caroline Tremaine has a house in London: I am sure she would be happy to meet the girl and look after her. And if your sister is still not strong enough for visitors, then Miriam can, of course, go to Longbourn or even come here. Although, as you are aware, Lizzie, I have invited my business acquaintance Baxter and his son to stay for a few days. Baxter is wishing to acquire some silk weaving business in the district and I thought they would be far more comfortable here than in lodgings in Lambton."

"Oh, not Gerald Baxter!" Bennetta dug her spoon viciously into a plate of marmalade. "He came last time with his father. He is the most annoying boy I've ever known. He follows one around like a puppy that expects to be kicked at any moment and he has clammy hands and his breath smells."

"Bennetta! Poor Gerald does not have good health. His looks are unimportant, he has a kind nature and excellent manners, which is more than I can say for you, Miss."

Elizabeth knew she was snapping, but the arrival of guests when her house was not running at its usual efficient levels of hospitality annoyed her.

"But, dearest, I fear you are missing the point. Look at the date on this letter! If Miriam took passage a few days after this was sent, then she might already have arrived in England. And if so, then where is she? What has happened to her?"

CHAPTER 4

So much noise, so many people! Miriam felt her head spinning, her heart racing as she was handed out of the small boat that conveyed passengers from the ship onto the stone steps that led up to the dockside at the port of Gravesend.

All around her a forest of masts stretched in each direction, rising and falling on the river that brought the ships up from the Channel, a river that stank, a river where all sorts of refuse floated and gathered in filthy swirls around the dockside.

The tide and wind had turned and the *Sea Sprite* would now wait until it changed again and it could sail further up to the docks where the cargo of silk and tea would be unloaded. But several of the passengers had arranged to disembark at the little town of Gravesend, in the county of Kent, where relations and carriages were waiting for them.

It was bitterly cold and Miriam shuddered as the east wind cut across from the opposite bank of the Thames, carving its way effortlessly through the cloak she was wearing. Although her mother had told her to expect cold weather when she reached England, she had never guessed at the severity of a winter in a northern clime. South Africa could get very cold in their winter, but nothing like this. She was reluctant to admit that Mr Sullivan, the First Officer, was right about anything, but his comment that her clothes were not warm enough was proving to be only too true.

The sailors were helping Mrs Poole, the Reverend and Delphine out of the boat, throwing their luggage onto the dry land, amongst all the other trunks and cases and bundles that the passengers had stowed on board ship.

Miriam staggered a little as she tried to walk: months of being at sea, with the deck always unsteady beneath her feet, meant that a surface that wasn't moving felt extremely odd. A hand reached out to steady her and she swung round to find Nicholas Sullivan at her side.

"Be careful, Miss Malliot. You will feel strange at first now you are back on dry land."

Miriam nodded her thanks and forced herself to stand on her own, bracing herself in case she swayed again. She was determined to be indebted to no one, especially this officer who always seemed so critical of her behaviour, although she had to admit there had been times on the voyage when his company had been a pleasure.

"Thank you, Sir. I am quite all right now. Pray do not let me detain you. I imagine you must return to your ship for the final leg of her voyage."

Nicholas gazed at the tall, red-headed girl who shivered in the cold wind. He was irritated that, even after his advice, she was not wearing a thicker cloak and could not even accept a helping hand without dismissing him immediately.

"The tide will not turn for several hours, when hopefully, the wind will be in our favour, too, and we can continue to our berth further up the Thames. Are you happy to have landed? It will all seem very strange to you, no doubt."

"I am sure I will soon become accustomed to everything, although Cape Town does seem a great many miles off."

"Your relations are meeting you, I believe you said. Can you see them anywhere? I will organize one of the men to convey your trunk to their carriage."

Miriam gazed round, trying to find anyone in the crowd of laughing, talking, excited people who could possibly be one of her Bingley relations but no one seemed to fit the descriptions she had received from her mother, although to be fair, she hardly expected to see a young handsome man, as Charles Bingley had been described to her many times.

The crowds of sailors and dockers were increased by men selling hot pies, cups of pea soup, jugs of beer, their cries for trade mingling with boys hawking newspapers, offering to clean shoes, or carry baggage. She was stunned by the noise, the motion, every face a different shape and colour, every nationality in the world seemed to be represented on the dockside.

Just then Mrs Poole hurried over, pushing through the crowds, her bonnet askew, her face a picture of worry. "Ah, Miriam, there you are. Excuse me, Mr Sullivan, I just need a word with Miss Malliot."

Nicholas bowed gravely and turned aside, to be immediately accosted by another passenger who was bitterly upset that some of his luggage had apparently been mislaid. When he turned back,

Miss Malliot and the Reverend's wife had moved a distance away and were, even now, hurrying towards the gates of the dockyard to where carriages were waiting in the tree lined road that led towards the little town. He supposed that the Bingley conveyance had been found and was surprisingly irritated that the girl had not even said goodbye to him, let alone wish him a safe journey.

Mrs Poole, thankful to the Almighty for having delivered her and her family safely to shore from the perils of the deep, was in a fever to be on her way to Canterbury. She had discovered that the mail coach from London to the cathedral city was shortly arriving at Gravesend and by the fortunate occurrence of their docking early, she could have her whole family safely at her sister's house before nightfall.

"Mr Poole and Delphine are already in the coach and our luggage is on board. Now I fear I must ask you to accompany us, Miriam, as I cannot leave you here unchaperoned. Your dear mama would never forgive me."

Miriam took a deep breath. She could see the mail coach, the horses stamping at the ground, eager to be away. The thought of travelling to Canterbury with the Pooles was more than she could bear. How would her relations ever find her? She would have to write and that might take days and days to sort out the muddle. And all the while she would have to be polite to Delphine and endure her stupid giggles.

"No, dear Mrs Poole, there is no need. Look - " She turned and although she quailed at lying to her chaperone, pointed at a smart dark green coach and four that was just pulling up further down the road. "I can see the Bingley crest on the carriage doors! That is my uncle, come to greet me. You can leave with a clear conscience and my heartfelt thanks for taking such good care of me."

Mrs Poole dithered, one foot on the step of the mail coach. The postillion was waiting impatiently to help her in, but still she hesitated.

"Oh dear, oh dear, I am sure your mama would prefer me to meet your relations and give them a report on our journey here. But it will be so convenient for Mr Poole to reach Canterbury today, so as to visit with the church officials there tomorrow. Well, if you are certain, Miriam, then I wish you a safe journey."

She allowed herself to be helped into the carriage and then pushed down the window to lean out once more. "I will write to your mother immediately, Miriam, and tell her of our safe arrival. Now hasten to your relations, child. Do not stand alone on the quayside with all these rough sailors around. It is dangerous for a girl on her own."

A shout from the driver and the horses broke into a walk and Mrs Poole, with a final squeal and a wave of her handkerchief, fell back into her seat, out of sight.

Miriam watched the mail coach vanish down the tree-lined road, then turned back to where her trunk was sitting on the dockside. The crowds were slowly diminishing; the green coach had driven away and soon the normal bustle of the dockyard returned as goods were carried to and from small ships, ferries hurried across to the far side of the Thames and the *Sea Sprite* lay in mid-stream, awaiting the tide to turn. A gentleman came out of the Customs Office, shut and locked the door and hurried away without so much as a glance in her direction.

Sitting on her trunk, she tucked her hands deep inside the folds of her cloak. The Bingleys were very late; surely they would have had no problem finding out when the ship was expected? She knew from the newspaper in Cape Town that arrivals and departures were always printed well in advance. Of course, storms and sudden calms could cause havoc with such announcements, but the other passengers had obviously been met on time by their connections.

She shivered; the wind was biting through her cloak and her bonnet was only calico, made for the hot African sun. And it was growing darker! From somewhere in the little town she heard a clock strike four. Dark at four o'clock! She had never imagined that.

Oh where were the Bingleys? She had gathered from many conversations with her mama over the years that the middle daughter of the Bennet family had been sadly overlooked and treated with disdain by all her sisters, but surely they would not leave a niece in peril, no matter what they thought of her mother.

"Miss Malliot! What in good heavens' name are you doing still here?" In astonishment, Nicholas Sullivan whipped off his hat and stared down at the girl sitting on a battered trunk by the side of the road. "Did your relations fail to arrive?"

Miriam bit her lip. She was tempted to snap back that, no, she *enjoyed* sitting in the cold and the wind, alone in a strange country, scared and lost, but she held back her hasty words and nodded instead.

"There has obviously been some sort of mishap - perhaps the carriage broke down or there has been a muddle with the dates. But it is of no consequence, Sir, I have the address to which I am headed. I intend to find a clean respectable inn where I can get a room for the night, and then tomorrow I will pay for transport into London."

Nicholas hit his hat several times against his thigh in frustration. Having spent the last couple of hours down in the hold, searching for a lost piece of luggage, he had come ashore, dirty and tired, determined to walk into Gravesend to enjoy his first hot bath for months, his first meal of meat that wasn't rancid and a plate of fresh vegetables.

To his surprise there had been mail waiting for him at the Customs Office from his father which to his frustration meant all his plans for the next few months were to be turned on their heads. He wanted to sit and think about the news he'd received: the last thing he needed was a problem with this young lady, who was no longer the company's passenger and so, in truth, was not his concern.

But of course he could not leave her alone on the dockside. He was well aware that several of the rougher elements amongst the dockers were staring at her. Why oh why hadn't the wretched girl gone with the Pooles until her elusive relations could be found?

Staring out into the rapidly darkening reaches of the Thames, he could see that lights were showing now on board the *Sea Sprite* but the wind was still not in their favour and he reckoned that they would not be under sail again until the next day.

"But did not the Pooles realise they were leaving you on your own?" he said, more sharply than he had intended. "I cannot believe they would do such a thing. It is not seemly for a young woman to be unaccompanied in such an area."

Miriam had the grace to blush and was glad that with her face turned down and the rapidly fading light, this burly sailor could not see her expression.

"I thought my relations had arrived at the dockside. It was my mistake, the Pooles were completely without fault." She shivered violently as a particular sharp gust of wind speared across the water and stood up. "I will not detain you further, Sir. As you know the town, if you can recommend an inn, I will be grateful."

Nicholas sighed. "This is a river-side town, Miss Malliot. Most of the inns have noisy clientele, rough and ready sailors and dockers. But just along the footpath lies The Three Daws, an ancient establishment. I have stayed there myself when waiting for a berth. The rooms are clean if spartan and I am sure you will be sensible and stay in your room and not venture down to the tavern area."

Miriam hesitated; she knew that it would be quite wrong to accompany him to an inn. Even though he spoke like a gentleman, he was, after all, just a rough sailor. She could almost hear her mama's shocked voice in her head, but at the same time, impulsively, without thinking any further, she was determined to prove to the world that she was an independent woman, capable of looking after herself. She hated to be indebted to anyone but was sensible enough to realise that she had to find shelter for the night as soon as possible.

"In the morning, I myself am taking an early carriage into London. You are welcome to share it with me. I appreciate that you are without a chaperone but in the circumstances, and as you have no maid in attendance...."

Miriam tossed her head. "Chaperones are considered very old-fashioned in Cape Town, Mr Sullivan. I am quite capable of securing a room for the night if you will direct me to The Three Daws and I certainly have no need of a maid. I am eighteen years of age, quite capable of doing up my own buttons!"

Nicholas gave a short bow of acknowledgement. He was without words; all the women of good character that he knew would have been horrified to have found themselves alone and unaccompanied in a foreign country. Miss Malliot seemed remarkably unconcerned. He didn't fully understand: he'd thought her a girl of good character. Was he wrong?

He frowned and whistled to one of the dockers, arranging for the trunk to be safely stowed on a barrow and trundled behind them as they walked along the cobbled path to the inn.

"You are continuing your journey by land?" Miriam was surprised.

"Yes, the Captain can manage the last part of the journey without me. The pilot will take *Sea Sprite* safely up river. Once I have made sure you are safe and sound, I will row out to the ship and tell him of my departure. I have to be in London tomorrow at the latest and cannot wait for the tide."

Miriam was puzzled: she didn't understand how Mr Sullivan could just leave his post in this way. Wasn't he employed by the shipping line? She was about to enquire further, then realised that his usually open face had darkened. Whatever had caused the First Officer to alter his plans and abandon his post on the *Sea Sprite,* it obviously brought him little pleasure.

A few minutes' walk brought them to the front of the inn. Even though it was only late afternoon, it was obviously extremely busy and Miriam could hear loud voices and singing coming from the rooms downstairs and the smashing of glass and shouts rang out.

She hesitated; perhaps this was not the correct thing to do, indeed she was beginning to regret agreeing to Mr Sullivan taking charge of her in this preemptory fashion. She realised that she should have made her way to the nearest church and sought shelter at the vicarage attached to it. But she had been so busy making sure he realised she was quite capable of looking after herself and needed no help that she was ending up in deeper trouble.

Nicholas Sullivan hesitated, too. On his last visit the inn had been a quiet, sleepy establishment but obviously at this time it was hosting the crews of many ships at anchor in the Thames, waiting for the tide. It was definitely not the place for a young lady. He sighed; he would have to find her an alternative lodging.

Miriam turned to tell him that she felt she must seek shelter elsewhere, her foot slipped on a cobble and his arm shot out to catch her before she could fall. At the same moment, the sounds of hooves and the cries of a coachman sounded and they stepped hastily to one side as a fine carriage rounded the bend and drew up beside them, the horses snorting and tossing their heads, their bridles decorated with medallions and feathers.

The postillion leapt down, opened the carriage door, unfolded the wooden steps and handed down a woman, dressed in the height of fashion, who stared around her in obvious disdain until her gaze touched on Miriam. She gestured imperiously.

"Come here, child. I do declare, are you Miriam Malliot?"

Miriam stared back in astonishment. "Yes, Ma'am, indeed I am."

"Thank heaven I have found you. Why did you not stay put at the dockside? What are you doing, wandering off with - with - " She gestured towards Nicholas who pulled off his hat and bowed.

"First Officer Sullivan of the *Sea Sprite*, madam, at your service."

The woman waved him away impatiently. "Sir, I do not wish for an introduction. I cannot understand why you have taken this young lady away to this dreadful place. I only wish my husband was here to deal with you, but as it is I can only say that we are all very displeased and if I had time, I would call in the authorities to have you taken into charge. Miriam, get in the carriage at once. Is that your trunk? It can go on top."

"But madam, who are you?" Miriam was startled and puzzled. Who was this woman who knew her name and why was she being so rude to Mr Sullivan?

"I am Mrs Caroline Tremaine, I am your Uncle Charles Bingley's sister and have hurried down from London to collect you. Your mother's letter telling of your arrival was most sadly delayed and I only received word this morning that you might have arrived. Thank heavens I got here in time. Now, please, Miriam, be so good as to get in the coach and let us leave this dreadful place at once before it gets too dark for the horses."

CHAPTER 5

Caroline Tremaine stared at the girl sitting opposite her as the carriage lurched into motion. She had only a vague memory of Mary Bennet - an exceedingly plain girl, singing and playing the piano very badly one evening, more than twenty years ago - the same girl in attendance when her brother married Jane Bennet and again when Mr Darcy threw himself away by marrying Elizabeth.

She could see no resemblance whatsoever to her mother in her present travelling companion. The tall, sturdy form, the dreadful bright red hair and the style of dress that had not been fashionable for many a year, all made her quiver with disdain.

"Lord, what a happy chance that I found you before that man had you hidden from sight!"

Miriam, unhappy that she had not even had the chance to thank Mr Sullivan for his help, stared back in dismay. "But he meant me no harm, madam. He is the First Officer of the *Sea Sprite,* and has kept me from danger at sea on more than one occasion."

Caroline leant forward and patted her hand. "Of course he did! You were valuable goods in his eyes, no doubt. My child, have you never heard of the White Slave Trade! Oh it is so very shocking. Young girls, just like you, whom men think are without protection, can be sold into...well, into slavery!"

"But Mr Sullivan would never do such a thing!"

"So why did he leave his ship? Why not send a messenger to the local church, pass you into the protection of a member of the clergy? No, he was taking you to a house of disrepute, I have no doubt. I shudder to think what might have become of you if I had been even five minutes later in finding you!"

Miriam fell silent. She was well aware that she knew nothing of the ways of the world outside of Africa and it had indeed been most odd that suddenly Mr Sullivan was going to take a carriage to London and not remain with his ship.

She shivered: she had always imagined that she was a good judge of character, but this had taught her a valuable lesson. In the future she would trust no one, except her own dear mama. And now she had to prepare herself for what lay ahead, meeting her relations who would probably look at her with the same disdainful expression as the woman sitting opposite her. It was quite obvious to Miriam that she fell far short of the lady's expectations!

"My dear," Mrs Tremaine said two days later to her own sister, Mrs Hurst, as they sat sipping hot chocolate in her ornate London drawing-room. "She sat there, a tall creature, tanned like a gypsy, a sullen, stubborn expression on her face, wild red hair coming loose under her bonnet, wearing the most odd, old-fashioned outfit. I almost expected her to produce a spear from under her chemise and shake it at me!"

"And had she really been about to enter the inn with a sailor?" Mrs Hurst, who was always bored with life, found a little enjoyment in the news and blinked herself more awake.

"Yes, can you imagine the disgrace? The sailor had his arm around her shoulders and was about to shepherd her into a most disreputable looking establishment. Just the sort of inn where white slavers might work. Thank heavens I got there in time, although Mr Tremaine was very displeased when the express letter arrived from Elizabeth, asking one of us to meet the girl at the port. The Darcys were worried that she might have arrived days earlier, because the letter from Africa had been so delayed."

"You had no choice but to go."

"Oh indeed, none at all. I should not care to offend Fitzwilliam and the girl is poor dear Jane's niece and so a distant relation of ours in a way, I suppose."

Mrs Hurst yawned and sipped her tea. "Did she have much conversation?"

"None at all - the girl is as dull as ditchwater - in that way she is very like her mother, as far as I can remember her. I explained that the Bingley London house is shut up at the moment and that she could not stay with me as Mr Tremaine and I were just about to leave for Bath as he needs to take the waters there - gout, you know."

Mrs Hurst, whose own husband suffered likewise, nodded. "So you dispatched her to the Darcys?"

"It was growing too dark to travel far, so we stayed the night at a pleasant inn just outside Dartford and in the morning I put her on a mail coach with a ticket through to Lambton. I explained that once there she is to find a local carter to carry her on to Pemberley. I sent an express letter to Pemberley, informing them of what I had done. No doubt Elizabeth will not think of reimbursing me for all the trouble this has caused, but then we must expect nothing more from her."

"Lord, what a to do. I wonder how the Darcys will cope with Miriam."

Caroline laughed. "As you know, I am very fond of Anne Darcy. She is a clever, strong-willed young lady. This African stranger will be kept very firmly in her place, of that I have no doubt."

The mail coach from London heading for Edinburgh, rolled into the little Derbyshire town of Lambton with a great clatter of hooves and the sound of the horn that the postillion carried, blaring through the chilly winter air. With cries to the horses, the driver brought the coach to a halt in fine fashion in the main square.

Miriam could hardly believe that her journey had ended. Exhausted, she ached all over from the constant jolting of the carriage. She had been determined to reach Lambton as soon as possible and had stayed in the coach every time it changed horses and drivers.

She had managed to purchase bread and cheese and a mug of ale when they had been forced to stop for several hours to repair one of the wheels and early in the morning she had left her seat to stretch her legs and use the rancid offices of a coaching inn.

Now she stepped down into a world very different from anything she had ever known. Her impressions of England had, so far, not been positive ones. The busy port, the bitter wind, Mrs Tremaine's angry demeanour, her doubts about Mr Sullivan's intentions and her own stupidity at believing he was a gentleman, all had left her feeling bruised, unhappy and homesick. She longed for her mama, their little African home, the hot sun, the giant mountain that loomed above Cape Town.

Now she stepped down into a picture from a storybook because it had been snowing, not heavily, but enough to cover the ground with a scattering of white, the first snow she had ever seen! And the air tasted different from that in the south of England - cleaner, fresher and much colder.

"Miriam! You are Miriam Malliot, aren't you?"

She spun round and found her hands grasped by a slight figure wearing red velvet trimmed with fur. Dark curls were escaping from under her bonnet and her sparkling eyes were full of welcome.

"Papa thought you would be on this coach or perhaps the one arriving tomorrow. We had an express letter from Mrs Tremaine this morning saying you were on your way. Oh, how lovely it is to meet you. Are you exhausted? I love travelling but you have come such a long way. I want to hear all about Africa. Have you ever seen a lion, or an elephant? We saw one a few years ago when a carnival came to town."

Miriam felt overwhelmed by the stream of words. "I...I'm sorry, yes I'm Miriam Malliot. And forgive me, you are?"

The girl laughed. "Why, I'm Bennetta Darcy, your cousin. One of your many cousins. You'll meet some of the others when we get home. Oh and this - " she turned swiftly and held out a hand to a man standing behind her, who pulled off his hat and bowed to Miriam.

"This is our guest at Pemberley, Mr Edmund Avery, the famous artist. He is painting a portrait of us Darcy children to hang in the picture gallery. Goodness knows why my parents wish for such a thing, but a portrait there will be in due time. But poor Jane is still suffering from a bad cold and is really in no fit state to be transcribed onto canvas, so our session has been cancelled and Mr Avery kindly offered to escort me to Lambton. I had errands to run for my mama and hoped I might be in time to meet you."

Miriam felt her head was spinning with the girl's chatter. Mr Avery was tall and slim, a dark eyed, good looking, elegantly dressed gentleman, carrying a silver topped cane. He bowed to her again, a friendly expression on his face as she curtsied, but apart from murmuring her name in acknowledgement, did not speak. A famous portrait painter! She loved to sketch and paint, although she knew her ability to be very limited; it would be wonderful to watch someone talented at work.

"We have our own carriage here and see, James, one of our footmen, has already rescued your trunk and installed it safely. If you are ready, we can set off for Pemberley. Mama is anxious to meet you. Goodness, how weird it is to think that our mamas are sisters. I wonder if they are alike. I know little about your mother, except that her name is Mary and she loves music and reading."

A little frisson of anger swept over Miriam. How typical that remark seemed of her Aunt Elizabeth: to tell her children nothing more about her younger sister than she liked music and reading! The same hobbies that would apply to thousands and thousands of women all over the world.

What about her mama's diligent care for the poor people of Cape Town, her deep understanding of many great works by learned men, her devotion to her husband? Were none of these values worth relating to her family? Well, Miriam thought crossly, she certainly wasn't going to give the Darcys the idea that Mary spent all her time thinking and talking about them!

"I'm afraid I know just as little about my aunts and their families," she said in an off-hand manner, huddling deeper inside the hood of her cloak, wondering if she would ever feel warm again.

"Oh!" Bennetta stopped to consider what she considered a most peculiar state of affairs. She had been brought up to believe that the Darcys of Pemberley were of the utmost importance as a family and that everyone was interested in what they said and did. Why, Mr Edmund Avery would not have agreed to paint their portraits if they had not been important. He had exhibited at the Royal Academy and even met the famous Mr Turner whose work her papa admired so much. Indeed he had paid many guineas only recently for a water colour of Venice that now hung in the picture gallery.

"Well, you will be meeting my immediate family very soon and I'm sure in the months to come you will get to know all your other cousins. Cassandra, Mrs Richard Courtney, lives just twenty miles away. She is our Aunt Lydia's daughter and my special friend. But she is not...." she cast a sideways glance at Edmund Avery who was pointedly not listening and whispered.... "going into company too much at the moment!"

"Oh, do you mean she is expecting a baby?"

Bennetta gave a little gasp. Edmund Avery was a very modern man, talented and artistic but he was not a member of the family and as such was not a person before whom you should mention a lady's condition so blatantly, even in these modern times of 1834.

"Look, Mirry, may I call you Mirry," she said hastily, changing the subject, "these are the Pemberley woods. We will soon see the house and be almost home. I love this view, especially when it snows. But I expect you have seen many wild and wonderful landscapes in your travels."

Mr Avery turned his head to stare out of his window, hiding the smile that was threatening to cross his face. It was wonderfully refreshing to hear a young woman speak out so plainly, without restraint. He sometimes got very tired of the conversations he was forced to have with the ladies he painted. Why even Miss Bennetta Darcy was prone to choose her words carefully when talking to him.

He wondered what this girl looked like - was she another blonde, like her cousins, Anne and Jane? He could only see the tip of her nose from under her hood and the side of a very determined chin, then she moved her head and he saw beautiful brown eyes set in a face stiff with cold. She wore no muff and her hands were, he noticed, square and tanned, not the hands of a fashionable young lady at all. He was intrigued. Her introduction into the Darcy circle would certainly cause some ripples.

Miriam realised that she had made some sort of social mistake by mentioning the arrival of a baby. How ridiculous, she thought crossly, her mind winging back to the African villages, the *kralls* as her parents called them, where her parents had gone to preach. While they were lecturing on Christian virtues, she herself had often escaped from her nurse and run wild with the local children and had, in fact, watched two babies being born before she was nine years old, although she had never admitted as much to her mother.

She glanced sideways and found that Mr Avery was staring at her, his dark eyes smiling warmly, almost as if he could read her thoughts and agreed with them. Colour flooded up into her cheeks, making her face feel warm for the first time in days. Quickly, Miriam pulled her hood even further forward; she didn't want the artist to see that she was bothered by his glance.

Just then the carriage slowed to a stop as the road rose steeply and the woods ended.

"There, Miriam, there is Pemberley. You can no doubt see why we love it so much."

On the other side of the valley stood the magnificent stone building, backed by wide gardens leading to parkland with many magnificent trees and finally more wooded hills. A wide stream, almost a river, ran in front of the house and as the coachman urged the horses onward, Miriam saw they were heading for a bridge that would bring them to the great front door.

As they descended the road, it began snowing again and with the wind blowing through the trees, to Miriam, it looked as if Pemberley was sailing through the air, like a majestic sailing ship.

Suddenly the memory of Nicholas Sullivan came into her mind and she wondered if his business in London was now finished and he was back on board *Sea Sprite*, readying the ship to sail.

Mrs Tremaine had convinced her that his behaviour had not been that of a gentleman, but Miriam still envied him his freedom. A picture flashed through her mind of the First Officer standing on deck, his dark grey eyes looking as stormy as the sea as he chastised her for some breach of shipboard etiquette.

But the carriage was drawing to a halt and she banished her thoughts of the man who might well have meant her harm if she had not been rescued in the nick of time.

She must still be on her guard because here was Pemberley and the Darcy family who had treated her own dear mother so casually and with such lack of respect. A family whom she must not ever think of in a friendly fashion.

The carriage drew to a halt and, before the footman - who had hair as red as her own - could help, Mr Avery had opened the door, holding out his hand to help Miriam descend down the steps. She murmured her thanks but refused to look up into his face: she was wary now that her forthright manners that had seemed perfectly normal in Africa, might be misinterpreted here in England.

She hesitated as Bennetta skipped down from the carriage and stood gazing up at the vast building, overcome by emotions. She had been told all her life that her mama had rich relations back home in Derbyshire, but even in her wildest dreams she had never imagined a house of this grandeur.

Against her will she recalled the small house in Cape Town where she had spent so many years - the ill-fitting windows that let in the dust and dirt, the heat that bleached the colour out of any drapes or blinds, the crawling insects that her mother could never eradicate completely.

Miriam brushed a tear away from her cheek, pretending it was a snow flake, as Bennetta ran up the steps and the great front door swung open before she reached it, manned by a footman in dark green livery who hastened to help James unload her trunk from the carriage.

The great hall of Pemberley stretched before her: a sea of shining black and white tiles, cherubs and angels in pink, blue and gold leaf on a wonderful painted ceiling that soared above her head, and a stone and marble staircase that wound round and up in an elegant spiral towards the first floor and beyond.

A tall woman, dressed all in black with white starched collar and cuffs was waiting to greet them, her hands folded quietly on her key laden belt.

"Miss Reynolds! Here is my cousin Miriam at last. Come in, Mirry, come in. Don't just stand there on the doorstep letting in all the cold air. Miss Reynolds is our invaluable housekeeper; she runs Pemberley for us and Mama often says she doesn't know what she would do without her.

"Oh, Mr Avery, I almost forgot you. My apologies, Sir. I expect you are longing to get back to your oils and brushes, but you must have some luncheon first. Where are my mama and papa, Miss Reynolds? I know they are anxious to meet Miriam."

"Welcome to Pemberley, Miss Malliot. I am very pleased to make your acquaintance. Mr Avery, luncheon is served in the small dining-room. Miss Malliot, I am sure you would like to be shown to your room. Mrs Darcy has not yet returned from visiting your aunt, Mrs Bingley, and a business acquaintance of Mr Darcy's has arrived and is waiting to see your uncle at present. I believe Mr Darcy has urgent matters to attend to at present with the head gamekeeper."

"Oh, the Baxters, I forgot it was today they were due to arrive! What a nuisance."

Bennetta had pulled off her bonnet, letting a cascade of dark curls fall to her shoulders. "Don't worry about them, Mirry, you will only need to speak to them at dinner. Mr Baxter is a kind, elderly man but his son Gerald is a silly person who annoys me intensely. I do hope Aunt Jane is not unwell again. It is unlike

Mama to be late for luncheon but Papa will be pleased to greet you.

"I trust you will not find a large family gathering too overwhelming. We no longer have a governess: Miss Smith, who was such a trial to me with her endless French conversation and of very little use as a chaperone, has gone to teach our cousin Harriet, down in Hertfordshire. And sadly, the lady who lately has kindly been acting as our chaperone when necessary, Miss Susannah Courtney, sister-in-law to our cousins Cassandra and Catherine, has returned to Wyvern Lodge to be of help to Cassie at this important time, so you will not meet her just yet."

Miriam pushed back her hood, wondering if her cousin ever stopped talking long enough to draw breath. She was quaking inside at the thought of meeting all these strangers, whom she knew would inspect her and find her very wanting.

Miss Reynolds' quick glance took in cheeks, pale beneath the tan from the sun, the shivers that ran across her body that she was trying to hide. Miss Bennetta meant well enough, obviously trying to make this awkward, silent cousin feel welcome, but she had failed to see that the other girl was almost collapsing with exhaustion.

"If you will come this way, Miss Malliot - I will show you to your room. You can rest before meeting the family. I will have a small repast sent up to you immediately and a maid later to show you the way to the yellow drawing-room where Mrs Darcy will expect to find you waiting."

Mr Avery bowed to Miriam, his expression one of warmth and admiration. "I am delighted to make your acquaintance Miss Malliot and I look forward to speaking to you much more in the days to come of Africa and your exciting life out there. It is a country I long to visit. An artist's dream, I have no doubt."

Miriam found herself ascending the great stairway behind the stately form of the housekeeper. Another flight of stairs led to a long corridor and a pleasant room, decorated in pale blue with drapes and bed coverings of a much darker hue.

To her delight there was a fire burning in the grate, a luncheon tray covered with muslin cloths and she could see steam rising from the water ewer next to the basin. She realised some maid must have been on the lookout for her arrival and had made the room comfortable for a weary, travel-stained visitor.

She felt so dirty and dishevelled and tried to remember the last time she had had the luxury of a bath. It must have been weeks ago when the *Sea Sprite* crossed the Equator and Mr Sullivan had arranged a canvas tent to be erected on deck and the female passengers had managed to pour great buckets of warm sea water over their bodies. But as refreshing as that had been, it had left her hair sticky with salt and she longed to soak it in fresh water.

"I will leave you to gather yourself, Miss Malliot. I have arranged for you to be maided by a young woman called Grace Frost. In the past the family have always used first names when addressing their servants, but Miss Darcy wishes the use of surnames to be followed at Pemberley, although Mr and Mrs Darcy prefer the old ways You may, of course, do as you wish; Grace will answer to both."

The housekeeper turned and hesitated in the doorway. "I hope you will allow me to offer my condolences on the loss of your father, Miss Malliot. From all I have heard, he was a good man."

Tears burnt Miriam's eyes and she blinked rapidly, determined not to show any emotion in front of a stranger. "Thank you," she said gravely and turned away.

Finally alone, Miriam took off her cloak, her cold fingers fumbling with the clasp and, as she did in every new room she entered, went to the window. It was still snowing and she could see little in the darkening afternoon but the whirling flakes and the tossing of trees in the distance. She turned back to her room; the maid had not yet appeared and although she was tired, she was too tense and excited to relax.

Washing her hands and face, she smoothed back a few errant strands of hair that had escaped her braid and pinched her cheeks until they glowed pink. What she wanted, more than food or drink, was to have her confrontation with her aunt and uncle, a meeting she was dreading, but one she knew she had to endure.

She had a letter to deliver to Mr Darcy from her mother: she was all too well aware of the contents, the request, almost a demand, for help finding a home back in England. The sooner the Darcys could find a small house for the Malliots to rent, then the sooner Miriam could be away from this overwhelming splendour and be secure in an atmosphere of plain tranquility.

Impulsively, she made up her mind: she refused to lurk up here in her room, waiting for the right time to be interviewed, as if she were a servant. She would go downstairs straight away - to the yellow drawing-room, if she could find it! Her appearance would be on her own terms, whether that was the polite course of action or not. Unfortunately, she was still wearing her traveling clothes. So be it. Miriam was not ashamed of them, even if they were fashionable and elegant.

She sat on the bed to gather her thoughts and summon up her courage. The warmth from the fire eased her frozen fingers and she could almost remember how it felt to be warm all over from the African sun. She shut her eyes for a second: thinking of home would make her doubly strong in the forthcoming interview with her aunt and uncle.

When Grace Frost knocked on the door and entered, carrying a pot of hot chocolate, she found the girl she was to maid lying fast asleep. She hesitated, wondering if she should make a noise and wake the visitor, but that would just mean a lot of work, helping her change her clothes and no doubt redo her hair.

Quietly, Grace unpacked the battered trunk, put away the clothes and laid out the best of what she considered a very poor selection of old-fashioned dresses. Irritated, she was quite determined to do as little as possible for this visitor.

Miss Malliot was not refined, not elegant and certainly not to be given the same consideration as one of the Darcy daughters. Grace hated being a maid; she was well aware that there was another world outside of Pemberley and was determined to do all she could to enter it. Grace had plans.

She stared down at the sleeping figure, resentment swelling inside her. She was prettier than this Darcy cousin; she was shorter, her figure was better and she knew she had a sharp brain even if she was lacking in education. Girls of her class were lucky if they managed to learn to read and write.

She tossed her head and glanced at her reflection in the cheval glass, biting her lips and pinching her cheeks to make them pinker. She knew men found her attractive; indeed her looks were her only weapon. Who knew what she might have done with her life if she had had an education and not been sent out to work as a scullery maid when she was ten years of age. But she would always be a servant here at Pemberley.

At one time Grace had had dreams of marrying one of the grooms, of living in a little cottage, of being poor but happy. Why, just the other day, Archie Sharp, the head groom, had asked her to go walking with him on her day off. She had been chasing Archie for over a year now and at last he was responding. He obviously felt it was time he took a wife and only a month or so ago, she would have been thrilled.

But - and she smiled to herself - she had now been given a chance to do much, much better than poor Archie with his corduroy breeches, smelling of horse dung and liniment. One day soon she would show the Darcys that she was just as good as any of them.

With a start, Miriam woke. To her horror she found she was lying on the bed, still fully dressed. The fire had been made up and a pot of what smelt like hot chocolate was perched on a trivet next to the flames, keeping warm.

She swung herself upright in a panic. What time was it? How long had she been asleep? Oh this was dreadful! Aunt Darcy would have been waiting. Had she sent the housekeeper or a maid to check on her? She must have done, for there was the chocolate. A small gilt clock on a table showed six - surely that would be almost dinner time.

She reached for the bell pull and then hesitated - did she really need a maid to help her? That someone had been in the room was quite clear because she realised her trunk had been unpacked: most of her clothes and belongings had been put tidily away but one of the dresses she had brought with her for evening wear lay across the arm of a chair, together with fresh stockings and shoes.

As swiftly as she could, she changed, unplaited her hair, brushed it and tied it back loosely from her face with a dark green velvet ribbon that had been a present from her dear papa on a long ago Christmas.

The huge house seemed cold as she left the warmth of her bedroom. Somewhere someone was laughing; it sounded like a young boy and it echoed down the passageway as she made her way back to the stairs. A footman stood on the landing, obviously surprised by her appearance, but in answer to her question, indicated the correct door.

Taking a deep breath, Miriam pushed it open and found herself in a small, comfortable room, paneled in a light wood with many book shelves. It was dark, the oil lamps yet unlit, just candles flickering in the gloom. A pretty painted desk stood in the window embrasure and the walls were hung with water colours and paintings of children at different ages. There was no sign of Elizabeth Darcy, but a man was standing with his back to the door, leaning with one hand on the mantlepiece, in the act of throwing a log on the fire.

Miriam's heart sank. Oh please, she prayed, please not Uncle Darcy, not until I have spoken to my aunt. Then she realised in the gloom that this was a young man, not her uncle. She took a step forward and then stopped, a gasp escaping against her will.

"You!"

The man had turned and looking at her with a frown was the man whose intentions towards her had been far from honourable, First Officer of the *Sea Sprite*, Nicholas Sullivan.

CHAPTER 6

Nicholas was tired, irritable and hungry. This whole urgent business journey to Derbyshire seemed like a waste of precious time. He was desperate to proceed with his mission but the weather was making that impossible. So here he was, trapped indoors in a house where dinner seemed ever distant and a host who was too busy to do more than send a message, begging his pardon for not being able to talk to him straight away.

He threw another log on the fire, deigning to ring for a servant to do a task he was quite capable of achieving. The flames curled round the dry wood, orange, yellow and a dark dark red that reminded him suddenly of a flag of hair, flying loose in the stiff wind, a face made beautiful by the joy in the girl's splendid brown eyes. He heard the door open behind him and turned - hopefully this was a summons to dinner - then,

"You!"

For a second Nicholas couldn't find his voice. There in the doorway stood the girl he had just been thinking about - which was impossible because this was Pemberley, home of the Darcy family and he had last seen Miss Malliot down in Kent being driven away towards London.

"Miss Malliot? Good Heavens, what are you doing here?"

Miriam clutched at the door handle, unable to step backwards or forwards. How could Nicholas Sullivan be here at Pemberley? Surely he couldn't have followed her? That was ridiculous.

"Mrs Darcy is my aunt, Sir. I was headed for the Bingley residence in London but there was a change of plans. Mrs Bingley is another aunt. I am well protected, as you can imagine."

Nicholas frowned, not understanding the last comment, then crossed the room in two swift strides, holding out his hand. Then he seemed to recollect where he was and bowed.

"Well, this is a rum state of affairs, I must say. A very strange coincidence but I am pleased to see you fit and well, Miss Malliot. You left Gravesend so quickly, with that other lady, that there was no time to say goodbye. Please, sit here by the fire. I am waiting a call for dinner but fear I may have been forgotten."

Miriam dropped a curtsey; she had no idea what to say or do. Mrs Tremaine had told her this man had evil intent in his mind when he had offered to find lodgings for her in the riverside inn. But now, gazing at his broad, deeply tanned, honest face, she found it very difficult to believe. But then she was just a poor girl from a foreign country. What did she know of this world of money and privilege and all the dangers that could befall someone as friendless as herself? How easy would it be to charm her?

"You have not said why you are here at Pemberley, Sir."

Nicholas frowned at her cold tone and her refusal to sit. Politeness insisted that he would have to remain standing as long as she did.

"My uncle, Mr Roger Baxter, is a gentleman involved with many business ventures in partnership with my father. He is half owner of the *Sea Sprite,* hence my position as First Officer. Uncle is keen to purchase a silk weaving factory here in Derbyshire or over the border in Cheshire. He is an acquaintance of Mr Darcy and that gentleman kindly offered him accommodation at Pemberley while he was looking at various premises for sale. But a few weeks ago, my uncle fell ill and my father wrote, insisting that I take his place until he recovers. The letter was waiting for me when the *Sea Sprite* docked."

"So you have given up your post as First Officer? You will surely miss the sea."

Nicholas smiled. "Only for a short while. A life as a factory owner is not for me. I was supposed to sail as Captain on her next trip, but that has been postponed until *Sea Sprite* returns to these shores once more in a few months' time. By then my uncle will no doubt have found a suitable replacement for me, one who understands the business world, not a sailor who is always looking to the distant horizon."

Miriam could find no reply to this: she was still confused and a little afraid. Mrs Tremaine had been sure that Nicolas Sullivan did not have her best interests at heart. She was an older woman, wealthy, well versed in the ways of the world. Why would she have said and acted as she had if she did not believe it to be true?

Just then the door opened and the tall, elegant figure of Edmund Avery appeared. Impulsively he held out his hand and clasped Miriam's.

"Miss Malliot! Well, how delightful to meet you once more. I was unhappy not to see you at luncheon but was told you were resting." He spied Nicholas, bowed briefly and said, "Edmund Avery, Sir."

Nicholas frowned: he disliked an excess of elegance in a man and there was a look of disdain on this fellow's face that irritated him. He had the feeling that the man had already worked out exactly how much his coat was worth and summed him up as not worthy of his attention.

"Nicholas Sullivan, Sir. At your service." He bowed but said no more.

"Hmm. Miss Malliot - " Edmund turned to Miriam. "I trust you will do me the honour of sitting close by me at dinner so you can relate stories of Africa and your long dangerous journey from that distant land."

"Not so very dangerous," Nicholas put in swiftly. "Miss Malliot was a passenger on my vessel and apart from one storm, we encountered no sea monsters, no mermaids, nothing of any great report."

Miriam glanced from one to the other, aware that there was a silence that needed to be broken, but not sure what to say. Mr Sullivan was right, of course, but it was very soothing to her ruffled feelings to see the warmth and admiration in Mr Avery's face. But before she could speak, there was a swirl of dark yellow plaid and an elegantly dressed woman swept into the room, holding out her hands to Miriam.

"Miriam! Oh my dear girl, it is so good to finally meet you. Have you slept well. I told the staff to let you rest; I was sure you needed repose after such a long journey. Let me look at you. Why you are nothing like your mother at all! Indeed, I can see no resemblance to any of your cousins. What lovely red hair. I am so sorry I was not here to greet you when you arrived, but I had to visit your Aunt Jane, who is longing to make your acquaintance and hear all about Mary and Africa. I do hope Bennetta made you welcome. Come, it is time for dinner. You must sit next to me and tell me everything. Oh we were distraught to learn about your dear father's passing."

She stopped suddenly, realising that other people were present, and advanced towards Nicholas who bowed politely.

"Mr Sullivan! My husband told me you were coming to stay for a few days - we were sorry to hear that your uncle has been taken ill and wish him a speedy recovery. I do hope your room is satisfactory? And you have made the acquaintance of my niece Miriam, I see? That is good. We do not stand on ceremony here at Pemberley."

"I already had that pleasure, Mrs Darcy. Miss Malliot was a passenger on the vessel *Sea Sprite* in which I had the honour to serve as First Officer."

Elizabeth laughed. "Oh, what a coincidence. I think that will amuse the family greatly. You must tell us all about it over dinner."

Nicholas bowed again. "I will no longer intrude on your family reunion, Mrs Darcy. I am sure I can follow my nose and find where dinner is being served!" He went to the door then turned and smiled at Miriam. "I look forward to renewing our acquaintance, Miss Malliot."

Edmund bowed gracefully. "I, too, will adjourn to the dining table. Miss Malliot - " he held out his hand, his gaze running over the cloud of dark red hair that was escaping from a velvet ribbon to cascade across her shoulders - "until later." He left, closing the door behind him.

"Aunt Darcy - "

Miriam stared at the woman standing in front of her - slim, sparkling dark eyes, looking not a day over forty, although she knew she must be. In her mind she saw a picture of her own dear mama, small, thin, her hair greying, her face lined by the constant sun. As much as it pained her, Miriam thought her mother looked more than ten years older than this woman and a flood of resentment coursed through her. Life was so unfair! Why should Elizabeth Darcy look so untouched by life and hard work?

"Yes, my dear?"

She hesitated... "That gentleman - "

"Mr Sullivan or Mr Avery, do you mean - yes, how strange that you are already acquainted with the former. We are delighted to have him at Pemberley. My husband speaks so highly of him and our boys are looking forward to hearing stories of his adventures at sea, especially Henry, our youngest. He wants to be an explorer when he grows up, although I am not sure how much of the world is left to explore!

"Mr Avery is a great favourite of my daughters. I am sure Bennetta mentioned that he is painting their portraits. Why, perhaps we can persuade him to produce a sketch of you. I am sure Mary would love to have one. Now, come and meet the rest of the family and take some refreshment; you must be so hungry."

She slipped her arm through her niece's and led her from the room, a footman leaping to open the door as she approached. Miriam was in a quandary, bewildered and confused. Everything was so different here - this vast house, so cold and strange. So many servants, so many manners and behaviours that she had no knowledge of at all.

For the first time since she had left Africa she felt truly alone. Whom could she talk to about her concerns regarding Nicholas Sullivan? There was no one. Aunt Darcy seemed all kindness and charm, but Miriam refused to be taken in by appearances. This was the same woman who had abandoned her sister to a life of hardship and toil. Why, just one of the emeralds on her fingers would have paid for all sorts of improvements to her parents' school in Cape Town and made her mother's life far easier.

She was hardly aware of her surroundings as she entered what her aunt called the small dining-room, only knowing that she could have fitted both of her African home's living rooms inside and still have some space over.

The heavy curtains were drawn against the dark of the evening, a log fire crackled, chasing away the cold and there was a lot of talking and laughing as footmen in green livery served dishes while the emptied plates were cleared away. Miriam kept her gaze down as much as possible, but there was no way she could not reply to her aunt's questions.

She gave a brief account of her father's last illness, assured her aunt that her mama was well in herself, although obviously very sad. Her youngest cousin, Henry, who was sitting opposite her, broke in several times with questions about lions and elephants.

Miriam's head was whirling with the noise, the number of dishes, the array of silverware, plates and glasses. She had never eaten a meal which was served by so many servants. At home there had been old Martha, an elderly lady who sang hymns just under her breath as she thumped the dishes down on the table and then bore them away to the kitchen when she decided the Malliots had eaten enough!

Twice Miriam reached to help herself from a serving plate, only to find a footman whisking the dish away and returning her a plate with a portion of meat laid out in a neat fan. The vegetables were all different, too, dressed in rich sauces which, she suddenly realised, were there to disguise the fact that the cabbages, carrots and turnips were all past their best.

There was an abundance of fruit on the table, nectarines and peaches, apples and pears displayed in a beautiful central silver epergne with three cut glass dishes.

"You are no doubt wondering how we manage such exotic fruit in these wintery conditions," her eldest cousin, Anne said, her tone bordering on insolence. "We have had hot houses here at Pemberley for many years. Something you are not used to, I imagine."

Miriam held her tongue. She could have said that she was used to platters of fresh fruit to choose from. Of picking oranges from a tree. This fruit would have been just about acceptable on any table in Cape Town! But the last thing she wanted to do was start an argument at the dinner table, even though this supercilious girl was making her quick temper rise.

Unfortunately, Edmund Avery was seated at some distance from her: he didn't have the opportunity of speaking but bowed his head towards her and smiled. The warmth of that took her by surprise and gave her a jolt of courage. Here, at least, was someone who appeared to like her, to treat her with respect. She wished he had been placed nearer, but Anne and Jane were on either side of him; Anne monopolizing his attention.

Nicholas Sullivan was seated at the far end of the table in earnest discussion with Mr Darcy, who had taken Miriam's hand when she entered the room and bade her welcome to Pemberley. Miriam had curtseyed, finding it hard to raise her gaze above the mother-of-pearl pin in his cravat. She was aware that he was tall and dark but a quick glance at his face told her that he was not smiling and seemed to have little genuine pleasure in her arrival.

"Thank you, Sir. It is very good of you to have me to stay. I have a letter for you from my mama. Perhaps I can give it to you after dinner?"

Mr Darcy frowned, then nodded. "Perhaps you would kindly hand it to your aunt for her perusal first."

Mr Darcy said no more, turning his attention to Nicholas Sullivan. He ate sparingly and finally turned to his wife and said, "My dear, I wish to show Mr Sullivan some figures I have drawn up for him to study. We shall join you in the drawing-room. Avery, would you care to join us? The figures will be of no interest to you, but there are one of two landscapes in my study that you might find worth your attention and I have a fine brandy to help keep out the cold."

When the gentlemen had gone, the rest of the family retired to a long, elegant room, furnished with taste and refinement. The two boys asked to be excused and vanished about their own concerns. Hot chocolate was being served and with her father out of the room, Anne Darcy felt she could ask whatever she liked with impunity.

"So, Miriam, do you intend to travel to visit our other aunts and uncles now you have reached our shores?"

All chilly blonde beauty, she leant back in her chair and surveyed her cousin. "Lord knows, there are enough of us in our extended family to keep you on the move for months without inconveniencing anyone for very long! Cassandra is not out in public much at the moment but I am sure she would be delighted to have a visit from you. Likewise you could stay with Aunt Bingley at Clifton

Park and be introduced to Beth and Sophia, more cousins! Both homes are a mere twenty miles away and I'm sure papa would let you have the use of the donkey cart."

Miriam felt her face flush. The tone of the girl's voice made it quite apparent that she thought Pemberley would be a far better place without poor relations cluttering up its many rooms and galleries.

"I would like to see something of Pemberley first," she replied, digging her fingernails into her palm, trying to stop her temper from rising to the surface.

"And we are delighted to have you here." Elizabeth Darcy raised an annoyed eyebrow at her eldest daughter who shrugged away the criticism. "You are not inconveniencing us at all. Your Aunt Jane is extremely anxious to hear all your news about Mary, but she does not experience good health at the moment and I fear she is not up to entertaining."

"Foo, Anne, anyone would think you were not happy to meet Miriam and learn about Africa and it's strange people and customs." Bennetta was tempted to flick her fingernail at her sister, just as she would have done when they were small, but she caught her mama's eagle eyed gaze fixed on her and desisted.

"There is no way Miriam could travel as far north to visit Aunt Lydia or our dear Catherine in Alnwick in this dreadful weather." Jane Darcy tugged a soft woolen shawl tightly round her shoulders and shivered. "I do declare it is getting colder and colder. We shall have more snow by morning."

Elizabeth cast an anxious glance in her direction, checking to make sure that she was not sitting in a draught. She worried about the younger twin all the time. Jane Darcy was not strong; she had been so tiny when she was born and her mother's terror at the thought of losing her had carried on into adulthood. So she had grown up cossetted and protected, even by her brothers and sisters, and had become timid and retiring, happier alone with her books than mixing in society.

Bennetta leant forward from where she was sitting. "Is this the first time you have seen snow, Miriam?"

She returned the smile. So far this cousin was the only person to have greeted her with any real show of warmth, except for Edmund Avery. She tended to believe that her aunt's welcome had been too well rehearsed to sound welcoming.

"Yes and I think it is wonderful. Mama has told me of snow, of course. She mentioned that she and her sisters used to have snowball fights, although - " she cast a glance at Elizabeth Darcy - "that is hard to imagine."

Elizabeth smiled and tried not to look surprised. Her memories of snowy days told her that Mary had always remained safely indoors, her nose in a book, and nothing would have induced her to throw a snowball at one of her sisters!

"Yes, wonderful until the roads become impassable and there is nowhere to go and nothing to do!"

"Benny, you have one of the largest private libraries in all England at your disposal. How can you say there is nothing to do? Do you enjoy reading, Miriam? I will gladly show you our book collection tomorrow. This is such a big house and you can wander for hours trying to find one particular room. Papa orders in all the latest titles for us, although sometimes I fear that Fitzwilliam and I are the only people who take advantage of that." Jane smiled at her cousin, wishing she could discover some common ground between them.

"You and Fitz are ruining your eyesight with all that reading." Anne sounded very dismissive.

"At least we can prepare for the ball." Bennetta yawned. "Lord I do hope it doesn't snow too heavily and we get shut off from the rest of the world. You see, Miriam, we are planning to celebrate the twins' nineteenth birthday which fell just before Christmas. But the twins were in London and then Jane went to Dorset, so there was no celebration.

"We thought it would be fun to give a ball for all our friends here in Derbyshire. I am not officially out until my birthday in May, but I am sure I can persuade mama and papa to let me attend. Have you a nice gown? If not, we can lend you one. I seem to spend my life lending cousins my clothes! Oh, you can dance, I suppose?"

"Perhaps our new cousin just knows strange African dances?" Anne said slyly.

Miriam felt her temper begin to rise; she found Miss Darcy a very objectionable girl. "I can dance, although I am afraid some of the newer tunes have yet to reach Africa. Mama was keen on my learning and I went to classes at home. And I am certain I can show you an African dance or two. They are very interesting! As for my gowns - well, I am sure they will suffice. I will certainly not need to borrow one, although thank you for the offer."

She tossed her head, determined that she would not borrow a ball gown, that she would wear one of her own, no matter how old and shabby it looked!

Mrs Darcy decided to intervene before the bickering grew more intense. "Well, tomorrow you must all gather in the room that your papa has put at Mr Avery's disposal. He is anxious to make progress with your portrait. And there is no point in frowning in that silly fashion, Bennetta. You know it has to be done so you may as well make up your mind to do so with a cheerful demeanour. The last thing your father and I want is to see you scowling out of the canvas every time we pass along the picture gallery!"

"Do you really think Mr Avery would consider doing just a very quick sketch of me that I could have framed for Mama?" Miriam asked wistfully.

"Well, let's ask him."

Nicholas and Edmund were just entering the room and Mrs Darcy smiled up at them.

"Mr Avery, I have another small commission for you. Do you think you will have the time to sketch a portrait of Miriam here? She would dearly love to give such an item to her mother and, of course, we would recompense you for your trouble."

Edmund Avery gazed at the young girl seated next to his hostess. She returned his gaze fearlessly and he felt his emotions stirred as he took in the dark eyes, the stubborn chin and the cloud of dark red hair that flared in the candlelight like flame. A sketch? No, he wanted to do more than that. He wanted to paint her in oils - he was already working on a piece that was to hang in one of London's private gentlemen's clubs.

His present model had been posing for him, lying on a couch - stretched out with bare shoulders, looking up at him, her hair in disarray, her eyes promising all sorts of wanton delights. But this girl with that face and hair! Of course, he knew for certain that she would never be allowed to pose in the way he wanted, but if he could sketch her face, he could add it to his painting.

"I would be delighted," he murmured.

Nicholas looked up sharply. He had heard something in the artist's voice, some hidden emotion, that he didn't like. He didn't trust Edmund Avery, especially where young women were concerned. He had met men like him before in London and knew only too well that their flattery and admiration could turn a young lady's head and lead her into all sorts of trouble. And for some reason, he was quite determined that that wouldn't happen to Miriam Malliot.

CHAPTER 7

Elizabeth Darcy sat in front of the mirror in her bedroom and shut her eyes: her head ached and she longed for bed. It had been a very long day for she had risen extremely early in order to travel to Clifton Park to visit Jane.

The snow had made the journey hazardous and she only hoped these first flurries did not herald a major fall when the road would be impassable. Her concern for her elder sister grew with each passing month. Jane should surely have recovered from Alethea's birth by now. Why the baby was now a chubby toddler, pretty and gentle, just like her mother.

She unclasped her earrings; sometimes being Mrs Darcy of Pemberley weighed heavily on her shoulders. Miss Reynolds was a treasure and ran the household with a rod of iron, but Miriam's arrival meant she herself had to see to the needs of three strangers that did not fall within the housekeeper's remit. Mr Avery was anxious to begin sketching and painting, Mr Sullivan needed to be escorted to view local properties that might be of interest to his uncle and Miriam could not, of course be left to her own devices.

Elizabeth recalled a comment in Mary's last letter about 'unsuitable acquaintances', 'a stubborn and willful nature'. The girl obviously had faults; she would need to keep a close watch on her; Bennetta was easily influenced, and whilst her recent firm friendship with Cassandra Courtney had calmed some of her riotous behaviour, her mother had a lurking feeling that her wild child was still there beneath the dutiful surface.

She sighed wearily; she had duties that extended outside of the house and grounds. There were certain poor families in the district who had to be visited regularly, especially in the bad weather and the new rector of Lambton had written, announcing his arrival in the district and saying he would soon call and leave his card.

Although that particular living was not one that her husband had in his power to bestow, all the civilities still had to be observed and the new rector and his family would have to be invited to luncheon at the very least.

Distantly she heard the murmur of voices, the click of the door as her maid left the room and then the touch of strong fingers on the back of her neck as her husband began to unclasp the necklace she was wearing.

Opening her eyes, she gazed lovingly at his reflection in the mirror. She could feel the heat from his body through his dressing-robe and wondered, not for the first time, why she should have been so lucky as to have fallen in love with Fitzwilliam Darcy and for him to have returned that love so passionately.

This little routine was something that he had started during the first days of their marriage. He would dismiss her maid and remove her necklaces and the ornaments from her hair. She smiled now, hearing him curse under his breath as the tiny clasp evaded his fingers.

"There! Got it. Confound it, Lizzie, why can't you wear jewellery with simple hooks?"

She leant back against him, relaxing as he placed the necklace on the table and returned to rub her shoulders, smoothing his hands across her skin, banishing the headache as if it had never been.

"So what is your impression of our visitors?"

"Mr Avery is a very elegant fellow and no doubt extremely talented, but he smiles too much for my liking. On the other hand, Mr Sullivan could well afford a new coat, the attention of a barber and smile a little more. As for Miriam, I must admit I am a trifle bewildered. At first I thought how different she is from our girls and all the other cousins, but that is only to be expected, of course."

Mr Darcy walked to the window and gazed out at the swirling snow. "It would indeed be strange with her upbringing if she was the same."

Elizabeth sighed. "I know, those first ten years of her life were so very odd. She had such freedom – why, I recall an early letter from Mary saying that she rarely saw the child all day, she was running around the villages with the African children. Even when Mary and the Reverend moved back to Cape Town and started their school, she was not an easy young girl.

"From what Mary has written in this latest letter, Miriam is very stubborn, tends to do exactly what she wants to do, is the champion of any underdog, whether the cause is deserving or not and refuses to listen to the advice of her elders and those who know better. She is also very mature for her age. I feel she has seen and knows things that most gently brought up young ladies do not."

"Another Lydia?" His tone was sharp and concerned. "Do you think she will be a bad influence on our girls?"

His wife got into bed and pulled the embroidered curtains of the poster to shut out the draughts. After twenty and more years of marriage, she could still not prevent her husband from having a window open a little at night even in the midst of a snow storm.

"No, she is not like Lydia. Although she does not favour Mary in looks, thank goodness, because even as her sister I am forced to say she was not blessed with an attractive face, I recognise a familiar sense of resentment in Miriam's demeanour. I cannot think what she has to be resentful about, but then I could never see why Mary was that way inclined. She won't make an impression on Anne, who is too sure of herself, or Jane who, for all her quiet ways, is a stubborn young woman with a deep sense of right and wrong. But as for Bennetta..."

Mr Darcy groaned. His youngest daughter was a sore trial to him and had been since the day she had been born when her entry into the world had nearly killed his wife.

"I believed that recently she had calmed her hoydenish ways. Having Cassandra living close by has been extremely beneficial. That sensible young woman, soon to be a mother, is an ideal companion for Bennetta. It is only a pity that circumstances do not allow them to meet up on a regular basis while Miriam is here."

"Mary writes that she wants you and Charles to find them a small house to rent. Perhaps it would be better if we looked for something closer to Kitty and Mama in Hertfordshire. In Meryton would be ideal. Mary knows the district well, of course, and there will be many acquaintances who will remember her. The only young person Miriam is likely to have regular contact with at Longbourn is Harriet Collins and, if I am honest, I don't think the Prime Minister himself could make an impression, good or bad, on that child! Yes, a house in Meryton would be ideal and the sooner the better."

"Well, if you think that best."

Elizabeth smiled up at him. "Put out the candles and come to bed, dearest. We must be the only people still awake in the whole of Pemberley."

But she was wrong. A floor above them on the other side of the house, Miriam was lying, unable to sleep, her head spinning as she recalled all that had happened that day.

How strange it had been to discover Nicholas Sullivan here in Derbyshire. She was determined to have as little to do with him as possible, but she did wish he wouldn't frown at her so. It was his behaviour that had been reprehensible, not hers! When, just before they retired for bed, Mr Avery had been arranging a time for her first portrait sitting in the morning, Mr Sullivan had been standing a few paces away, glowering in a most frightening fashion.

She turned over, unused to the softness of the bed or the closeness of the hangings that the Grace, the maid, had pulled round her before leaving the room. Miriam had never had a personal maid and found it awkward to have this girl, who was about the same age as herself, helping her undress, tidying the room, bringing a warming pan to slide between the sheets.

Trying to strike up a conversation had failed; the girl, although polite, had replied with terse, brief sentences. Miriam had the distinct impression that here was someone else who wasn't pleased by her presence at Pemberley. Perhaps it meant a lot of extra work because she seemed in a great hurry to leave the bedroom.

But at least there was the pleasing prospect of speaking more with Mr Avery in the days to come. His friendly smile and the pressure of his fingers on hers when he had bade her goodnight had warmed her and she knew her cheeks had turned pink as she returned his grasp.

Miriam sighed, only wishing she could disentangle her feelings about her Aunt Elizabeth. She had been kind, warm and caring; not the type of woman who would turn her back on a sister in need or try to take all of a beloved father's attention to herself alone. It was bewildering and puzzling.

Three days passed and Miriam settled into an uneasy routine at Pemberley. She woke early but however early that was, the fire in the grate had always been relaid and lit. Snug behind the heavy damask hangings that surrounded her bed, she never saw or heard the housemaid whose task that was and could only wonder, with a sense of guilt, at what time that little girl started her day's work.

As the room grew warmer, Miriam lay in bed, waiting for Grace Fox to knock and enter, bringing a large ewer of hot water with her. With her maid's help, she washed and dressed and let Grace braid her thick red hair into its long plait and coil it to the back of her neck. The girl had quick, nimble fingers, although Miriam was shocked to see that she had dreadful chilblains that must have been so painful.

"It's from the washing, Miss," Grace explained. "And the cold in our rooms. There was frost on the inside of the window pane last night."

"You have no fire in your room?"

Grace smiled at her reflection in the mirror as she fastened the last pin. "Miss Reynolds won't hear of servants having fires, Miss! I shares a bed with Susan Briggs, who is Miss Anne's maid. We're warm enough at night cuddled up together, but washing in cold water is cruel at this time of the year. It freezes in the ewers overnight, of course, and by the time you go down to the kitchen in the morning for hot, it's time to start work."

Miriam fell silent, her thoughts swirling. Out in Africa the Malliots had only had one servant, Martha, who was cook, cleaner, washerwoman and maid. She lived in a tiny room off the kitchen but Miriam realised she had never given any thought as to the elderly woman's basic requirements, if she had a family and where they lived. She wondered now why it had never occurred to her before.

"Does Mrs Darcy know you have no hot water, Grace?"

The maid gave her an odd glance from under her lashes. "Why, Mrs Darcy leaves the managing of the household to Miss Reynolds, Miss. We get a good wage, three meals a day and free clothing for when we are on duty. One day a fortnight off and every other Sunday, although the master and mistress like us all to attend church on Sunday morning."

"So Pemberley is a good place to work?"

Grace shrugged. "I've been here since I was ten, Miss. I know no other, but I'm told it is a fine place to work." And a fine place to leave, she said to herself. She was determined that she would not remain a servant for the rest of her life.

During breakfast that first morning, Mr Avery had suggested that Miriam sit for him for twenty minutes before he continued with his portrait of the Darcy children. Miriam had been delighted that he would take the time to spend on something that would bring him no public credit. She knew how much her mama would treasure such a sketch.

She was making her way through the great house when she came face to face with Miss Reynolds, who gave her a distant nod and went to walk past. Miriam suddenly remembered the maid's poor fingers, covered in chilblains. Surely that wasn't right, surely something should be done. Full of a desire to help, that her father would have recognised, she said, "Oh Miss Reynolds, may I have a word, if you are not too busy."

The housekeeper turned, her face blank, hands folded quietly over the heavy keys she wore on her belt. "Yes, Miss Malliot. How can I assist you?"

"It's about Grace."

Miss Reynolds frowned. "You are not satisfied with her work? I would be sorry to hear that. She is a bright girl. Perhaps you are not used to a maid of her quality? I imagine it must be difficult for your mother to find staff in Africa with the relevant experience."

Miriam fought to keep her temper but she was well aware of the thinly disguised insult towards her mother. "Grace is a good maid, I have no criticism of her work. I am more concerned with the conditions in which she has to live, especially during this very cold weather. She tells me there are no fires in the servants' rooms. This seems very wrong to me."

The housekeeper was speechless for a second or two. No one had ever before queried how she ran the servants' hall. The staff were well fed and clothed and working at Pemberley was known to be a much looked for position.

"There have never been fires in the servants' bedrooms, Miss Malliot. They are hardly used except for sleeping and there would be a considerable waste of time in carrying wood, coals and ashes, up and down stairs."

"But surely there could be some relaxation of the rules during this bitter weather?"

Miss Reynolds shook her head. "I shouldn't worry yourself about it, Miss. These girls are hardy creatures, well used to a little discomfort. I will have strong words with Grace if she has been complaining to you."

"Well, I think it's disgraceful," Miriam burst out, unable to keep her temper under control. "I have a fire in my room and I'm sure my cousins do as well. And Grace has not complained to me. Please do not chastise her because she is not at fault. I just cannot see that it makes for a comfortable household when you don't even have hot water to wash with every morning! Do you have a fire in your room?"

There was a silence until finally the housekeeper said in a distinctly chilly voice, "If that is all, Miss Malliot, I have a great deal of work to do."

"Certainly. I am sorry to keep you from your chores. I will speak to my aunt directly about the whole situation. I am sure she will be able to think of some way of rectifying the matter once it has been brought to her attention."

Miss Reynolds watched as the girl nodded briefly and continued her progress up the stairway to the top floor of the house. What a strange creature she was. A frown broke through her blank expression. Mrs Darcy left the running of the house entirely in her hands, but if this niece with her wild ideas made herself heard....

Miss Reynolds made her way down to the kitchen. Perhaps she had better have some thoughts of how to make the servants' rooms warmer before the mistress asked to speak to her about the problem.

When, hot and bothered from her argument with the housekeeper, Miriam arrived at the large room on the top floor, not far from the servants' quarters, she found the artist already at work, his shirt sleeves pushed back to his elbows. The room faced north and even on this dull, dark day, light streamed in through the uncurtained windows.

Even though it was a place of work, with rolls of canvasses and supplies of paint and brushes in abundance, there was a comfortable sofa in the middle of the room and a table laden with bottles of wine and plates of cheese and cold meats. She noticed, too, with a flicker of irritation, that a large fire burnt in the grate. Obviously the housekeeper had no problem with Mr Avery being warm and comfortable!

He turned, smiling. "Come in, Miss Malliot, welcome to my studio. Not as spacious as my one in London, but it will suffice while I am here at Pemberley. Pray, sit here, with the light from the window on your face."

"This is very good of you, Sir. Are you sure it is not an imposition?"

Edmund Avery smiled down at her and shook his head. He raised his hand and she flinched as he picked up her long braid and pulled it teasingly over her shoulder, his fingers almost caressing her face. She felt hot colour flood her cheeks; to be touched in such an intimate fashion seemed wrong, but then, she reasoned, Mr Avery was an artist and would obviously have no time for her girlish inhibitions.

"Why confine all this lovely red hair so tightly?" he said laughingly. "I am sure your mama would much prefer to have a sketch of you with it loose. That is certainly how she must think of you."

"Well, if you are sure." Reluctantly, she unbraided her hair and shut her eyes as he teased it out to lay over her shoulders. She was only glad that she had chosen to wear a dress with a high collar that morning. She didn't think that her mama would have wanted a gentleman's hands on her bare shoulders, not matter how great an artist he was.

For ten minutes she heard only the scratch of his charcoal on paper until the sound of voices and footsteps outside heralded the arrival of the five Darcy children.

"I believe I must now attend to my other work," Avery said as she rose to go. "But please come again, Miss Malliot. I shall need several sittings to do you justice. I will send a note by your maid as to when I am free. And leave your hair unbraided, please."

She dropped a curtsey just as the girls hurried into the studio.

"La, Miriam, you look quite wild," Anne said lazily. "What a sight you are, to be sure. You had best go and tidy yourself. I thought Bennetta's curls were bad enough but your mop is most unladylike. You'll frighten the servants, looking like that!"

Miriam bit her lip and said nothing: she refused to leave the room just because Anne Darcy wanted her to and sat quietly in a corner, watching as Mr Avery grouped the three girls on a sofa with Henry on the floor at their feet and Fitzwilliam standing behind them in the centre of the picture, as was his right as heir to Pemberley.

The quiet, dark eyed boy smiled at her and Miriam wished she could get to know this cousin better. She was beginning to realise that he wasn't proud and standoffish as she had first imagined, just rather shy.

Suddenly she smiled to herself; Henry had produced a mouse from his pocket and was stroking it, unseen by his sisters. He looked up, caught her looking and shook his head at her, pleadingly. Miriam got up and left the studio before she began to laugh, but the outraged screams and screeches from her cousins followed her down the many twisting stairways.

She thankfully saw little of Nicholas Sullivan during the days that followed. The snow showers had stopped and she gathered from Bennetta that he was away from Pemberley just after dawn, inspecting various properties that might interest his uncle to purchase. At dinner he had always been seated at the far end of the table from her and apart from a polite bow, he had spoken not a word to her.

Just once, in the evening, when Mr Avery was standing behind her as she sat on a sofa, inspecting a book of interesting bird pictures, had she thought Mr Sullivan was about to speak to her.

As Mr Avery had leant over her, pointing, the velvet of his evening coat against her ear and neck, murmuring that he thought that particular drawing very fine, Nicholas Sullivan had stood up and started across the room towards them. But then Anne had imperiously claimed Mr Avery's attention from the pianoforte and as he moved to her side, Nicholas had returned to his own seat, frowning.

The long winter days seemed endless: it was too cold to walk outside and Miriam couldn't remember a time in her life before when she had been shut up in one place for so long. She ached to be outdoors, for fresh air and freedom.

She had had two more sittings for her portrait but when they were over she was left to roam the great house, discovering different rooms and corridors every day. She wandered along the great picture gallery, stopping to stare up at the portraits of Darcys and Fitzwilliams who gazed down at her with, she was sure, a critical eye. She even explored as far as the kitchens and then felt awkward when everyone stopped what they were doing when she entered, the cook politely asking if there was anything she required.

Miriam shook her head, praising the meals she had had so far and then left. It was all so different from the casual atmosphere in her African home. Martha, their one elderly servant had always welcomed her into the kitchen, often letting her stir a sauce or weigh out the ingredients for a cake. But at Pemberley it was obvious that members of the Darcy family, no matter how remote, were not expected to enter the kitchen.

Aunt Elizabeth was extremely busy, constantly sending notes to enquire after her sister's health and to find out if Cassandra Courtney was keeping well. She had a myriad of charitable tasks to perform for the staff on the Pemberley estate and in the surrounding villages. Miriam had tried talking to her about the servants' bedrooms, but felt she had achieved little by so doing.

"My dear Miriam, I appreciate that our ways here in England are strange to you, but I pride myself on the knowledge that the conditions here for our staff are as good as any in the land. The maids and footmen spend most of their time downstairs and although Pemberley can be a cold house in the winter, the kitchens are always warm."

Elizabeth had laughed, her eyes bright with humour. "La, I should think that for most of the day, Grace is warmer in the servants' hall than you are in our great rooms! Indeed, Mr Darcy does not allow our boys to have fires in their rooms. He believes it ruins their constitutions, although I also think, where Henry is concerned, it is to stop Pemberley from being burnt to the ground one dark night!"

"But Aunt..."

"Now, Miriam, please don't upset Miss Reynolds - not with this wretched ball being planned! If it will make you any happier, I will look into the matter myself."

And with that she had to be content, although she felt irritated with herself, knowing that her dear papa would not have given in so easily if he thought there was a wrong he could right.

The days slowly passed: Anne was having private art lessons with Edmund Avery, Jane vanished into the library after luncheon every day and Bennetta spent all her spare time making endless plans for the ball she and her sister were determined Pemberley should hold once the weather changed.

Everyone was kind and polite if not friendly, but left Miriam feeling lonely and homesick. All the fine food and beautiful pictures, the myriad of elegant rooms and countless servants could not make up for her mama's smile, the hot African sun and the freedom she now realised she had enjoyed living in Cape Town. She was certainly not a prisoner at Pemberley, but it was accepted that she would inform someone if she wished to leave the house, even to walk in the gardens.

She wrote a long letter to her mama, telling her of her journey and sending the necessary compliments from Elizabeth Darcy. But even as she handed it to one of the footmen for posting, she wondered if her mother would receive it. Surely she must be on her way to England by now. If the sale of the school had gone through to Reverend Ogden, then there was nothing to keep Mary in Africa.

Three weeks after she arrived, Miriam woke and discovered it had snowed heavily again during the night. All the fine trees dotted across the parkland outside her window at the back of the house, were laden down with a thick white blanket. The sun was shining faintly now but the temperature had fallen overnight and great icicles were hanging from the stone surrounds of the terrace border. Under her window, two gardeners were already hard at work clearing the pathways.

She was almost ready to descend to the breakfast room when a knock at the door heralded Grace.

"A note from Mr Avery, Miss." The girl gave her an odd smile and it flashed through Miriam's mind that the maid might think this was a *billet-doux* from the artist, some flirtatious nonsense and she was quick to dispel any such notion.

"Thank you, Grace. Open it, if you please and read it to me."

Grace looked startled and for one awful moment Miriam wondered if the girl was embarrassed because she could not read, then she broke the seal and after a few moments said, "Oh, it just says that your sitting with him this morning has to be postponed, Miss." She sounded oddly pleased.

"Ah, I see. Well, I expect Mr Avery is very busy with the big family portrait. My little sketch must be almost finished by now and there is no urgency for it. My mama will not be here in England to see it for several weeks yet, even if she is already on her way."

"Yes, Miss." Grace busied herself with tidying the room. "He's a very clever gentleman, isn't he, Mr Avery? And wealthy, I have no doubt."

"Mr Avery is extremely talented, but I have no idea of his fortune. It is not something a gentleman ever discusses."

"No, of course not, Miss. But I have heard from his valet, Fletcher, that he owns a big house in London and gives extravagant parties." She smoothed down her apron over her hips. "Must be very exciting working in such an establishment."

Miriam smiled. "More exciting than Pemberley, you mean?"

Grace shrugged. "Pemberley is a fine house, of course, but very quiet. The Darcys do entertain, of course, but nothing is ever done on a lavish scale. Sometimes I just wonder about London. A girl could make something of herself down there."

"You do not intend to remain a lady's maid for ever, then?"

Miriam was intrigued; she could sense the ambition and frustration in this young woman who had to be about the same age as herself and wondered just how she could alter her station in life. It would be almost impossible. Grace had not been born the daughter of a gentleman, so her role in the world was fixed. She might well become a housekeeper or a cook, if she stayed unmarried, but even the role of governess would not be open to her because of her lack of education. If she no longer wished to stay in service, then she would have to look at finding a position in a factory or, if she was very lucky, working as an assistant in a shop.

"I have plans, Miss. If I see an opportunity to better myself, I intend to take it."

"You have no beau?"

Grace dropped a shoe she was carrying and bent to retrieve it. She pushed the thought of Archie, the head groom, out of her mind. He had a roving eye but until recently she had been quite sure that she could bring him to the point of asking for her hand. But now...her voice was muffled as she said,

"No, Miss Malliot, no beau. It's all right for some, but I don't wish to live in a tiny cottage, washing and cooking for a man all my life, producing endless children, destined for near poverty. Any dreams I have would be swept away and I would have to live the life he wanted us to live."

Miriam was still thinking of those words as she made her way downstairs. She was well aware that she would never have to wash and cook for her husband, if she ever found someone she wanted to marry - even the poorest of gentlefolk could afford the few shillings needed to employ a maid - but Grace's words held a ring of truth. A husband would provide for her, both materially and forge the path they would lead through life - but it would be his path. She was sure her mother had never dreamt of living most of her life out in Africa, but she had married a missionary and so had had no choice.

She felt a flare of resentment that women were treated so differently to men in this world. Men and money - they were the two things that controlled your life, from beginning to end, and she could see no way of changing that.

"Cousin Miriam!"

She was startled out of her thoughts by Henry racing up the stairs towards her. She smiled at her young cousin, who had reached that strange age in boys where they seemed to be all long arms and legs.

"I am glad to find you alone. I have been meaning to thank you for not giving me away up in the studio that day - about the mouse, I mean, but I have had no chance to speak privately."

Miriam tried to look severe and failed. "It was very wrong of you to scare your sisters. I could hear them screaming all the way down the stairs. I'm surprised your papa did not appear to question the noise."

Henry ran fingers though his untidy thatch of blond hair. "Oh that was Anne wailing. She hates mice. Jane just went pale and Bennetta laughed: she thought it amusing. Mr Avery wasn't too pleased, though. The sitting had to be abandoned - Anne didn't feel well enough to go on and insisted that Mr Avery escorted her outside to walk on the terrace to get fresh air."

Miriam looked at him severely. "I have the strongest impression, Henry Darcy, that you planned that on purpose."

The boy grinned. "I do so hate sitting still, Cousin! But if we get more snow tomorrow, Fitz and I can go sledging! Mr Sullivan has said he will join us, but Mr Avery has refused. Mr Sullivan has said he will make a sail to fix to my sledge so I can go faster downhill than Fitz! He knows all about sails, of course, being a sailor. I love sledging - It is so exciting when you reach the steepest part of the hill. You could almost be flying like a great bird."

Miriam felt a pang of envy. "And do your sisters not take part?"

Henry looked puzzled. "Ladies don't go sledging. It's dangerous, you know. What would happen if you fell off?"

"Surely the snow would cushion your fall?"

Henry just shook his head. "When we have really cold days, the lake will freeze and there is skating. You tie the blades to your boots - I'm sure you will not have seen that before out in Africa. Ladies are allowed on the ice as long as they are accompanied by a gentleman."

Miriam was still wondering why sledging was forbidden but skating was allowed for young ladies as she took her place at the breakfast table. A fire was crackling in the grate, but it was making very little impression on the chill in the room.

Elizabeth Darcy, well wrapped in a shawl of the softest green, looked up from a letter she was reading.

"Ah good morning, Miriam. I trust you slept well? The girls are not down yet, as you can see. They tend to stay in bed for as long as possible in this cold weather and I believe they have asked for their breakfasts to be served in their rooms. Luckily their father left early on estate business otherwise I fear we may have had arguments about their lazy behaviour during luncheon! Mr Sullivan ate earlier but I'm afraid Mr Avery is also not joining us and keeping to his room. He fears he may have a cold coming."

She gestured to a footman who carefully poured out a cup of hot chocolate and placed it in front of Miriam.

"Good morning, Aunt. Yes, I slept well, but I had hoped to speak to my uncle today, regarding my mother's letter," Miriam said. "Do you think it will be possible to find a house for us soon? It doesn't have to be very big, a small cottage to rent will do quite well."

Elizabeth sighed. It was obvious that her niece had no idea of the actual requests in Mary's letter. She did not want to live in a cottage and she could see no reason that the combined fortunes of the Darcys and the Bingleys should not provide her with a home she considered suitable.

"We thought it would be a good idea if we looked somewhere close to Longbourn, so that your mama could be near our mother and our sister, Kitty. There will be lots of acquaintances who will remember her as Mary Bennet and, of course, with Mr Collins' connection to the church, she will no doubt find a great deal to occupy her time. Mr Darcy has, I believe, already made enquiries and if we get some suitable replies, we will travel down to our house in London so as to be closer to investigate as soon as the weather allows."

Miriam watched in silence as the honey dripped off the spoon onto her bread. She was quite certain that her mother had no desire to live near Aunt Kitty; she had told Miriam many times that she did not have a good relationship with that particular sister. She expected to reside near the Darcys and Bingleys, but obviously they were only too anxious for her to live hundreds of miles away!

As for her own situation, here at Pemberley she had five cousins. Nearby resided Cassandra Courtney and all the Bingley family, whom she had yet to meet. Down in Hertfordshire there would be her grandmother, her aunt and a very small child. Miriam could not imagine that there would be any great social life at all. Her mama, on a very small income, would be at the mercy of the rest of the extended family, always having to be thankful for their charity. And that would be her fate as well.

She was beginning to realise, with extreme clarity, that she and her mama were the poor relations of the family and for all the kind words that had been spoken to her, so they would always remain.

CHAPTER 8

After breakfast Miriam wondered how she was to fill yet another long morning at Pemberley. She missed her morning art session in the studio with Mr Avery. Although she found sitting still just as difficult as young Henry, she had persevered without complaint, knowing that her mother would be pleased with the finished sketch.

Obviously with the Darcy girls keeping to their rooms and Mr Avery fearful of having caught a cold, it was obvious why he had cancelled the sittings.

Miriam turned towards the library, then hesitated. She still had not seen the sketch: Mr Avery had insisted that she only saw the finished piece. But the studio would be empty now: it would take just a few minutes to run upstairs to take a quick glance. It would hurt no one and Mr Avery need never know.

Without thinking further, she ran up the curving stone stairway that gave way to much simpler wood steps as she reached the third floor where the servants' quarters and the art studio were situated.

She was just about to open the door when she heard the distinct sound of a girl laughing inside the studio and the deeper reply of a man's voice.

Swiftly, Miriam hurried back to the top of the stairs. She turned as she started to descend and, to her astonishment saw her maid, Grace, come out of the studio, smoothing down her skirts, laughing back over her shoulder at some remark the man inside was making.

Retreating silently down the stairs, Miriam knew her cheeks were flushed. Regardless of the problems she had encountered with Nicholas Sullivan when she landed in England, she was not a completely naive young woman; her upbringing had exposed her to all sorts of situations between men and women.

It was quite obvious that despite declaring that she had no beau, Grace was involved with a young man, probably one of the footmen. The grooms and gardeners would not be allowed any further into the house than the kitchen; they would certainly not have dared to have an assignation upstairs.

Miriam smiled to herself as she reached the first floor. The fact that Grace was daring to have a life of her own pleased her. A young woman was attempting to escape from the bonds of servitude that bound her. And suddenly, remembering all she had heard, Miriam decided impulsively that the man was probably Mr Avery's valet, Fletcher! She had seen him around the house; a tall, thin young man with a supercilious expression, but good-looking enough to attract a girl like Grace who was determined to make something of herself.

That was obviously what Grace had meant when she had talked about moving to London. It was very romantic. Perhaps they would marry and, although Miriam knew it was very rare for husband and wife to work in the same household, Mr Avery was a kind man and one, she thought, to whom the rules of society meant very little.

She found herself wishing that all Grace's dreams would come true. At least she had dreams: Miriam was well aware that she never allowed herself to think of the future, beyond living with her mama somewhere in England. The years that followed were dull and misty. She could not imagine romance coming into her life and even if it did, she knew her mother in the future would depend on her and marriage would be out of the question. The vow she had made to her father was still clear in her mind. He had relied on her taking care of her mother.

Miriam was still thinking of Grace when she realised she could hear someone playing the pianoforte in the small music room. Standing outside the door, she listened in pleasure. The touch and feeling in the music was far superior to anyone she had yet heard play at Pemberley. Jane was the best performer in the evenings, but this person was considerably above her in ability. It must be Mr Avery!

Pushing open the door, she intended to sit quietly and listen, but stopped in astonishment, unable to stop an exclamation of surprise, for it was Nicholas Sullivan sitting at the pianoforte, not Edmund Avery.

He looked up at the sound and smiled at her as he continued with a tune that conjured up pictures in Miriam's mind of waves and clouds and the *Sea Sprite* speeding across the dark green water.

Without realising it, she moved to stand next to him, amazed that those broad, tanned hands which she had seen hauling on ropes, could coax such lovely music into being. With a final soft chord the piece came to an end.

"That was lovely. You play very well, Mr Sullivan."

"You sound surprised, Miss Malliot."

"Indeed, I think I am. The art of piano playing seems..."

Nicholas smiled up at her. "Not the pastime of a rough sailor?"

Miriam felt her cheeks redden. "I am quite aware that you are not just a sailor, that you hope to captain *Sea Sprite* one day and that you have many business ventures here in England and abroad. But I suppose I think of you as a practical person, not one who would enjoy or partake in the more artistic side of life."

"Such a person being one like Edmund Avery, I suppose?"

"Mr Avery is an artist of great reputation. I have no idea if he can play the piano."

For a second or two Nicholas gazed down at his hands, still resting on the keys. Edmund Avery was a name surrounded by gossip and innuendo in London. Nicholas had no way of knowing how much was true, but he was sure that it couldn't all be false. But there was no way he could tell Miriam Malliot that her tendresse was being given to a man with extremely dubious morals.

"He certainly has a reputation! Of that there is no doubt. And sometimes an apparent friendship is not all it seems to be." Closing the piano lid with a snap, he stood up. Miriam took a step backwards; she always forgot how tall and broad shouldered he was.

"So you think of me sometimes, Miss Malliot?"

She walked away to the far side of the room to glance out of the window trying to understand the remark he had just made. What did he mean by 'an apparent friendship is not all it seems to be'?

He had never suggested that there was a friendship between them. She was confused.

"I would find it difficult not to think of you because I spend many hours recalling my voyage to England and how wonderful it was to be so free, running before the wind. That piece of music reminded me once again of the journey from Africa."

"It was a good, fast voyage. The winds were in our favour. But sometimes, when you sail far to the south you meet dreadful gales and seas so high the waves tower above the top of the masts. Vast creatures lurk below the surface, birds with giant wingspans float above the ship and sometimes huge icebergs rear into view. You think they should be white, but in fact they have every colour of the rainbow inside them."

Miriam shut her eyes for a second, imagining the beauty, wishing with all her heart that she might see them one day. When she opened them, she found Nicholas standing quite close to her, his eyes as grey as the skies outside. A shudder ran through her and she took a step backwards. Nicholas frowned.

"Sometimes you act as if you are scared of me, Miss Malliot. I thought we were friends on board the *Sea Sprite* but since arriving in England, you seem to have changed your opinion of me."

She took a deep breath; Nicholas was a guest here at Pemberley, as she was herself. She was unsure of the etiquette involved in accusing a gentleman of evil intentions when there was no proof, just supposition, although that was offered by a lady such as Caroline Tremaine who was a woman of the world and knew a great deal about life.

"I am but slowly getting used to England, Sir. Our free and easy way of living on board ship can not be replicated here in Derbyshire."

She turned back to the window once more. "More snow is falling! I believe you are to go sledging with Henry and Fitzwilliam tomorrow. The girl who travelled on the *Sea Sprite* would have been pleased to have joined you in such an exciting game. Unfortunately, the Miriam Malliot you see before you now must stand on the sidelines and watch."

Suddenly she realised that what she was saying was not just an excuse, it was the truth. The Miriam who had lived in Cape Town, the Miriam who had boarded the ship, had roamed the decks, glorying in freedom that sailing gave, who insisted on going on deck during a storm, that Miriam had been lost for the past weeks, overwhelmed by the vast house, the different way of life and the Darcy family.

Nicholas frowned. "Yes, because sledging can be a very dangerous pastime. The younger boys are only allowed to slide when an adult is sitting behind them, ready to brake if they think they are going too fast. Fitzwilliam is a cautious lad and, for all his absentminded manners, he is quite aware that he is heir to Pemberley and will act accordingly. He will not court danger. Young Henry on the other hand..."

Miriam tossed her head. "Henry has a spirit of adventure that I find admirable. Surely you cannot err on the side of safety at every turn in life?"

"Children take risks because they do not fully recognize the dangers that surround them. As adults, we must behave with more caution. That is doubly so for young ladies, of course."

"Of course! Sometimes I forget that social graces are all important and that women must always do what is expected of them, whether we want to or not. And we must never forget that our reputations hang by a thread even in these enlightened times!"

Nicholas laughed. "Well, I don't think your reputation would be broken by sledging downhill in the snow, but your arm or leg might well be if you fell off at speed!"

"So you would not offer to partner me on a sledge?"

"No, Miss Malliot, I would not." A look of concern crossed his face. He could sense a stubborn streak, a wilfulness in this girl that alarmed him. "And you would surely not worry your aunt and uncle by doing anything that could put you in the way of harm whilst you are under their protection?"

Miriam fell silent. She was quite certain that her aunt and uncle would not be bothered if she had an accident, except for the inconvenience it would cause. But if she did injure herself, even in a minor fashion, it might delay them travelling to London to begin looking for a house she and her mama could rent. That was something she wanted more than anything.

"Are you planning a long stay in Derbyshire, Sir?" she asked, changing the subject.

Nicholas returned to the piano. "No, I have now seen several properties my uncle might find of interest. My involvement is now ended until he has inspected them himself. I know little about the silk industry - only how beautiful the finished material is when I ship it home from the East."

"I expect you are anxious for the *Sea Sprite* to return to England so you may take up your role as Captain."

"Indeed. I have been waiting for that day with barely controlled impatience."

There was a little silence and finally he continued, "And do you think your mother is already on her way? I am sure you miss her as she must miss you."

Miriam dropped him the smallest of curtseys, but refused to discuss her mama. She had had no letter from her since her arrival, but there could be a multitude of reasons for that and at the back of her mind lurked the thought that Mary Malliot would not miss her daughter that much at all.

Before she could speak, the door opened and Bennetta stood gazing at them before hurrying into the room, her dark curls flying as they escaped from her tortoiseshell hair clasps.

"There you are, Mirry! I have been looking all over for you. And Mr Sullivan! I fear we have been neglecting you. I do hope my cousin has been rectifying that mistake."

Nicholas' eyes twinkled and he tried to stop from smiling; the youngest Darcy girl had a joyous approach to life that he found difficult to resist. "Miss Malliot has been very kind."

"Oh I am pleased, but I must spirit her away now as the date for our ball has now been settled and there is much to discuss."

She caught Miriam's hand and ran with her out of the room, giggling. "Oh, you should see your face, Mirry! You don't have to thank me for rescuing you. It was a pleasure. I like Nicholas Sullivan, but I fear he is too much the bluff sailor to be socially agreeable to me. I could see from your face when I came in that you were bored and longing to escape."

"I wasn't bored," Miriam replied honestly, although she knew she would be hard pressed to find the words to describe how she felt in Nicholas' company - irritated, rebellious, envious, they all made sense but she had no idea why the sea captain should have this effect on her. "He is an interesting man."

"La, I will take your word for it, but personally I prefer the company of Edmund Avery! Such a handsome man and so elegant.

He always dresses in the latest fashion. I do wish Papa would wear coats with tight waists. He tells me he is no popinjay but being elegant is important. Poor Mr Sullivan's coat is at least two years old! But I fear Papa would not countenance an alliance between me and Mr Avery, even though he is a celebrated artist.

"I find flirting with him very satisfactory, especially as it annoys Anne so much. She is determined to come first in his regard, although I am beginning to suspect that poor Jane is badly smitten by our good-looking artist.

"She sits and sighs a lot lately, as if she is thinking of a certain gentleman. It must be Mr Avery as she never mentions anyone she has met in London and she certainly has met no one around Pemberley! There is a dreadful dearth of young men locally. Well, Jane will do well not to let Anne know, because that will make her double her efforts to gain his attention."

She stopped for breath, but before Miriam could reply, she raced on, "Now listen, Mirry, Mama has been chastising me, saying I have been neglecting you but I know you will understand. Anne and I are anxious for this ball to go ahead and have been making all sorts of plans with Miss Reynolds and our head cook. Mama says she does not have the time to organize anything at the moment, so she has left it all to us."

"It sounds exciting. When will it be? We are supposed to be going to London when the weather improves to seek out a home for my mama and myself."

"Oh, Mama will not leave Derbyshire until Aunt Jane feels stronger. I am sure she will as the weather becomes warmer. This cold is debilitating when you feel unwell to start with. So I am sending out invitations for an evening in March.

"Mr Avery says he will have finished the portrait by then and will need to return to London, but I think he likes the idea of a ball and I suggested he gives the picture its first showing in one of the little side rooms off the main ballroom. He was in agreement that that was a splendid idea."

"So we shall not be heading south for at least three weeks! Why, my mama might well be in England by then."

"Oh don't look so worried, Mirry. If she arrives early, there is plenty of room for her here at Pemberley! Why, she might well like to have a say in which house to live in. I know I should hate for someone to choose for me.

"Now, come upstairs and help me look at my ball gowns. I had a new one last year, so I don't think I can expect another so soon. Papa says I am becoming extremely extravagant, although I did point out that last year I had to take a great many of my belongings north to give to our cousin Catherine who had been sent to Northumberland with no more than a change of underwear and a couple of dresses! That was before she became Lady Courtney, of course."

She darted away in a flurry of petticoats and white stockings. Miriam followed more slowly: she had to admit she was intrigued by the thought of attending an elegant ball. No such thing had ever happened in Cape Town. There had been the occasional dance given by friends but her mother had always been asked to play the piano and Miriam had usually spent most of the evening at her side, turning the pages of her music. Refreshments had been a very plain fruit punch containing no alcohol and a few plates of cake and biscuits. She was sure that this ball would be a far grander affair.

And as she sat on Bennetta's bed, watching as gown after gown was pulled from a closet and laid out for her inspection, to her annoyance she found herself wondering if Nicholas Sullivan could dance as well as he played the piano. But then, surely he would no longer be at Pemberley: he had told her his work for his uncle was finished, so he would be leaving to travel south, no doubt. She should have been feeling pleased at this deduction, but instead was annoyed with herself all over again at feeling extremely disappointed.

"So what will you wear, Mirry? Do you have a special evening gown?"

Miriam started; she had been lost in her musings regarding Nicholas. She stared at the beautiful dresses thrown so casually across Bennetta's bed, knowing that she had nothing in her portmanteau that came even close to the level of elegance and fashion her cousins would show at the ball. But she was determined they would not feel sorry for her, offer to lend her clothes. That would be so demeaning.

"Oh, I have a couple that I think will do splendidly. No one will be looking to see what I am wearing."

Bennetta began to contradict her, then stopped. She was not at all sure if she really cared for Miriam or not. Her red-headed cousin was so different from any other girl she had ever met. She wanted to like her: she envied her the life she had led out in Africa, the fact that she had travelled such vast distances, seen so many wonderful things. But there was something wild and untamed about her.

"I have noticed that Edmund Avery seems very irritated when we all arrive for our sitting and interrupt his work on your sketch. Perhaps he has feelings for you? Why, Mirry, I do believe you are blushing! Can you see yourself as wife to a famous artist?"

"Don't be silly! He is just a very pleasant man who is being kind."

"But you must wish to be married one day?"

"Do you?" Miriam countered.

Bennetta held a white dress edged with yellow frills in front of her and stared at her reflection in the mirror. She had witnessed two marriages recently, that of her cousins Cassandra and Catherine. She had been pleased for both of them as they both seemed ridiculously happy with their husbands, but did she want to follow in their footsteps?

She couldn't imagine meeting anyone she would like enough to give up the freedom that was hers as a wealthy young woman. She was a Darcy of Pemberley; she did not need to get married to have an interesting life. But she was not naive; she realised that very few girls were in such an enviable position. A thought struck her - the freedom she valued came at a price: living at Pemberley she would always be under the control of her father.

Bennetta's fingers clenched at the yellow frill, not realising she was pulling it loose. She adored her papa but had always known that he did not care as much for her as he did for the twins or the boys. Every time he looked at her she could see irritation in his eyes and a sense that he was always waiting for her to cause him trouble.

She knew from gossip she had overheard since she was little that her birth had almost killed her mother. It was only since she was old enough to make the connection that she guessed this was why her papa's love was tinged with unease.

Realising suddenly that she was tearing her best dress, she laid it carefully back on the bed and pushed all the thoughts that upset her so much to the back of her mind. She would not think of her future now. There was a ball to plan.

She caught a glimpse of Miriam in the mirror... to be fair her cousin was tall and striking with that vivid red hair. But she sometimes had a mutinous expression and no doubt a quick temper. What was worse, Miriam had no money and no prospects. She was an only child and as such she would be expected to spend the rest of her life living with her mother, caring for her as she grew old. Obviously the Darcys and Bingleys would provide an annual income for the Malliots but on Mary's eventual demise, what would become of Miriam?

Bennetta frowned, then turned her mind to happier thoughts. Perhaps there would be some young man at the ball who would find her cousin attractive? And there was always, of course, Edmund Avery. Had she mistaken the expression on his face when he looked at Miriam? Perhaps it wasn't the same as the way papa looked at mama, when he thought no one was noticing, or even how Richard Courtney gazed at Cassandra, but it showed the artist was not completely indifferent to the girl he was sketching.

She puzzled as to what his expression meant: if she had been forced to give it a name, she would have called it hunger. Which was, of course, ridiculous: Edmund Avery didn't want to eat Miriam! She wished she was a little more cognizant as to the way gentlemen thought about ladies. It was something she needed to improve before she came out officially into society on her eighteenth birthday in May.

She hugged her thoughts to herself: if Edmund Avery had a genuine affection for Miriam it would annoy Anne and annoying Anne was always a plus as far as Bennetta was concerned!

CHAPTER 9

During that night, the snow that Henry Darcy longed for fell heavily and the inhabitants of Pemberley woke to a silent world of silver and white. At breakfast the boys could talk of nothing else but sledging down the slope that led from the lake towards the great park.

"You see, Cousin Miriam, the path is cleared from the house up to the lake so it is easy for us to reach. Then we race down the other side. It is an area of grass, free from bushes and trees that might impede the sledge." Henry's eyes shone with excitement. "And Mr Sullivan is to fix a sail to the back of my sledge. This year I will beat Fitz, just you see!"

"So we are allowed to watch? We are not in any danger from doing that?"

Nicholas looked up sharply at the tone he heard in her voice. It held a hint of challenge that disturbed him.

"Oh yes." Fitzwilliam thought the question quite unremarkable and smiled across the table. "The men have been clearing the snow and putting down cinders and sand on the pathway. It is a gentle climb - much steeper on the other side of the hill, of course. You will have a fine view of us from up there."

"Well, I for one, have no desire to wander around in the cold." Anne shivered dramatically, then glanced across the table at Miriam. "I suppose you will go to see the spectacle, Cousin?"

"I only wish I could take part."

Anne laughed. "Surely not even a young lady brought up in the wilds of Africa would believe such behaviour to be suitable?"

"I don't think it has anything to do with where you were brought up," Bennetta said, always keen to argue with her sister. "I've always longed to fly down the slopes but realise it is too dangerous. I know I will be envying the boys. Perhaps you need an adventurous spirit to understand that, Anne!"

"Girls! Girls! You are giving me a headache with your bickering." Mrs Darcy rapped on the table for attention, glad her husband had already left the room. "Miriam, you will need your warmest clothes and strongest boots if you wish to watch the boys this morning. Mr Sullivan, I thank you for your help and trust you will not make Henry's conveyance too fast. His father will not thank you for broken bones and smashed teeth!"

Mr Avery had sat silently eating, but at last spoke. "I shall bring my sketch pad and accompany you ladies, if you will allow. I am afraid, I too, do not have an adventurous spirit but I admire those who do." He smiled warmly down the table at Miriam who felt herself blushing.

Anne glanced up, her eyes very bright. "I am sure you would face danger with as much courage as the next man, Mr Avery! I think I will change my mind and accompany Bennetta. It is far too cold for Jane to be outside, but I am in need of some fresh air."

Later, Miriam was standing on top of a hill, gazing down the snowy slope towards the great park. Below her it stretched away into the distance where the woods began. A wonderful sight: she had, of course, known that the estate was large, but until you saw it from up high, you had no idea of how much land the Darcys owned.

A grim smile crossed her face as she remembered the little earth yard outside her African home where her mama tried to grow flowers in pots - enjoined in a battle against the sun and insects she could never win.

Miriam was shivering with cold because none of her dresses and coats were fit for the rigours of an English winter day, but she was happy to suffer the chill air that caught in her throat. To be out in the open, away from the stuffiness of the house, filled her with bliss.

She did, however, envy Bennetta and Anne their muffs and bonnets. Even Mr Avery was wrapped in a cloak lined with fur. Her own woollen gloves were already soaked through, although her fingers found warmth in her pockets from two large baked potatoes that one of the footmen had handed out to the family as they left the shelter of the house.

The boys had already made two surging runs down the slope, whooping and yelling as they went. If the little sail that Nicholas Sullivan had fixed to the back of Henry's sledge helped, it was hard to deduce, but he seemed happy, as did Fitzwilliam. Miriam was delighted to see the heir to Pemberley acting like a boy, all his reserve and good manners forgotten in the joy of speed.

"They are enjoying themselves, Sir," she said as Nicholas approached, brushing snow from his knees. Hatless, his face ruddy from the wind and cold, little snow crystals clung to his fair hair, glinting in the weak sunlight.

"Indeed, I envy them. The sail works very well, but perhaps not as well as Henry had hoped! But at least I shall not occur Mr Darcy's displeasure."

"I envy them, too," Miriam said under her breath and was aware that he gave her a sharp, frowning glance.

He was about to speak, to remind her of how dangerous this sport could be, but then Henry appeared, pulling both sleds to the top of the hill, calling out that Fitz had been summoned back to the house by their papa but hoped to sledge again in the afternoon.

Nicholas turned his attention to looking for damage to the wooden runners as Anne told her brother the next run must be his final descent.

"It is growing late. Soon it will be time for luncheon. Mama will expect you there, clean and dry!"

"Poor Mr Sullivan," Miriam murmured to Bennetta. "I fear he would like this sport to continue all day. Stopping for luncheon must seem like a poor excuse to him. He is used to days full of action."

Mr Avery looked up from where he was standing with his sketch pad open. He shivered and pulled his cloak tightly around his shoulders.

"I do declare it grows even colder. I think I will walk to the bottom of the hill and watch them descend. I will attempt a sketch of the sledge moving. It should make a pretty picture for your mother, Miss Anne. Can I escort you? And Miss Bennetta?

Miss Miriam?" He laughed. "I only have two arms, I fear, but I am sure Mr Sullivan will also oblige to help you young ladies back to the house."

"Oh, don't worry about Mirry and me," Bennetta said cheerfully, her eyes full of mischief. "We can support each other and if I am not very mistaken, Mr Sullivan wants to use Fitz's sledge for the final run!"

Edmund Avery hesitated, then doffed his hat and held out his arm for Anne, whose cheeks were suddenly very pink at his attentions, and together they moved away down the path.

"You read my mind very well, Miss Bennetta," Nicholas Sullivan said with a grin.

"Oh no, Sir. Please do not attribute such powers to me. My cousin was the one to point out what is your heart's desire at this very moment."

"My heart's desire?" Nicholas' voice as he turned to gaze at Miriam, was very low, almost confused, as if she had asked him a question to which he had no clear answer.

"Sir! Sir!" Henry lunged cheerfully through the snow to their side. "I have had a good thought. If you were to sit behind me this time, then surely my sledge would go even faster, because of your weight! Isn't that the science of it, Sir?"

Miriam watched as the sailor's eyes gleamed and he agreed. Linking her arm with Bennetta's they stood on the edge of the slope and watched as the sledge, now heavily laden, was pushed away from the summit and careered down the slope at a tremendous speed, snow flying from under it as Henry's joyous shouts echoed back up the hill.

"Oh how wonderful that looks!" Bennetta echoed Miriam's own feelings. "It is so unfair that we are not allowed to take part, just because we are women."

Just then, through the clear, crisp air came the sound the luncheon bell being rung.

"We will be late for lunch. Aunt Elizabeth will be displeased."

"Unless we go down very, very quickly!" Bennetta's eyes were sparkling and Miriam gazed at her for a second, then laughed joyfully as they rushed across to the other sledge. Skirts and petticoats hampered them for a few seconds but at last, casting all doubts aside, Miriam found herself sitting behind her cousin, with her arms wrapped round her waist.

"Hold tight!" And with a shout she pushed off with her feet as she had seen the boys do and then they were sliding, faster and faster, almost flying through the air. She could hear Bennetta screaming and her face was burning with cold speed, she was alive once more.

Then all was tumbling, choking snow as the sledge turned over and she was flung out into a drift. Half laughing, half sobbing, she struggled to free herself and then hands were under arms, pulling her upright and Nicholas Sullivan was there, brushing the snow from her hair for her bonnet was long gone. And on her other side, Edmund Avery was all concern and consideration.

"Miss Malliot! Are you all right? What possessed you to do that? You could both have been killed."

But Miriam could tell from the expression on the sailor's face that he was not that angry; that he admired their spirit and determination.

Before she could reply a shadow fell across them. Mr Darcy had rescued Bennetta from the snow, his face dark with annoyance.

"Thank you, Sullivan, Avery. I am glad they are unhurt, but please, I do not wish to keep you from your luncheon. I will bring the girls back to the house in a moment or two."

Nicholas hesitated, but faced with his host's implacable expression, he could do no more than bow and retreat back along the path. Edmund Avery started to speak, then he too bowed and return to where he had left Anne standing, looking shocked.

"Bennetta! I am ashamed of you. How dare you do something so reckless, to put yourself and your cousin in danger?" Hands on her shoulders, Mr Darcy knew he was being too abrupt, too condemning, but his heart was still racing from seeing his youngest daughter being thrown from the sledge like a raggedy doll.

Why did this child of his manage to arouse such mixed feelings in him? She was the only one who could make him so angry because at the back of his mind was his memory of Lydia Bennett, the way she laughed at life, her self-centred ways and how she had nearly ruined all their lives by her behaviour.

Miriam cast a swift glance at her cousin's face. She had been laughing only moments earlier, now her normally bright cheeks were white and she seemed to flinch from her father's anger like a puppy that was about to be reprimanded. Impulsively Miriam stepped forward.

"Sir, please do not be angry with Bennetta. It is all my fault. She tried to stop me but I wanted to sledge very much and persuaded her to accompany me. I thought it would be safer than being alone, but I am very sorry to have caused you any distress."

Her uncle turned to her. "Miriam! You are saying you were at fault? That this was your decision? Then I apologize, Bennetta, for blaming you but you should have done more to stop your cousin. She is very new to this country and our ways. It was rash of you."

"Yes, Papa. I am truly sorry," Bennetta whispered.

"Well, no permanent damage has been done it seems. Run along now, both of you, into the house and change for luncheon. Mrs Darcy will be wondering what has become of us and when Anne tells her what has happened, she will be worried."

The two girls scurried away to the house. Miriam was shaking with cold; she was soaked through, snow had sifted inside her boots and down the neck of her dress. Bonnet and gloves had all disappeared.

"Thank you, Mirry," Bennetta said softly as they reached the door. "You need not have spoken up and lied in such a fashion. I am quite used to Papa being angry with me."

"Oh la, I do not care what your papa thinks of me. I fear I will never be his favourite niece! But wasn't the sledging the most amazing sensation? I do not regret a second of it. Not a single second." She swept inside the house and hurried upstairs to change out of her wet clothes.

Bennetta followed more slowly. She had twisted her ankle a little when she fell out of the sledge but would never tell anyone. Her father's anger did not surprise her; she only hoped Anne had not painted too bad a picture of the accident to her mama. But the image she recalled most as she brushed out her black curls in front of her mirror was that of her cousin, standing covered in snow, bright red hair gleaming, with a gentleman on each side of her, glowering at each other like two dogs with one bone.

CHAPTER 10

Nicholas Sullivan strode through the woods surrounding the great park of Pemberley, his strong boots making light work of the melting snow that lay all around. The thaw had come unexpectedly, much to the disappointment of the Darcy boys who had hoped to sledge again. Now all the streams that trickled from the surrounding hills and woods were in full flood, racing towards the river that usually meandered gently past Pemberley but could now be heard roaring and splashing on its way east.

Annoyed at himself, Nicholas tightened his fists as he strode back towards the house. Up at dawn, forgoing breakfast, he'd walked for miles, glad to be outside where the cold wind could freshen his mind. He was so unused to being indoors, he felt imprisoned, even in the luxurious apartments of Pemberley.

A few days previously, before the thaw, he had been determined to return to London but for some reason had lingered in Derbyshire, telling himself that it was pointless leaving before he heard from his uncle that there were no more likely silk factory premises for him to inspect. But he had the nagging sensation that that was just an excuse.

He admitted to himself that he felt in some way responsible for Miriam Malliot, which was ridiculous. He had looked out for her on the *Sea Sprite* - because the irritating girl was always in danger of falling overboard - and tried to help her when she landed in Gravesend, there was no reason to believe she was in need of any assistance from him now. No reason at all. Her complete disregard for her own safety, illustrated by her behaviour in the snow, had shown him that she cared little for anyone's opinion.

But even though she was surrounded by relatives, living in luxury, Nicholas had the oddest feeling that the red-head was completely and utterly alone in the world, with her mother so far away, and that her cousins, aunts and uncles did not have her best interests at heart. If they had, surely they would have seen that Edmund Avery's regard for her was not suitable.

Unobserved by either, Nicholas had watched the artist's manner grow more and more familiar as the days passed. He could see that Miriam thought this was friendship, but he suspected that Avery had far more than friendship on his mind!

'If she wasn't so damnably stubborn, I could perhaps speak to her, warn her not to get involved with someone like him,' he thought savagely. But he was concerned that if he once mentioned it, she would, out of sheer contrariness, fling herself even further into a relationship that wasn't just unsuitable but dangerous.

He strode out of the woods, down a path towards the river: in the distance he could see Pemberley on the far bank, the morning light gleaming golden on its elegant walls. Fed by the snows from the higher slopes, the normally gentle river was now a foaming torrent, threatening to spill over its sides; branches and leaves tossing in the spray.

Nicholas frowned. There had been a simple wooden plank footbridge that crossed the stream here; he had used it in the early hours of the morning, but since then it had obviously been swept away by the flood.

If he remembered correctly, there was a shallow area quite close to the house where large stepping stones spanned the river. Hopefully they would still be above water, otherwise he was going to have to wade across. That held no fears for him as he had tackled far worse torrents in his time at sea, but it would make him very late for luncheon and very wet, although luckily that was no great hardship as far as he was concerned!

He strode along the bank and then, as it curved towards the house, his sharp eyes caught sight of a figure on the far bank - a girl, her skirts held up over her boots, red hair showing from under her dark winter bonnet, standing on the edge of the river, gazing at the fording stones. He began to run...

Miriam had been bored and irritated all morning. Edmund Avery had cancelled their sitting in the studio yet again: Grace had delivered another note from the artist, and although she had said nothing as she handed it over, Miriam knew from the expression in the maid's eyes that she was, for some reason, delighted.

Mr Avery wrote that he had some finishing touches to make to the portrait of the Darcy children before it went on show at the ball. Miriam could quite understand that; she was sure her sketch had been ready for days and although it seemed the essence of vanity, had wondered if her early morning visits to the studio had been because he enjoyed her company!

As Grace helped her to dress, she wondered why the maid had seemed so pleased that Miriam would not be ascending to the art studio that morning. Could it be that she had arranged yet another clandestine meeting with Fletcher, the valet?

Miriam watched the girl's reflection in the mirror as she stood behind her, braiding her hair which this morning would obviously not be worn loose, as Mr Avery usually required.

There was no doubt that Grace was pretty. She had bright blue eyes, a wide mouth with very red lips and even under her maid's uniform, Miriam could see that she had a good figure. She would surely have no trouble in attracting a follower, but Miriam wondered if Fletcher was indeed the right sort of partner for her.

When she had first suspected that there was an alliance, she had thought it romantic, indeed she had not reported the liaison to her aunt as she should have done, but now...there was something about the valet that she found disturbing.

She had only ever spoken a few words to him in all the time she had been at Pemberley, but recently she had caught him looking at her whilst Edmund was sketching and she hadn't cared for the expression on his face. She had a very strong feeling that Fletcher was not a kind man and she would hate for Grace to have her heart broken. Surely continuing the relationship would be folly indeed.

On an impulse she said, "Tell me about your beau, Grace! I am sure you have one, even though you once said you did not."

For a second the other girl looked startled and Miriam could have sworn that she almost looked angry. Then her normal blank expression returned.

"I think I told you before that I have no beau at present, Miss Malliot. I was walking out with Archie, the head groom, but I no longer have plans in that direction."

With a final flick of her fingers, the thick red braid was secured, and she turned away to tidy the bedroom: Miriam felt she could ask no more, only hope that the girl's commonsense would prevail. One thought was comforting; Mr Avery and Fletcher would both be returning to London directly after the ball and it was unlikely they would ever return to Derbyshire.

The long, dull morning dragged by: Miriam wandered the great galleries and rooms, knowing she was in a bad mood but not knowing how to shake off her miseries. She wished she enjoyed reading as much as Jane and Fitz, so she, too, could find sanctuary in the library.

Anne, Bennetta and Aunt Elizabeth had left after breakfast to take charitable supplies to some elderly villagers. She would have been happy to have helped them, but it had obviously never occurred to them to ask for her assistance. It was just another indication that they saw her as a visitor and not part of the family and that saddened her.

There was no way she was going to disturb Mr Darcy in his study. Miss Reynolds informed her, with her usual thinly disguised disdain, that the Darcys were expecting visitors for luncheon and she did hope Miss Malliot would be on time.

She tried to concentrate on some embroidery, but what she wanted, what she needed desperately was fresh air, the wind in her face, being able to walk and run as far as she could.

At last she could bear the inaction no longer and pulling on a bonnet and cloak, slipped out of a side door and made her way down towards the river. A short walk would do her the world of good and she would still be back in time for luncheon.

She was well aware that she was breaking one of the rules that her aunt insisted on ever since she and Bennetta had scandalized everyone by sledging down the hill - that someone should be aware of where she was at all times - but surely an hour on her own was not going to do anyone any harm. She felt a surge of rebellion against all the regulations she had to live under.

She had apologized to her aunt for upsetting her and had to admit to herself that they had been very lucky to have escaped without mishap to life and limb. But oh, that was what had made it so exciting! The speed, the danger! She had felt alive for the first time in weeks.

The river was in full flood from the thawing snow and Miriam stood marvelling as the usually smooth ripples were hurled into brown and grey waves that smashed against the banks. Oh, it was so wonderful to be out of the house!

Taking a deep breath, she stared across the river to where the parkland stretched out towards the distant woods. Once amongst the trees, she could run and run, no one would see her and her black mood would vanish.

The big black stepping stones that led to the other side were almost covered by the rushing waters. Miriam was quite convinced that although her boots might get wet, she could jump from stone to stone easily to reach the far bank...but...if she slipped and fell, it would cause all sorts of questions to be asked. She would have to explain why she was in such desperate need of freedom to relations who seemed to have no such desire.

She was about to turn away when something caught her gaze. There, clinging to the middle stone amidst a litter of twigs and leaves was a tiny scrap of very wet fur. Even as she watched, a small pink mouth gaped open and she realised it was a kitten. Obviously swept downstream, it had reached a sort of refuge but not one that would last much longer. All doubts put aside, Miriam slid down the muddy bank into the water...

Nicholas' heart was racing as he reached the ford; even as he watched, to his horror Miriam leapt onto the first of the great flat stepping stones, the foam from the racing river splashing up over her feet.

"Miriam! Stand still! Don't move!" he yelled in a voice that needed to be heard by men at the top of tall masts in the midst of a storm at sea. She looked up, a mutinous expression on her face, gathered her skirts and jumped forward on to the middle stone.

The second Miriam landed, she knew she was in trouble. She bent and plucked the kitten from its twiggy nest, pushing it under her cape, inside her jacket where she could feel the water from its icy little body against her warm skin. But now the water was well over her boots, up to her ankles, splashing and drenching her heavy winter skirt and she was alarmed at the power of the rushing waves.

Staggering a little, she fought to keep her balance, calling on all the skills she had learnt as a child, running wild around the African villages. She feared she did not have the strength to get back to the bank and she could see that more and more large branches and piles of rubbish were being swept downstream towards her. If one of the larger branches hit her, she doubted she could remain upright.

"Miss Malliot - Miriam! Are you all right? Stand still. Don't try and move. I'm coming to get you. Don't be frightened."

"I am not frightened, Sir," she shouted back crossly. "Just getting very wet."

Nicholas fought back a grim smile as he plunged into the river and began wading across, the water up to his knees. He couldn't imagine any other girl he had ever met being brave enough to snap at him in this direst of situations. Most would have screamed and fainted, although to be fair, most would never have tried to cross the river in the first place!

At last he reached her and knew they would have to move quickly. The water was above his knees now and soon even he would be thrown off balance by the forces of nature.

"Miriam - listen - you need to jump off the rock towards me. I will catch you. Do you trust me?"

Miriam stared down at him. Trust him? Of all the men in the world, she knew he was one she shouldn't trust. She could still hear Mrs Caroline Tremaine's voice in her head, explaining that Nicholas Sullivan had meant her great harm, that once she had entered the inn he had chosen in Gravesend, anything could have happened to her! He was a sailor, not really a gentleman, as her cousin Anne had said on many an occasion.

But - but her own heart told her otherwise. This was a man who had cared for her on board ship and surely there would be an explanation for his behaviour when they landed. All she knew for certain was that she trusted him implicitly, whatever anyone else said.

Taking a deep breath, she leapt towards him, feeling strong arms crush her to him as he lifted her up and strode through the water, his feet struggling to find a grip on the river bed, until the bank was in reach and he lifted her up and she lay in the muddy grass until Nicholas was once more at her side, wet through but grinning like a small boy. He pulled her to her feet.

"Are you hurt, Miriam. I mean Miss Malliot!" He was still holding her hands, as if he was scared to let them go.

"I think we can dispense with Miss Malliot in the circumstances," she replied, realising she had lost her bonnet, again, to the river and her braid had come loose, letting her hair cascade down over her shoulders. She was wet and dirty but safe. "I must thank you for your assistance. I fear I underestimated my abilities."

He looked startled, then reluctantly letting go of her hands said gravely, "I am sure we all do that at times, but I also fear you are squeaking, Miriam."

Even as he spoke, a small tabby head appeared from under her cloak and hissed at him. He put out a finger and needle sharp teeth dug into his flesh. "You have a strong protector, it seems. Was it for him you risked your life?"

He offered her his arm and they began to walk slowly up the path towards Pemberley. Figures appeared on the steps: obviously someone had seen what had happened and the alarm had been raised.

"Miriam! My goodness, my dear girl. What has happened? Surely you are not in trouble again? I fear I must not let you out of my sight for a second. What would your mama say?" It was Aunt Elizabeth, her face all worry and concern.

Miriam swayed for a second, allowing Nicholas to relate the whole adventure, realising that he was minimizing his own role, making it sound as if the whole affair had been nothing more than a minor difficulty encountered on their morning walk. And she was pleased, because the last thing she wanted was an inquisition into her actions.

"Goodness gracious me! Can it possibly be...why yes, Mother, Father, look, it is Miriam Malliot! And - Mr Sullivan!" The horror in the tone showed that the speaker had taken in the wet, dirty, bedraggled spectacle that confronted her.

Miriam raised her eyes to stare around her in disbelief. There, just stepping down from a carriage were the Reverend and Mrs Poole and, standing gazing at her in horror, Delphine Poole, a vision of blonde loveliness in pale blue velvet, the white fur trim on her bonnet gleaming in the weak sunshine.

CHAPTER 11

"A cat! My dear Lizzie, are you telling me that Miriam put her life in danger once more to rescue a cat?" The disapproval in Mr Darcy's voice was quite clear to his wife.

"To be fair, my dear, it was a kitten. I'm sure no self-respecting cat would have got itself into such a perilous position! And Miriam's life wasn't in any great danger, although Nicholas Sullivan seemed to think it was."

She glanced sideways with raised eyebrows at her husband who was busily sharpening one of his quill pens, but her eloquent look was not noticed.

"Ridiculous child! If she'd drowned, that would have been a fine letter to have written to your sister, wouldn't it? And all for a damned cat."

Elizabeth smiled and touched his cheek. Twenty years of marriage had taught her that she could tease her husband about a lot of things but sometimes you had to know when to keep a still tongue. She had often found their house cat, an arrogant, green-eyed creature who kept the Pemberley mice population at a reasonable level, ensconced on Mr Darcy's desk, being stroked absentmindedly, but this perhaps, was a fact she would not mention at this moment.

"Don't forget her father was full of missionary zeal. His aim in life was to help people - whether they wanted him to or not! Perhaps there is more of his character in Miriam than we appreciate. I remember Mary telling me in a letter many years ago that the girl was always rescuing injured birds, lost dogs - she even brought home a small pig once!"

"She is certainly nothing like her mother. Indeed, she is nothing like any young girl I have ever known. I sometimes feel we are harbouring one of those wild, exotic birds in the house and must approach it with care. I can forgive her for trying to rescue the kitten, but she left the house without informing anyone that she was doing so, after I had expressly asked her not to after the sledging incident; that is what I am annoyed about. There is still snow on the ground and accidents can happen quite easily on the steep slopes and in the woods. She might not have been missed until it was too late."

"Where is she now?"

"I sent her and Mr Sullivan to wash and change. The Poole family is waiting for us in the yellow drawing-room and we will all have luncheon together. The rest of our family have vanished to the four winds. The thought of a meal with the Reverend Poole did not appeal to them, apparently!"

"It is a strange coincidence that the gentleman charged with Miriam's safety on board ship is to have the Lambton living."

Elizabeth nodded. "Yes, it makes for a much stronger connection than perhaps we would have wished for. I can see, for example, that we must ask them to be guests at the ball next week. I am sure Miss Delphine will be only too pleased to attend. She is a pretty little thing and apparently out, even though she is only sixteen."

"Have they, perhaps, heard from Mary? It seems strange that we have not had a letter, telling us her plans and the name of her ship."

Elizabeth shook her head. "No, they wrote, obviously, informing Mary that their charge had been met by the Bingleys at Gravesend. Of course they did not realise exactly what had transpired. Luckily, all was well. But their letter might not even have reached Africa yet and may miss Mary altogether. Indeed, she may well be on the high seas at this very moment and the next we hear will be her knocking at our door."

She turned to go, then turned, her eyes gleaming with mischief. "Oh and although I am sure you are not interested, my dear, the kitten is in the stables where there is a mother cat who has a litter and has happily accepted another baby."

But as she made her way downstairs to take up her role of hostess, she wondered again why Miriam was so very different from her cousins, why there was no likeness to anyone in the family.

Suddenly a memory of a garden wilderness, a chill breeze and as clear as a bell, a voice she had not heard for years, that of her husband's terrifying aunt, Lady Catherine de Burgh, echoed inside her head..."Obstinate, headstrong girl..."

Luncheon was a very quiet, sedate affair. Miriam felt rushed and flustered. There had been no sign of Grace when she went upstairs to change out of her wet clothes and a query to one of the footmen brought no information. She knew she could have just rung the bell and Miss Reynolds would have appeared, but that would have meant getting Grace into trouble.

It was, indeed, very late for luncheon; perhaps the girl had thought she could sneak away and have a tryst with her beau, Fletcher, up in Mr Avery's studio. There was no way Miriam wanted to do the young girl harm by reporting her absence, so she pulled on the first dry clothes she could find, towelled her damp hair into a curly mane and hurried down the long stairways to the dining-room, aware that everyone was waiting for her.

Miriam sat at the long dinner table, her cheeks burning, eyes cast down, aware that the Reverend and Mrs Poole were looking at her with grave displeasure. They had recovered from their astonishment at finding her and Nicholas Sullivan here at Pemberley, listening to the explanations and exclaiming at the coincidences that had brought everyone together.

Mrs Poole had made it clear in a quiet aside that Miriam should have mentioned the Darcys to them instead of just talking about the Bingley family. Their annoyance seemed to be centred on what they obviously considered her lack of manners in not talking of her very wealthy relations and her extremely unseemly behaviour down at the river. They apologized profusely to her aunt and uncle, as if they were in some way responsible for the way she had acted.

Miriam fought to keep her temper under control. A confrontation with the Reverend and his wife would be considered unacceptable behaviour to their guests by the Darcys.

She wondered what they would say if she told them she had lied to Mrs Poole on the dockside in Gravesend. That she had always known the dark green carriage she had spied in the distance had not belonged to the Bingleys and that Mrs Caroline Tremaine had been forced to rescue their charge from a situation that could possibly have led Miriam into unbelievable dangers.

Delphine was sitting across the table, next to Nicholas, demure and pretty in blue velvet, cut in the very latest fashion, the skirt full, the waist tight, sleeves billowing down to tight wrist bands, a fine woollen shawl covering the fairly low cut bodice.

Miriam was amazed that a Reverend's daughter could afford such clothes. Her own dear papa had never had a spare penny to spend on a wardrobe for her. She wondered if decking out her daughter in such finery was a deliberate ploy by Mrs Poole. That lady had made it quite clear to Miriam that finding Delphine a husband was one of the most important tasks in her life.

Miriam watched the girl now, one golden curl flicking against Nicholas' broad shoulder every time he bent his head to speak to her: she was finding difficulty in peeling an apple and he had taken over the task, using his own pocket knife, a fearsome implement, instead of the silver fruit knife one of the footmen had offered.

Delphine was giggling as he attempted to take all the peel from the fruit in one long curl and Miriam thought crossly that she had never heard such an aggravating sound. She recalled that Nicholas had always seemed very attentive to Delphine on board the *Sea Sprite,* was obviously delighted to be reacquainted with her once more, and had no idea why that should annoy her so much.

From the other end of the table, she could see Mrs Poole gazing at the couple with a look of contentment on her face. Indeed, Nicholas Sullivan would be considered a great catch for her daughter.

Edmund Avery was seated next to her and with the absence of all the Darcy children from the table, turned his attention to Miriam. "I was deeply distressed to learn of the danger that befell you this morning, Miss Malliot. Especially as you had just recovered from your accident on the snow slope."

She could hear the depth of feeling in his tone and felt warm colour flood into her cheeks. Here was someone who was thinking about her safety, not just her behaviour. "I fear the danger has been greatly exaggerated, Sir, but I thank you for your concern."

"It always surprises me when people tell me that London is a dangerous city - during my visit I have noticed that far more alarming events can occur here in the countryside or - " he smiled courteously across the table at Nicholas - "on board one of your sailing ships, Mr Sullivan."

"Oh, you are so correct, Sir," Delphine broke in. "I was terrified for most of our journey home from South Africa. The vessel and the men who sailed her were so rough - apart from Mr Sullivan, of course!" she added hastily, recollecting who was sitting at her side.

"Surely a little danger gives a certain spice to life," Miriam said, remembering how much she had enjoyed being on deck as the *Sea Sprite* battled through rough weather.

Edmund smiled at her, his dark eyes gleaming. "Ah, I know from your recent exploits that you are a young lady who might well appreciate taking a risk. Indeed, the face that I saw before me when I started your sketch is that of a young woman keen to experience adventure, to explore sensations. The sketch is finished now; I shall be happy to show it to you. Perhaps we can make a time for you to come up to the studio?"

"Thank you, Sir. My mama will be delighted to receive it. But as for your other remarks, I fear the life of a young woman even in this day and age is too constrained to encounter many risks."

"That is true and we gentlemen do everything in our power to keep you ladies safe." He bowed round the table. "But if you were ever offered an opportunity to - say - cast off the ropes of caution that bind you in society, would you do so? Believe me, the sense of freedom that such an action can give is beyond price."

Miriam smiled back, uncertainly. There had been a strange tone to his question that she did not truly understand, but even the thought of freedom of speech, freedom of movement and action fizzed through her veins like hot wine.

She was about to speak when there was a crash opposite her and Nicholas was on his feet, apologizing, as the peeled apple he had been holding had fallen to the table top, along with his knife, smashing the dessert plate in front of him.

"My abject apologies, Mrs Darcy, for my carelessness. I trust I have not spoilt your dinner set."

"Pray, do not worry, Mr Sullivan. These minor mishaps are part and parcel of life when you have a large family and a son as clumsy as young Henry."

A footman soon cleared away the broken pieces, Nicholas returned the knife to his pocket and the conversation reverted to the weather. The meal progressed without further incident, but Miriam could not help but wonder. She had watched Nicholas Sullivan for many weeks as they travelled north from Cape Town. In all that time she had never known him be clumsy or careless, especially whilst holding a knife.

The Pooles' departed after lunch, all effusive politeness to their hosts, obviously delighted to receive an invitation from Mrs Darcy to attend the Pemberley ball on the coming weekend.

Miriam made her goodbyes, shutting her ears as best she could to Mrs Poole's admonishments to behave in a way of which her dear mother would approve and was hastening back to her room when Nicholas called after her.

"Miss Malliot, Miriam, if you will allow because I find I cannot call you Miss Malliot since our escapade in the river and I trust you will see fit to call me Nicholas. But you seem well and not upset by the cold and wet."

"Not at all - Nicholas. I am no delicate flower that needs protection from the elements."

He raised an eyebrow at her fierce tone. With flashing brown eyes and her mane of red hair, she was a sight to stir the blood of any man. "Indeed, I am certain that 'delicate' would never be a word I would associate with you."

Miriam remained silent and turned away. She was well aware that she was taller than any of the Darcy girls and could certainly only come off the worst in any comparison to Delphine Poole, who was small, slight and with her long white neck and yellow curls, the epitome of a delicate spring flower. In comparison, with her untidy red hair she felt she resembled one of the great clumps of weeds that grew along the river bank.

But even though she harboured no great delusions regarding her looks, it was never pleasing to be reminded that most gentlemen would find her physical demeanor unattractive to their eye.

Steeling herself, Miriam turned back to her companion. "I must, however, thank you for your assistance at the river. I do not think I was in any great danger, but the current was, I admit, faster than I had imagined."

The First Officer fell silent. He disagreed, he thought she had been in very great danger. If she had fallen, she could easily have hit her head on one of the stones and been swept away. But her actions had been governed by her headstrong character, an impulsive nature, the same nature that had encouraged her to sledge down the hillside with her cousin, that allowed her to make decisions about people and be loathe to change them.

He had been worried about Miriam before today, because of her obdurate belief in Edmund Avery's good character. Watching and listening to him at luncheon had only confirmed Nicholas' concern that she might well be in danger from the worldly-wise artist. There had been a lasciviousness in Avery's expression when he had spoken of risks and danger that set alarm bells ringing.

"We can all get carried away, by feelings as well as floods."

The words were spoken before he had thought them through and suddenly he realised that the torrent of feelings he had for this girl were threatening to overwhelm him. When had he fallen in love with her? He didn't know, only that he was, and although it was ridiculous to think she could or would ever return those feelings, he knew he would do anything in the world to protect her.

"Miss Malliot – " It was Edmund Avery, coming towards them, smiling. "Would now be a good time for you to inspect the sketch? I am quite at your disposal."

Miriam hesitated: she wanted to see the sketch, but how could she be sure that Grace was not still up in the studio with the valet? "Thank you, Sir, but perhaps another time? I am fatigued and would rest."

She was aware of Nicholas sending her a sharp glance, almost as if he didn't believe her, but Edmund just bowed, elegantly, and left the room.

"Miriam, my dear." It was Mrs Darcy. "I have received a letter from my sister Jane, who is feeling a lot stronger and would love to meet you. She will not be coming to the ball on Saturday, so I thought you and Bennetta could perhaps travel to Clifton Park tomorrow. It is just twenty miles, easy driving on the turnpike. You should be there in time for lunch and back home again in the evening."

"Oh, that sounds wonderful." Miriam was delighted that she was at last going to meet her Aunt Jane, the one sister whom her mother had truly liked.

"Unless you have made other arrangements, I will be quite happy to accompany the two young ladies," Nicholas said abruptly. "Indeed, I do have a little business to conduct with Mr Charles Bingley on my uncle's behalf. He owns property in Lambton that might be of interest."

Elizabeth Darcy hesitated but, even though she had her own ideas as to his reasons for wanting to accompany Miriam, there was no reason to forbid him. And, after all, Bennetta would be with them as chaperone. What could possibly go wrong?

CHAPTER 12

"So are you ready to meet more of our family?" Bennetta leant forward as the carriage jolted along the road, swaying from side to side. She was sitting opposite Miriam, wrapped in a fur rug against the cold, even though their feet were resting on stone bottles filled with hot water to keep away the chill of the early spring morning.

Miriam was enjoying the journey; she could hear the head groom, Archie, shouting encouragement to the horses and knew that Nicholas was sitting next to him on the box. He had smiled as he'd handed her into the carriage, his touch warm through the material of her glove. His smile warmed her, too, and she found it hard to concentrate as he said that he always preferred to be outside in the fresh air when possible and by so doing would leave more room for the two of them inside.

She thought it must be very cold, both for the coachman and Nicholas but imagined the thrill of the movement diminished any feelings of discomfort. She only wished that she had a chance to travel like that herself, sitting next to Nicholas as they sped along the road behind the cantering horses. The inside of the carriage was dark and luxurious but Miriam hated being shut in, longed for the fresh air in her face, being able to stare out to far distances, rather than just watch trees and bushes pass by through the window.

She realised suddenly that Bennetta was gazing at her strangely and replied with a guilty start, "Of course I am anxious to meet our Aunt Jane, yes. Mother always speaks highly of her." She realised that her cousin might well ask whom her mama did not speak well of, but luckily Bennetta was not paying attention.

"Aunt Jane is a saint. The loveliest person I know, apart from my own mother, of course. And, to be fair, she is prettier than mama! Although I would never dream of saying that to anyone but you."

"I am sorry to learn that she has such ill health. Aunt Elizabeth always looks so concerned when speaking of her."

Bennetta sighed and wrapped the rug closely round her legs. "She was always well when we were children. Why, she and Mama used to take us on picnics up on the hills, or drive into Lambton to shop or visit the travelling fair every year. Then to everyone's surprise - Mama and Papa were really shocked, although they pretended they weren't - she gave birth to little Alethea, who is nearly two. Our youngest cousin - until Cassandra has her baby, who will be a second cousin, I suppose. Goodness, we have such a large family. I have a notebook in which to keep a record of everyone's birthdays!"

"Cassandra is our Aunt Lydia's daughter, isn't she?"

"Yes, as you know, she lives with her husband, Dr Richard Courtney at Wyvern Lodge, which is next door to the Bingley estate. Cassandra is my closest friend in all the world. I fear I am far fonder of her than I am of Anne! I love Jane dearly, but Anne annoys me so much.

"Our Aunt Lydia lives in Newcastle which is a large town a great many miles away in the north. I like her a great deal; she is funny and lively and makes me laugh with the outrageous things she says and does. Papa does not approve of her at all! He abhors Mama asking her to stay, although of course sometimes it is only courteous to do so. But I fear she and her husband, a Colonel Allerton, disapprove of Cassandra's marriage and Aunt Lydia has only been to stay with them once in all these months."

Miriam was anxious not to get involved in that conversation, although she had a fellow feeling for her Aunt Lydia. She was quite certain that Mr Darcy did not approve of her, either! "And we have Bingley cousins, of course."

"Lord, yes. Beth - we call her Beth, although she was named Elizabeth after mama - is just a few days younger than the twins. She was nineteen on the 1st of January and a sweet, kind girl. Then there is George who is a few months older than me. He will not be at home; he is a scholar at Oxford University, although I have no idea why because he is not very clever. Then comes Sophia who must be nearly fourteen and the baby, Alethea."

Miriam sank back in her seat, trying to keep all the names straight in her mind. It would be interesting to meet her cousins, of course, but she knew with a weary sort of certainty that she would have nothing in common with Beth and Sophia Bingley.

They had been born into a gentle life of luxury, as had Bennetta. What did they know of making every penny count, of wearing shoes that had paper thin soles because there was no money for new ones, of having enough to eat but nothing fancy or extravagant, not enough in the bank to purchase books, to own a horse, to learn how to ride? She had seen her aunt's face this morning when, over breakfast, Miriam had confessed that she had never learnt to ride.

She had felt like crying out - where do you think your sister could find the money to buy and stable a pony? Where would the guineas come from to pay for her daughter to have riding lessons? Has it never crossed your mind over all these years that we were poor out in Africa, with no great incomes to spend as the mood took us?

She tried to chase away the thoughts that surfaced so often in her mind - that her aunts and uncles could well have helped her own dear mama much more in the past. "Will the Bingleys attend the ball on Saturday?"

Bennetta shook her head, dark curls escaping from her bonnet. "No - Aunt Jane and Uncle Bingley will certainly not come, Sophia is not out yet. As for Beth..." She fell silent.

"As for Beth?"

"She has been asked, of course, and I know Mama invited her to stay with us at Pemberley for a few days. But she said she could not leave her mother or Alethea. I don't know what will happen when I have my official coming out party. My birthday is at the end of May and the ball will happen some time after that.

"Mama and Anne wish it to be held in London - and I must agree there are a great many eligible young men in town who would be invited to attend. We know everyone around here already. Why there will not be a single strange face to be seen on Saturday, which could prove boring."

Frowning, Miriam turned over these words as the carriage swayed on. She sensed there was a lot that Bennetta was not saying, a lot that she disapproved of, but it would be wrong of her to comment without knowing the whole situation. And one short visit was not going to make that much difference to her understanding.

"Oh, stop! Archie, Mr Sullivan. Please stop the carriage!" Bennetta hammered on the roof and there was a shout of alarm as the horses were pulled to a walk and then to a stop. A thud from outside and Nicholas appeared at the door, opening it, his face a mask of worry.

"Miss Bennetta, Miriam - are you all right? Is there a problem?"

"No, I'm sorry, I didn't mean to leave it so late to tell you, but look, we are in Clifton village - and just here is the little road that leads up to Cassandra's house. I've decided to visit her. No...no, don't interrupt, Mirry. You can have Aunt Jane all to yourself. I can see her any time and you might well be living away down in the south of England very soon."

As she was speaking, Bennetta jumped out of the carriage in a flurry of amber velvet and rouched petticoats. Confused, Miriam followed her.

"Archie! Archie, tie down the reins and leave them to Mr Sullivan. I am sure he is quite capable of driving the carriage the rest of the journey. You can come with me and when I have finished my visit, you will accompany me to Clifton Park. The gates to the Bingley house are about a quarter of a mile down this road, Mr Sullivan. You can't miss them. There is a lodge and an elderly servant and his wife who live there - just call out and they will come: you will not have to dismount to open the gates. Give my regards to my aunt, Mirry. I'll see you all in a little while."

And before Nicholas or Miriam could reply, she waved and ran off down the track. Archie flung a distraught glance at Nicholas, then turned and hurried after her.

There was a silence, broken only by the stamping of impatient hooves and the sound of birds high up in the trees that lined the road. Then Nicholas laughed - "Your cousin is the most extraordinary young lady it has ever been my misfortune to meet."

Miriam tried to look shocked, but found herself smiling. "In the short time I have known her, I have realised that she does like to get her own way."

"Heaven help the man who bravely decides to make her his wife!" Nicholas grinned and sprang back up into the driving seat.

Miriam hesitated, surprised and hurt that he had not helped her into the carriage, but remembering suddenly that he was not a proper gentleman.

"Give me your hand, Miriam."

She looked up to find Nicholas leaning down, the reins in one hand, the other, broad and tanned, reaching towards her. "Surely you would prefer to ride up here in the open air, rather than be shut inside, even if it is for just a short journey? Or is the climb too steep for you?"

Miriam tossed her head, and ignoring his outstretched hand, picked up her skirts and climbed neatly up the metal rungs, onto the driving seat next to him. "Not so steep, Sir!"

Nicholas laughed and slapping the reins, urged the horses into a steady walk that quickened into a trot. Miriam gasped as the jolting was more severe than when you were inside the carriage. She clasped the side of the box and found herself smiling as the clean wind reddened her cheeks. She filled her lungs, thinking she could never have enough of this exhilaration.

All too soon the gates of Clifton Park came into view in the distance; there was the lodge as Bennetta had explained and

Nicholas was drawing on the reins, slowing the horses to a walk, almost as if he did not want the journey to end.

He turned his head; Miriam's bonnet had slipped down her back, held round her neck by its wide ribbons. Her glorious red hair was trying to escape from its thick braid, curling round her face in little flicks of flame. "I fear we must turn in here. Your aunt will no doubt be anxiously waiting for you. Of course..."

"Of course?"

"The horses are not tired and it is a clear road ahead for about a mile, as far as I can see. Shall we let them have their heads?"

She gasped. Every sensible bone in her body told her she should say no, that they should pass through the gates and amble slowly up the long drive to the house. But she knew that this was probably the only chance she would ever have to ride with Nicholas in this fashion. Soon he would be away to his ship and she would be journeying down to the south of England, to find a little cottage where she and her mother could spend the rest of their lives, the poor relations of the family. And, she wanted to rebel, to speed with him through the clear spring morning, free of all restraints.

Nicholas took one look at her face and didn't wait for a reply. With a shout and a slap of the reins, the horses were gathered up and broke from their walk into a canter. It was the most reckless thing he had ever done. Even as he heard the girl next to him laughing with delight, he knew they were being completely irresponsible, but he didn't care. He had never heard her laugh so happily before, never seen that reserved expression alter into one of pure happiness and joy.

At the end of a mile, he slowed the team, carefully steered the carriage round a small green triangle where two roads met and headed back the way they had come. He was aware that Miriam was holding his arm and although he knew it was to stop her from falling off, he delighted in the feel of her hand on his sleeve.

"Shall we tell them the horses bolted?"

He glanced at her and realised she was smiling, her expression full of mischief. What a girl she was! Wild and tempestuous, no milk and water maiden, there was no way she belonged in this green and placid country. Was this what Edmund Avery saw, he wondered. Would this show in the sketch he had drawn, when they were allowed to see it. If so, it would cause quite a stir in the Darcy family.

"Hopefully no one will enquire! Look, the lodge keeper has heard us and is opening the gates. We must put aside our rebelliousness and become good and staid citizens once more."

Miriam dropped her hand from his arm and struggled to pull on her bonnet and tidy herself in order to meet her new relations looking as respectable as her mama would have wished if she had been here.

But she knew now that her feelings for Nicholas, this flood of emotion that coursed through her body, was not just the effect of the headlong carriage ride. She had to admit that she was falling in love with the sailor. And she also knew that would lead to heart-break. Nicholas would soon vanish back to his ship; he had no possible interest in a wife and even if he did, she was certain that he would choose someone meek and compliant, such as Delphine.

Nicholas liked to look after people; that was obvious. He had often become impatient with her attempts at independence and although he might well admire her strength of character, it would a docile, pleasantly agreeable girl he would want as his companion in life, not Miss Miriam Malliot!

As the day slowly progressed, Miriam realised that the whole way of life at Clifton Park was centred on her Aunt Jane and she could well understand why. She had never before met a woman with such a beautiful face and even though she was lying on a chaise and looked thin and pale, nothing could deter from her gentle manner and fine features. From her chaise she controlled the whole household with a sweetness of approach that brought instant loyalty and obedience from her servants and the obvious devotion of her husband and children.

Mr Bingley proved to be a civil, well-mannered gentleman with an open, honest face, marred only by a constant worried frown. He, had welcomed Miriam warmly to his home, hoped she was finding England everything she had hoped, exclaimed at her height, the redness of her hair, asked after her mother and then vanished into his study with Nicholas.

Jane had held out her hand, drawing Miriam to her, to sit on the chaise at her feet. She seemed delighted to meet her and pleased that Mary would soon be with them in England. Putting her niece at ease with the kindest of questions, Miriam could well understand why Bennetta called her Aunt Jane a saint. There was none of Aunt Darcy's crisp tones and words, just a lovely nature and a belief in the goodness of people and life.

It was puzzling: Aunt Jane was obviously a good person - had she not seen the unhappiness of her younger sister? How Mary had been excluded, mocked by her father, tolerated by her mother? Or did her very good nature mean that she could never have imagined such a thing happening?

Miriam was introduced briefly to little Alethea before the child was taken away by her nurse. Her cousin Beth was nearly as pretty as her mother, with fair curls and ringlets that fell to her shoulders, but she frowned a great deal and her expression was worried and thoughtful. She sat close by, on the edge of her seat, ready to hand Jane Bingley a glass of water or a handkerchief, a book or a piece of embroidery the second she asked for it.

"So tell me, Miriam, do you think Mary will enjoy living in England once more?"

"I think so, Aunt Jane. Obviously it is an entirely different way of life, but then Mama spent her childhood and younger years in Hertfordshire, so I am sure she will soon get used to everything once more."

"I am told by Lizzie that she and Mr Darcy are hoping to find a cottage for you near to our own mama and Kitty in Meryton. It is a small town, to be sure, but a cheerful one full of good people. And with Mr Collins, Kitty's husband, so well placed in church circles, I am sure you and Mary will be very happy there."

Miriam gazed round the well-appointed drawing-room, not as large and lavish as those in Pemberley, but in comfort a world away from the little house she had lived in with her parents in South Africa. She hated to ask these relations - even one as kind and good natured as her Aunt Jane - for more favours, but was forced to do so for her mama's sake.

"Will the cottage be furnished, do you think? If not, I fear I must ask you and my aunts for a few pieces of furniture, crockery, kitchen utensils and such like."

Jane Bingley looked puzzled.

"Well, of course Lizzie and I will provide anything that Mary wants and I am sure Kitty and Lydia will help within their means. But Miriam, surely your mother will have packed up your African home and have arranged for it to be shipped here to England?

"I suppose it would be a nonsense bringing carpets and curtains as they may well not fit, but your beds, chairs, books - indeed, I am sure Mary has a favourite dinner service she would like to use over here for entertaining. But perhaps it has been decided that the cost of shipping everything is more than what it will be to have everything new. I can see that argument very clearly. It is one I would make myself."

Miriam bit her lip and gazed out of the window. At the end of the path that lead to an orchard she could see the familiar figure of Nicholas Sullivan. How she wished he was here; his support would have been invaluable.

"I think that your ideas of how we live in Africa are far from reality. To be blunt, Aunt Jane, we are poor. The only income my father had was from the church and he tended to give away most of that to people he thought needed it more than his family."

Jane struggled to sit up, her pale cheeks flushed pink and her daughter bent over her, anxiously rearranging the pillows until she was comfortable once more.

"Miriam, I do not understand. I can well believe that you did not live in the same state as the Darcys, or even as we do here at Clifton Park, but your parents had an annual allowance from both our families, as our way of helping their charitable work. And there was one large sum that was sent out to Africa so your dear father could start his own school, buy the building, desks, books, etc. He was to take in paying pupils and make a reasonable income in that way. So why have you been living in such a poor fashion?"

Miriam stared at her in complete confusion, her mind whirling. This would explain how her papa had bought his school, of course, but she had seen no sign of extra gifts of money arriving over the years. Her parents would not have felt it necessary to tell her when she was a child, but surely as she had grown older, it would have been mentioned?

So where had the money gone? It certainly hadn't appeared in the form of food on the table, or on their backs in the way of better clothing. Their home had been shabby and in bad repair; no guineas had been spent there.

A cold thought crept through the heat of her confusion. Had her mama known of the money? She recalled the bitterness that had been evident in her every conversation about the Darcys, Collinses and Bingleys. Bitterness that Mary had been forgotten, overlooked, once again become the child who had no friends, received no affection.

Jane Bingley could see the distress her words had caused and chided herself for speaking before thinking. She and her sisters had had no idea of the conditions in which Mary lived. Her infrequent letters had made no mention of her life style, although they had sensibly realised it must be less than theirs.

"Your papa..." she began.

Miriam, her cheeks flushed with shame at the thought of being disloyal, broke in swiftly.

"Papa was the most generous man I have ever known. He read the Scriptures daily and his biggest belief in life was that you should give everything you could spare to the deserving poor."

Jane sank back onto her cushions, exhausted by her sudden outburst, well aware that the rest of her family would find that explanation annoying. Mr Darcy and her own husband had sent packages of guineas out to Africa every year for the comfort of the Malliot family. To think that it had all been given away was laudable, but she wondered if Mary had even known. The sister she remembered would surely have made certain that even if they had not lived in luxury, her daughter's life was as easy as possible.

"Mama, you look tired. You should rest." Anxiously, Beth placed a handkerchief soaked in lavender water on her mother's forehead. "I am sorry, Miriam, but Mama must have quiet. She is not strong."

"Of course. I am so sorry, Aunt Jane. I will walk in the gardens until Bennetta arrives."

"Beth, you must accompany your cousin. I will sleep for a while. There is no need for you to sit with me. The fresh air will do you good."

Reluctantly, Beth fetched her cloak and bonnet and the two girls walked out into the gardens that were beginning to show all the signs of Spring. The afternoon sun was warming the air, pushing back the chill of winter.

"I am sorry if I have caused your mother distress." Miriam swung her bonnet by its ribbons, declining to wear it, enjoying the feel of the breeze on her face. She felt she had to apologize, although she believed the distress she was feeling far outweighed that of her aunt's.

Beth sighed, her beautiful face marred by worry. "She gets tired very easily; Papa and I are concerned about her all the time."

"But she has a good doctor, I am sure. What does he say?"

"Our doctor here in Clifton is a Doctor Marchwood. He says that having Alethea was a strain on her health, but that Mama will get stronger as the months pass. Papa believes him but, oh cousin, I do not! I wish she would consult Richard Courtney - I believe he is a very fine doctor with modern ideas - but Papa says it would not be advisable as he is part of our extended family now.

"I fear she grows weaker, not stronger, and we try to keep any sad or distressing news from her. I fear she will be most unhappy when she recounts your conversation to my father. She has always believed that Aunt Mary led a happy life out in Africa, one of piety and service to others: she always told us that that was part of her sister's character."

Miriam glanced at the girl by her side. "Oh then you must tell her that you spoke to me and I insisted that our lives were happy, because they were. Indeed, I may not have had much in the way of possessions, but I enjoyed far more freedom than any of the cousins I have met so far."

Beth smiled her thanks. "But you can see why I choose not to leave Clifton, even for a few days. I would love to attend the ball on Saturday, for I enjoy dancing, but I am needed here. Sophia is not yet fourteen, a mere child still in many ways. I cannot expect her to attend to Mama. I believe we are all given a role in life to play and this is mine."

At the end of the path they were walking, a gate lead into an orchard and in the distance Miriam could see Nicholas talking to Bennetta. "I understand and I am certain the Darcys do as well."

"I am not so sure about that, but I can feel that you have a fellow feeling for me. After all, you will be your own mama's sole help and support in the years to come, won't you? In fact your situation is probably worse than mine because I, at least, have a father, brother and sisters to support me. I am more sorry for you, Miriam, than I can say, because you will have to face that task all on your own."

Under the apple trees that were just showing the first budding of curled leaves, Nicholas found his attention drifting away from Bennetta's chatter. He was gazing back up the pathway to where

Miriam stood talking to the oldest of the Bingley girls. Her hair, uncovered, blazed like a flame against the pale stone of the house. His vision, sharpened by constant viewing of distant horizons, made it clear to him that she was unhappy. Whatever the other girl was saying, it had brought a frown to her face and that was something he hated to see.

Bennetta glanced up sharply at her companion, although her chatter did not cease. She had seen that look on gentlemen's faces before: her papa when sometimes he looked at her mama and didn't think anyone was paying attention, Richard when he looked at Cassandra and Sir Robert Courtney during his wedding ceremony to Catherine. It was an expression that made the sternest face soften. So, she thought, that was interesting and probably very sad because she was certain Miriam had feelings for the artist Edmund Avery.

Bennetta suddenly declared crossly that she had caught her shawl on a rose bush that clambered over a trellis and would Nicholas please detach it for her. She watched as he recovered himself and attended to her problem, his blunt, tanned fingers seemingly impervious to being scratched. Yes, he certainly did not have the hands of a gentleman, she thought, but there was something about his brisk, forthright, nature that appealed to her.

"Tell me, Mr Sullivan," she asked innocently, "if you were a married man, would your wife accompany you on board your ship?"

Nicholas looked down at her but Bennetta was turned away from him and he could not see her face. "Well, it does happen, yes, but only if the lady in question enjoys travelling and the shipboard life. It is a very hard environment for a woman."

"Oh, I am sure it must be. When I was younger, I wanted to run away from home and become a pirate, but as I have grown old, I realise that I like my comforts too much."

Nicholas released the shawl and found himself smiling. "Of course you are very old now, Miss Bennetta, I appreciate that! So perhaps the life of a pirate is not for you."

"And do you wish to find yourself a wife who would travel with you?"

There was a long silence, then, "What I would wish for myself and what would be appropriate behaviour are two very different things. If my ship was trading round the Mediterranean, then possibly. But I sail to Africa and the China seas; I could not ask a lady to share such a dangerous life with me. It would be entirely unfair."

"Indeed," Bennetta murmured, watching Miriam's face as she walked towards them, swinging her bonnet, apparently enjoying the breeze in her face. The frown that had creased her brow suddenly disappeared when she drew near to Nicholas and Bennetta stored away that information with a secret smile.

CHAPTER 13

Miriam had never experienced anything like the growing sense of excitement and anticipation that surrounded Pemberley as the day drew nearer for the ball. The house reminded her of a giant beehive, everyone except her seemed to be continually busy; the servants running from place to place, trying to follow orders from several people at the same time.

All was noise and confusion, indoors and out. Arrangements were in place to care for the many horses that would be arriving with carriages and room had to be allocated for the actual carriages themselves. Their drivers would need food and drink, of course, just an extra responsibility for the kitchen staff who were already in a state of turmoil as Anne and Bennetta kept thinking of additional items of food they had to have appearing on the supper tables.

Indoors, the vast ballroom had been polished and decorated with towers of spring flowers and foliage. Miriam peeked in to watch the chalk being laid down in swirling patterns on the shiny wooden floor, so that dancing shoes did not slip and bring woe to their wearers. Adjoining rooms were prepared with tables covered in lace edged linen, ready for the copious amounts of food and drink that the kitchens were trying their best to deliver on time.

The musicians, who had come all the way from the large town of Derby, had been given their own rooms on one of the higher floors and their practicing could be heard all through the day, much to Mr Darcy's annoyance.

A small room adjoining the ballroom had been set aside for the presentation and display of Edmund Avery's painting of the Darcy children. It stood against the back wall on a large easel, covered with a velvet curtain, ready to be displayed to an admiring audience. A new work by such a distinguished artist was a very important event.

Miriam had still not seen her own sketch but she guessed that Mr Avery was very busy with the final little details on his great portrait and didn't like to bother him over such a small affair.

Miss Reynolds, usually a housekeeper whose demeanour was always smooth and serene, now wore a permanent frown and could not be parted from the notebook that she wrote in endlessly. She was constantly in consultation with the cook, a redoubtable lady with a fierce temper which was being raised to boiling point by the demands being made by the young ladies of the house.

Elizabeth Darcy was everywhere, organising, cajoling, settling arguments, trying to keep everyone calm, discussing which of her many jewels her daughters would be allowed to wear, determined that Pemberley should be at its very best.

Mr Darcy and Edmund Avery, had sensibly retired to the billiards room and Nicholas realised that walking through the great park, even in the rain, was far more enjoyable than being asked his views about music or flower arrangements.

He had intended to leave for London once he returned from their visit to the Bingleys but the Darcys had insisted that he stayed for the ball. He had agreed, although he knew in his heart of hearts that he only stayed, not out of politeness to his hosts, but because he wanted to dance with Miriam. He wanted to take that memory with him, wherever he went in the world.

For the Darcy daughters there was not enough time in each day for all they needed to do to look their best. Even Jane, who usually could not have told you the colour of her dress if you had asked her to shut her eyes and remember, was busy with Tabitha, her maid, working on a lace overthrow of her cream silk.

With an impatience that drove her own maid to distraction, Anne had tried several new hair styles, all of which took at least an hour to achieve, before returning to the one she knew suited her blonde beauty the best.

Only two people found the hectic preparations boring: Miriam and Fitzwilliam Darcy.

Miriam eventually sought sanctuary in the library on the Friday morning. She still had not received any word from her mother and although her aunt had told her not to worry, that mail from Africa often took months and months to arrive, she was writing once again, hoping that her uncle could send this letter express on the fastest ship he could find.

She was beginning to have a real concern over what was happening at home. She knew her mama would have begun a letter the second *Sea Sprite* cleared the harbour breakwater, carrying Miriam away to England. It seemed so odd that nothing had yet reached her.

Miriam had left Bennetta agonizing over which dress to wear the following evening: several beautiful, costly gowns, mostly white with pink or yellow ribbons and trim, were laid out on her bed.

To Miriam's untutored eyes they all looked similar, but choosing the right one was obviously causing her cousin a great deal of distress. She seemed to have completely recovered from the disgrace of the sledging incident and now was in a state of heightened excitement waiting for their cousin Cassandra to give birth.

Elizabeth Darcy had laughingly told her daughter that babies came at their own speed, that this one was probably a few weeks from making an appearance and running to the window every five minutes to see if a messenger was in sight was not going to quicken the procedure!

Miriam hoped it would be soon; she was anxious to meet her cousin, the mysterious Lydia's daughter, whose life was already touched by scandal and gossip. She was only sorry that the circumstances had made it impossible. She was sure that Cassandra would have been only too happy to have received her, but she was reluctant to approach her uncle with a request for transport to Wyvern Lodge.

Her own choice of dress for the great occasion had been very easy: she only had one halfway suitable ball gown. It was a dark yellow muslin and very old-fashioned in cut and design. No waist, no skirt with several petticoats, but a pretty neckline that showed off her shoulders, so that was something to be pleased about.

Even a day ago Miriam would have worn it with head held high, proud to be the poor relation who was determined to take as little help from her relatives as she could. But the knowledge that her aunts had indeed sent money out to her parents in Africa and that it was not their fault that her father had used most of it for his charitable concerns, meant that her attitude towards them had altered. Especially her reluctance to take any gift from Aunt Elizabeth.

She knew that if she had asked to borrow a dress, one would have been found for her. But it was too late now. She had been forced to bury her pride when Grace Frost had gathered up the garment and carried it away, muttering that she would see what she could do to make it wearable, an expression that Miriam hoped was not disdain on her pretty face.

She looked up now as the library door opened, then muttered a very unladylike word she had learnt from the boys who roamed the docks in Cape Town as a drop of ink fell and blotted her page.

"I'm sorry, Cousin Miriam, did I startle you?"

"Fitzwilliam, no, I am just clumsy with a pen. I am sure your skills at writing far outpace mine."

"Well, Henry and I have had tutors since we were babies. We have Mr Charlton at present, of course. He is a very clever man. Papa insisted that we learnt to make our letters by the time we were six. And I go to school, of course, where you have to write neatly or else you are beaten."

"Does Henry not go to school?"

Fitzwilliam shook his dark head. "There always seems a reason for him to stay at home with Mr Charlton. He often falls sick when the new term begins and plans are made for him to come later, but somehow he has always managed to avoid it. But Papa is quite determined he will accompany me next term, although I have heard rumours that Papa is thinking the navy might be a good life for him. He does so like being outdoors and active."

Miriam turned her face to hide her smile. She could quite believe that Henry Darcy would do everything in his power to avoid school. "You are not involved in all the preparations for the ball?"

The boy picked up a book and riffled through the pages, then - "I have to attend!" he burst out, with more emotion than Miriam had ever heard him use before. "Mama and Papa insist. They say that as heir to Pemberley and now I am nearly sixteen, I must play my part as host to those attending."

"Yes, I can see that that would be one of your responsibilities. I take it you do not care for dancing?"

Fitzwilliam gazed at her from dark eyes very similar to those his father had once admired many years before.

"I think it a very silly occupation. Papa says he used to feel the same, but that one day I might meet someone I want to dance with, but I can't imagine that. I've had to learn, of course, but I keep tripping over my feet and I am scared I will tread on my partner's toes!"

Miriam nodded. "That is indeed a worry. But perhaps if you just dance with one of your sisters, or even me, it will not matter if our toes suffer."

The boy smiled. "To be candid, Cousin, I am more concerned by a dance called the waltz that Bennetta and Anne are so determined will be performed tomorrow. I haven't learnt that at all, and I fear to look foolish and embarrass Mama and Papa."

Miriam jumped to her feet. "I have only learnt it recently myself from Bennetta, but can show you the basic steps. Come, here is an empty piece of floor. Give me your hand, now place your other hand on my waist."

She watched as Fitzwilliam went very red. "It seems remarkably rude to touch a lady's waist," he said.

"Well, you may not have to dance this at all. Or if you do, you can come and find me. But it is wise to know how. Look, I step backwards as you step forwards and you move your feet like this - one, two, three, turn, one two three, quite quickly in time with the music."

She stepped back, Fitzwilliam moved forward tentatively but with the wrong foot and their feet tangled and they began to laugh as they struggled to stay upright.

"I can see that neither of you would be adept at dancing a hornpipe on deck during a storm!"

Miriam gasped and dropped Fitz's hand, aware that she was blushing but unable to stop herself. Nicholas was standing in the doorway, laughing at them.

"My cousin was kindly showing me how to waltz," Fitz said cheerfully. He liked Mr Sullivan and knew his laughter was not laced with malice.

"So I presumed. Perhaps you would learn faster if you watched closely. If Miss Malliot will allow...?" He held out his hand and smiled at Miriam.

Before she could stop to think and decline, she found her fingers warmly clasped, a broad hand on her waist and the pressure of his body guiding her backwards as he hummed a tune and guided her around the shining library floor.

For long seconds she didn't dare raise her gaze but then she realised she was being a coward, and lifting her head, found herself staring into the dark grey eyes that haunted her dreams at night and most of her waking moments, too.

The look in his eyes spoke more than words could possibly say and Miriam felt the world toss and turn and settle back in a new way that she realised would alter her life from this day forward. For several more spins around the floor she pretended that she could love this man, be part of his life, then reality broke into her happy dreams. Nicholas had said nothing to her, she was making up romances from the look in his eyes, the pressure of his hand on hers.

And she was in no position to do so. Her life was already arranged; she would live with her mother, caring for her as she grew old, as she had promised her papa she would, being a useful member of society in whichever town they found themselves living.

She would attend her cousins' weddings, no doubt admire their children, but she would remain a spinster, one of the poor relations who would be invited to luncheon and tea and the occasional dinner party when another person was needed to make up the numbers. Marriage, even a love affair, was not and never would be for her. One other thing was clear, if she felt like this about Nicholas, then she could never marry anyone else, even if she was asked some time in the distant future.

She was suddenly aware that Fitzwilliam was clapping and laughing. "Thank you, Cousin Miriam, Mr Sullivan. That is most useful. I can see what I was doing wrong now."

'So can I,' Miriam thought bitterly and pulling her hand free, she stepped back from her dancing partner. Nicholas looked a little startled, then bowed gravely.

"Perhaps we can continue this dance tomorrow evening?"

"I am not certain if my mama would consider the waltz proper in the setting of a ball where so many people will be strangers. In the privacy of a private party, perhaps, but I fear I will have to sit it out tomorrow. However, I am sure there will be plenty of young ladies who will be only too delighted to stand up with you, Sir."

She dropped a curtsey and headed for the door, eager to be on her own, to sit and reflect on what had just happened.

Nicholas bowed again. He didn't understand - one minute she was relaxed and compliant in his arms, enjoying herself, telling him with those dark brown eyes that she cared for him and the next she was cold and distant, treating him as if he were a servant, no worse than that because he didn't think any servant would be chilled through by such an icy stare.

"I am sure you are correct, but unless your dance card is already full, then I would hope to have at least one dance with you, before I head back to sea."

Miriam spun round. "The *Sea Sprite* has returned to her home waters already? That was surely a fast voyage."

"She only sailed to the island of Madeira and back on this trip. She needs new sails and some general refurbishment before I take her down to Cape Town and then on to the East. She is docked in London and I will travel there after the ball."

"Correct me if I am wrong, but surely you will be gone for several months, Sir," Fitzwilliam said. "I trust you will visit us on your return and relate all your adventures. I know my brother, for one, will be so pleased to hear them."

Nicholas smiled at the grave dignity in the young boy's voice. Fitzwilliam Darcy might not yet have all the social skills such as dancing that behove him as heir to Pemberley, but he was learning fast. "Indeed, it would be an honour, Master Darcy."

Miriam, who had felt a sense of loss that was ridiculous when she had nothing and no one to lose, found her voice once more. "You are obviously anxious to be on your way, Mr Sullivan."

"Are we to be formal again, then? I trust not. Why, Miriam, it is my profession. Do you agree, there is nothing and no one to keep me here?"

Confused and flustered, she couldn't reply, just curtsied again and left the room for the sanctuary of her own room.

Nicholas stared after her; he felt bewildered, he was a man of action, of straight speaking. This luxurious world he found himself in irritated him. Miriam's manner towards him changed from one second to the next. Hot, cold, hot, cold, he didn't understand women at all and wished fervently that he was back on the quarter deck of his own beautiful *Sea Sprite*. At least there, even in the midst of a terrible storm, he had some idea of what was going to happen next; here at Pemberley he was at a loss.

CHAPTER 14

On a warm Spring evening, Pemberley *en fete* was a beautiful sight. In the early dusk, golden light streamed from its tall windows and the great porticoed front doors stood open as the carriages, curlicues and phaetons stopped outside to allow their passengers to alight.

Two footmen in the dark green Darcy livery stood either side of the steps to help if needed and once inside the great hall with its wonderful painted ceiling, their cloaks and overshoes were deftly removed and taken away by a series of maids.

The ladies were escorted to a room that had been set aside with mirrors and tables and the chatter and laughter rose as they made minute adjustments to their elaborate hairstyles, pinched their cheeks to bring up the colour and surreptitiously glanced around to see who was wearing the most fashionable and expensive dresses. Jewellery was silently assessed and snippets of gossip carefully stored away for enjoyable retelling later to friends who had not been privileged to attend the ball.

The air was thick with the scent of powder and perfumes, battling with the aroma from the beautiful flower arrangements that decorated every table and alcove. Slowly and surely the noise level rose as more and more guests arrived and then the footman at the bottom of the circular stairway stepped aside and people began to move upstairs to be welcomed and greeted by Mr and Mrs Darcy who stood in the anteroom to the ballroom.

During a pause as a particularly elderly lady slowly climbed the stairs towards them, leaning heavily on her companion's arm, Mr Darcy sighed. "As this ball was Anne and Bennetta's idea, I think it only fitting that they should stand here, being polite to people they don't care for and hardly know."

Elizabeth fought to keep her face pleasantly blank. "I agree, my dear. Indeed, I know that Anne is longing to play her part as Miss Darcy. Jane would hate it, but will do her duty. Perhaps we will not ask Bennetta, though. If she begins to flirt with every young man who appears up the stairway, the ball will never begin."

Her husband frowned but had to admit there was truth in her remarks. "She looks astoundingly pretty tonight," he said, breaking off to welcome the elderly lady and her companion and usher them towards the seating at the side of the room, clicking his fingers to summon a footman with a tray of champagne.

"I know. I fear our youngest daughter has put her sisters well and truly in the shade. So let me summon Anne and Jane. They can take over this duty and Anne, at least, will be happy that we have excluded Bennetta."

Mr Darcy raised an eyebrow at her less than maternal words regarding her first born child, but knew Anne had the power to irritate and worry her mother. She had the same effect on him. He could see too much of himself as a young man in her manners and outlook on life. The young man he had been before he came under the influence of a certain Miss Elizabeth Bennet.

He turned to see the Reverend Poole and his wife and daughter advancing towards him, all smiles, and they reminded him of Miriam. He wished the girl didn't make him so uneasy. There was already a rebellious streak in Bennetta and he feared Mary's impulsive daughter would fan that flickering flame into a fire one day.

He wondered why his niece was not at the ball: he was certain he had not seen her yet and with that brilliant red hair he knew she would be hard to miss.

The subject of his thoughts was sitting in front of her mirror at that moment, staring at her reflection. Her dark gold muslin with the paler yellow lace cap sleeves did, indeed, look old-fashioned, but it's simple style suited her and she was wearing round her neck a string of carved beads that Martha, who had looked after Miriam and her mother in Africa, had given her as a going away gift. They looked odd and exotic, a far cry from the pearls, diamonds and sapphires that the other ladies would be wearing.

Her dancing slippers were old and she had forgotten until she took them from the closet how shabby they looked with one rose gone and one heel split. But then she doubted she would be dancing a great deal and she had nothing else to wear.

Grace, had helped her dress earlier but the maid had left the room on some errand and never returned. She had been aware that the girl was angry about something but all her gentle questioning had brought forth no response.

She wondered if Grace had had a lovers' tiff with Fletcher, the valet who attended Edmund Avery. She was sure they had formed some sort of alliance in the past weeks. But, of course, after the Darcy portrait was revealed during the ball, Mr Avery's work would be over and he and his servant would be leaving for London during the coming week.

Miriam knew she had to speak to him before he left because he still had not given her the sketch he had made of her. She was anxious to have it framed before her mother arrived from Africa and their life in England began in earnest, far away from the luxurious setting of Pemberley.

Miriam sighed: she could only guess how Grace was feeling at Fletcher's departure because if it was anything like the way she was suffering, knowing she would shortly be saying goodbye to Nicholas, then it would be heartbreaking indeed.

But a broken heart was not the sort of reason that Grace could give to Miss Reynolds to stop her from working. Miriam's hair still lay in a red cloud over her shoulders, brushed and gleaming but free from all restraint. There was no way she could contrive a decent style by herself. The braids and curls that Grace managed to force into her hair were way beyond her capabilities. But if she rang the bell a third time and no one answered, then Grace might get in serious trouble with the head housekeeper.

"Well, I don't know why you are fretting," she murmured crossly to herself. "As the poor relation of the family, no one will be looking in your direction."

A tap at the door and her cousin Jane entered, looking elegant and fine in cream silk, although privately Miriam thought a darker colour would have suited her very fair complexion better, although this evening her usual pale cheeks were rosy and her eyes were bright and sparkling.

"Miriam - goodness, you are not nearly ready. What a slow poke you are, to be sure. Mama has sent me up to fetch you down to the ball. The dancing will begin soon and she is keen that you enjoy yourself. This, after all, is your first official outing at Pemberley."

'And likely to be my last for some time,' Miriam thought swiftly, but knew she must keep her regrets at her future life to herself. Sympathy, pity indeed, were both things she would hate to receive, even from someone as gentle as Jane.

Her cousin had taken up her hairbrush and was busy pinning up the long red hair. "Grace Frost should have done this for you," she said crossly. "That girl - I have heard nothing but complaints about her for the past few days and now she has left you to get ready on your own."

"I expect she had other duties," Miriam said diplomatically, not wanting to mention Fletcher and that this night was probably the last time the two lovers would have to be together.

"You look very well tonight, Jane. Surely it is not just the thought of a dance that has made you so happy?"

Jane smiled shyly and shook her head. "La, I have no idea what you mean, Miriam."

"Is it possible that there may be a guest you are very pleased to see."

Her cousin smiled again and Miriam wondered how it was possible for twins to be so alike and yet so different. When Jane smiled it lit up her face; Anne's smile never seemed to reach her eyes.

"Oh Miriam, I know it is stupid of me, but Sir Digby Frobisher has arrived, I saw the Frobisher carriage from the window. He is here with his parents."

"And?"

"It is silly of me, I'm sure he is not really interested, but we had such a long and heartfelt conversation about the plays of Shakespeare when we met at Catherine's wedding last year. We danced and...and he made sure I had a glass of mulled wine and..."

She paused, the comb still in her hand. "I met him again in London, before Christmas. Time has gone by so fast. I felt we had...a connection. We discussed many things but there was no time for us to become closer. I had already promised to visit Colonel Fitzwilliam down in Dorset. But oh, Miriam, I have since received such wonderful letters from Digby. Warm and kind, but very proper. No sense of false familiarity.

"I didn't know Papa had invited him tonight. I didn't even know he was in Derbyshire, he lives in London, but apparently he is visiting his parents who have a lovely home across the border in Cheshire. But please, do not speak of this to anyone."

"Jane, you have a beau and you never told anyone!"

"Oh I am sure Anne guesses how I feel, although we have not discussed it. After all, there is nothing to discuss, but I am hopeful that tonight will be an opportunity to further our acquaintanceship. He is exactly the type of man that interests me."

"I wish you joy," Miriam said warmly and, with a sigh, stood up as Jane finished pinning her hair. She was aware that her cousin was looking askance at the yellow dress but didn't care. She had no beau waiting for her in the ballroom.

An hour later, Bennetta declared the evening a success. The heat in the room had increased as the dancing progressed. The musicians were playing well and the whole atmosphere was agreeable. She had danced every dance - her card could have been filled three or more times over.

Flickering through the crowds like a small white bird, her glossy curls escaping the flowered headband that held them away from her face, she spotted Miriam sitting at the side of the room, holding a glass of lemonade and flung herself into the chair next to her.

"Goodness, Mirry, there you are. I have been watching and you haven't been dancing and I am sure there are many gentlemen here who would happily partner you. La, I am so hot! I have begged Mama to open the windows but she is worried by cold draughts on our hot skin. I truly believe Mama is getting more old fashioned with every passing day."

"She looks very beautiful, though."

Bennetta gazed over to where her parents were standing, talking to the Reverend Poole and his wife. Mrs Poole, who looked every inch like a very fat cabbage, in her opinion, did not compare well with the elegance in blue lace and silk of Elizabeth Darcy.

"Why yes, I must admit Mama looks well for her age. And whoever told Mrs Poole to wear that hideous colour green should be taken out and horsewhipped!"

"Bennetta!"

"Well, it's true, you can't say it isn't. But look - Fitzwilliam is dancing!"

Miriam's mind flashed back to those few wonderful minutes in the library, held close in Nicholas' arms when the young boy had been watching. "Oh, I am glad. He was so dreading the ball. Is his partner one of the twins, I can't quite see?"

"No, it's Delphine Poole. Oh poor boy, he looks quite besotted. I shall tease him so much at breakfast tomorrow and just wait until I tell Henry!"

Miriam watched as the young couple made their way up the long-ways dance. Fitzwilliam obviously had eyes for no one but the tiny blonde girl in pale blue at his side and a quick glance over at Mrs Poole brought a smile to her lips.

The Reverend's wife looked like a cat who had just spotted a cream jug left unattended on the table. Of course he was a few weeks shy of his sixteenth birthday, but Delphine was only a month or so older. Perhaps Mrs Poole was hoping that this would sow the seeds of a future alliance, although Miriam thought that very unlikely. Surely there was no way the heir to Pemberley would be allowed to marry the daughter of the local vicar, no matter how pretty she was?

She frowned; her uncle had married her aunt, after all. Elizabeth Bennet had been the daughter of a gentleman, that was true, but even Miriam's own mother had to admit that their family had been very undistinguished and that the marriage had been the talk of society for years. So, perhaps Mrs Poole was not so much without hope as might be imagined.

"And there is Anne, flirting with Sir Digby Frobisher! She is naughty. Mama will be very put out. She hates it when we flirt in public but he is very good-looking, isn't he? I love his moustache. Do you think it would make a difference - being kissed by a man with a moustache! Do you think it tickles?"

"Bennetta, what a question! I cannot possibly guess." Miriam was puzzled: from her angle she couldn't see through the crowds in front of her. "Surely he is dancing with Jane?"

"Jane? Oh no, it's definitely Anne. She's wearing very dark pink and Jane's dress is cream. I haven't seen Jane for ages. She's probably slipped out and retired to the library to read one of her silly books. She isn't keen on meeting strangers. Look, the dance has ended and Digby is escorting Anne out, probably for champagne. He seems very attentive, but then I suppose Miss Darcy of Pemberley would be a good alliance for the Frobishers. I expect they met when she was in London. There are so many interesting men in town. Just you wait till Mama and Papa take you there - you will have beau waiting on you at every turn."

"Miss Bennetta, Miriam."

Miriam's worries about Jane vanished in a flash. Nicholas was standing in front of them, looking tidier and smarter than she had ever seen him before, bowing and holding out his hand towards her. "I believe the musicians will play a waltz next. We have to finish the dance we began."

Bennetta jumped to her feet. "Oh the waltz! Wonderful. I am promised to Mr Adler and I can see him coming towards us. I do believe that in the next interval he will finally unveil his portrait. It is already in position in the small ante room. I dread to think what I will look like, but we all have our crosses to bear! I will speak with you later, Mirry. Enjoy the dance. Don't step on her toes too often, Mr Sullivan!" And with a flash of white petticoats and silk stockings, she was gone to meet the artist.

Miriam allowed the sea captain to pull her gently to her feet and as the music changed, she felt one hand firmly on her waist and her own clasped with a pressure that surely was unnecessary to guide her around the floor. Several couples had declined to take part in this new dance and Miriam felt everyone in the ballroom was looking at her. Then Nicholas squeezed her fingers and she raised her gaze to his and the rest of the room and everyone in it fell away.

"So are you looking forward to London and a plethora of beau? Miss Bennetta seems to think you will soon have young men at your beck and call."

"My cousin is still very naive. I think she sees everything through rose-coloured spectacles."

He whirled her round, his hand tightening on her waist. "You didn't answer my question, Miriam. Do you look forward to an alliance with a suitable man, to marriage, to children?"

'Only if the marriage was with you, if the children were ours,' she wanted to cry, but forced back the words. "I think most young women wish to marry but I will not be one of the many who accept the first proposal I receive just to have a roof over my head and the respect that a married woman is entitled to receive."

Nicholas' gaze seemed to sear her skin. "You would follow your heart, not your head?"

"Yes," she whispered. "I would follow the man I loved to the end of the world!"

"The end of the world can be a very scary place, Miriam. I know, I've sailed there!"

"But if you trust someone, you can face any danger."

"Miriam, my dear Miriam..."

She glanced up, saw in his eyes what he was about to say and knew she must stop him before the whole situation became shrouded with embarrassment and regret.

"But sadly my circumstances will always prevent that happening. I am afraid my life is very much set out for me already. I am my mother's only child and as such I must be at her side as she grows older. I made a vow to my dear father on his death bed to take care of Mama."

Nicholas' grip on her hand became almost painful, it was so tight. She felt herself being swirled round again and again as the music grew louder and the people watching began to clap the couples on the floor who were attempting this new, extraordinary dance.

Suddenly Miriam realised he had steered them out of the ballroom into the side room where, surrounded by flickering beeswax candles, Edmund Avery's shrouded canvas stood waiting for its audience.

Dropping her hand, Nicholas said, "Listen, Miriam, your mother is not an old lady! Surely your aunts would be able to find her a suitable companion if...well...Miriam, I must tell you how much I admire your bravery, the fearless way you look at the world, your sense of adventure."

"Nicholas - !"

"Listen, Miriam - "

Before he could continue, the door to the ballroom was thrown open once more by a footman and Mr and Mrs Darcy, with Edmund Avery in close attendance, came into the anteroom. A crowd followed them, the Darcy children, friends and relations, all laughing and talking.

Nicholas and Miriam were swallowed up in the crowd and she was only thankful that he hadn't been holding her hand. But he stood behind her, so close that she could feel his breath on her bare neck.

Her thoughts were a torrent of discord - he had said he admired her! Had he been about to declare his love? To propose marriage? But that was not possible: she had no doubt that a companion for her mama could be found easily enough; there were many gentlewomen, thrown onto hard times, who would be eager for such a position. But she had promised her father that she would care for her mother. Promised as he lay dying! That was not something she could easily renounce.

She forced herself to be calm. Nicholas had said he admired her, that was all. He probably admired Delphine Poole, too. He always seemed happy in her company.

She hardly listened as Mr Darcy introduced the artist to those who had not met him. All Miriam wanted was for this to be over, for her and Nicholas to somehow be alone again so he could finish what he had been saying.

Then Edmund Avery was stepping forward, grasping the cloth that lay over the portrait and pulling it free. Clapping and polite cheering broke out for the painting was magnificent. The five Darcy children, grouped together naturally and happily, gazed out of the canvas in a fashion that caught your attention and left you wishing to know them better.

Mr Darcy was shaking Edmund Avery's hand and Anne had hurried forward to examine herself in the portrait, exclaiming at how good the likeness was. Bennetta seemed delighted and even Fitzwilliam managed to tear himself away from Delphine to admit that the artist had managed not to make him look a complete fool. Only Jane, paler than usual, stood stiffly apart, replying to compliments with lips that seemed reluctant to move.

Miriam found herself clapping and then Nicholas was bending forward to whisper in her ear. "Come, we have unfinished business. No one will miss us."

They turned to make their way through the crowd when suddenly a strident voice rang out. "Goodness me, it's the white slave trader!

The sailor from Gravesend. My word, Sir, what are you doing here? Darcy! Elizabeth! Come quickly. This man should not be here at Pemberley, frightening Miriam again."

There, in the doorway, stood Mrs Caroline Tremaine, dressed in the height of fashion, the diamonds at her neck and wrists flashing in the candlelight, with a look of great censure on her face.

CHAPTER 15

"La, what a comedy of events!" Elizabeth Darcy sipped from her glass of champagne and laughed. "Poor Mr Sullivan! There you were, being a Good Samaritan to poor Miriam in Gravesend and being mistaken for a White Slave Trader. Why it is too funny!"

"My dear, I fear Mr Sullivan does not share your sense of humour. I must admit I think, I too, would not care to be branded with that name, especially in front of a large audience." Mr Darcy reproved his wife gently.

"Well, how was I to know the gentleman in question is a well-respected sea captain and man of business?"

Caroline Tremaine fanned herself and gave a little laugh and everyone joined in. She enjoyed being the centre of attention; she had only attended the Pemberley ball at the last moment.

Arriving unexpectedly to stay with her brother at Clifton Park, she had not realised that such a prestigious event was taking place. Jane and Charles had already said they would not attend, but Caroline had decided that it was uncivil for no one from the Bingley family to make an appearance whether they were invited or not.

Miriam stood in the background, her fingers clasping her glass so tightly that she feared it might snap. Nicholas had looked at her only once since Mrs Tremaine had made her astounding announcement and all the explanations had followed on. But that one look had been enough. In it she had seen how wounded he was that she had believed what she had been told. That their friendship, based on the weeks spent together on board ship, had immediately been queried, found wanting and thrown aside. That she hadn't trusted him, had made no attempt to defend him either by word or deed.

She knew she would never be able to forget the expression in his eyes as he listened to Mrs Tremaine rattling on about how she had rescued Miriam from his clutches and how thankful she had been to be rescued. She could see anger, injured pride and disappointment. Sadly she also thought she could see relief; perhaps he was realising that if he had declared his love, he would have been coupled to a girl who had thought him the darkest type of villain.

The rest of the Darcy family had returned to the ballroom and once the excitement had died down, the other guests, once they had admired the portrait of the children, had followed. Bennetta had been slow to leave Miriam's side; she guessed something was wrong, but had no idea what that could be.

She had joined in the general amusement at the thought of Mr Sullivan being a wicked kidnapper, but even as she laughed, she had realised that neither Nicholas nor Miriam was smiling. But at last her mother had prevailed on her to see to their guests and with a quick touch on Miriam's frozen hand, she had returned to where the music had started again.

At last Miriam and Nicholas were alone. He gave her a curt bow and turned to leave. With a little cry, she thrust out her hand to stop him, catching his sleeve and holding it tightly, regardless of how inappropriate that was.

"Mr Sullivan...Nicholas...wait...please listen. Let me explain."

Nicholas stopped - he could hardly pull his sleeve roughly out of her grasp - but he refused to look at her. He was angry, bitterly hurt that Miriam could have ever thought so badly of him, and confused by the affection that he thought she had recently been showing him. Being laughed at by the Darcys and their friends had been extremely irritating but he could even have taken that in good grace if it hadn't been for Miriam. They had no idea how close the two of them had grown over the past weeks.

He had noticed Edmund Avery's smirk of derision, the way he had looked Nicholas up and down as Mrs Tremaine was telling her story, as if the artist would have expected no less from someone who was, in his opinion, obviously only just a gentleman.

"I would not want to force you to be in the company of someone you so obviously do not trust, madam."

"I do trust you," Miriam whispered.

"I think not. Over the past weeks, I sometimes thought I was imagining your reluctance to be in my company, but I now see that even though we had spent that long voyage in close proximity, you were more inclined to accept Mrs Tremaine's opinion - who had never met me - than your own judgement."

Miriam's temper, always quick to flare when she was accused of a fault when she knew she was in the right, bubbled to the surface and she dropped his sleeve and stepped back.

"I profess, Sir, that being alone in a strange country, not knowing anything or anyone, I was at fault and not best able to make sensible deductions. Everything happened so very quickly and, of course, I did not know I would ever see you again."

Nicholas stared into the brown eyes that gazed fearlessly into his own, realizing once again that this was no meek and mild girl who would retreat at the first sign of conflict or argument. No, Miriam would step forward, not back, she would have her say and do what she felt was right. He honoured her for that and was angry now with himself for behaving in such a childish, ungentlemanly fashion.

"Miss Malliot...Miriam..."

There was a polite cough and then, "Mr Sullivan." The door had opened and a footman stood, the noise of the ball flooding in around him. "Mrs Darcy requests the pleasure of your company."

Nicholas swore under his breath, hoping that Miriam didn't hear. "Mrs Darcy must be obeyed," he said with a smile. "But we will talk again this evening. We have several unfinished subjects to discuss. I will, with your agreement, come and find you."

He bowed over her hand and as he raised his head and gazed into her eyes, Miriam caught her breath at the expression on his face. It said so much, promised heaven and a safe harbour from all of her worries.

Miriam watched him turn and be swallowed up by the noise, the laughter and music and sound of dancing coming from the ballroom. Then the door swung shut and she was left alone in the candlelight, the Darcy children staring down at her with their painted eyes.

She glanced up; sure that even in oils, Anne was looking at her in a mocking fashion, Jane with pity, the boys with boredom and Bennetta - the sparkling dark eyes seemed to say, "You can have everything you want if you are brave enough!"

But the portrait also showed them as a family. No matter how much they fought and argued, they were together and she was alone. She didn't belong here, in this luxurious house with its countless rooms and grand galleries. She wanted a very different sort of life and, up until an hour ago, perhaps that had been just within her reach.

Could she now repair her friendship with Nicholas or had her lack of trust ruined her future? When he had said they would talk again, had he meant as friends - or, if she was reading his expression correctly, something more, much more?

Although, and her heart sank, if he was offering more - how could she possibly accept? Why, even as she stood here, her mother was probably on the high seas, travelling towards England, looking forward to their new life together. And Nicholas was soon to set sail for the other side of the world. Marriage was certainly not something he was in a position to offer.

Bringing Mary to mind, Miriam realised she still hadn't seen Edmund Avery's sketch of her. Perhaps he had forgotten all about it, after all it must seem a very trivial trifle compared to this wonderful portrait of the Darcys. How talented he was: she knew she could admire the artist now and not the man. She was almost embarrassed to think that she had once thought him an interesting person. Now he seemed a vain peacock compared to the eagle that was Nicholas Sullivan.

She had tried to see the sketch before, of course, when she had been stopped by hearing Grace and her lover in the studio. But now - she opened the door slightly and could see to where a long-ways dance was in progress. Edmund Avery was partnering Anne, all elegant flourishes and head tilts. Miriam could tell from the music that the dance had just begun, so he would be occupied for some considerable time.

With all the servants on duty or having their own dinner before the guests left and their night-time tasks began, this would be the perfect time to slip upstairs and collect the sketch. She would give Grace a note to slip to his valet telling him that the artwork was now safely in her possession and thanking him profusely for all his kind attentions. He would surely be heading down to London after the ball and there was no need for their paths to cross again.

She picked up a small oil lamp from a nearby table and found a door that led her out into a windowless corridor that stretched the length of the house. No fine carpets, portraits or tapestries here, just cold stone and bare walls. This was the way the servants would come through to the ballroom, so that the guests need not see them.

A few dim tallow candles flickered on their sconces as Miriam sped towards the end of the passageway where she guessed the stairs led up to the floors above. Her yellow dancing slippers made not a sound and she shivered from the chill air that felt as if it had never, ever been warm. Her shadow danced along the wall beside her, enjoying the adventure.

She met no one, it was as if this side of the great house was asleep whilst all the gaiety was happening elsewhere. Guessing the direction of the corridor correctly, she fled up the stone steps towards Mr Avery's studio, her shoe with the cracked heel sliding where candle wax had dripped to the floor.

Trunks and bundles had been stacked in the passageway, obviously awaiting their transport downstairs. Tentatively, she tried the door; all her plans would come to naught if it was locked. But obviously with the Darcy portrait now on show, Mr Avery considered there was nothing of any great value to protect.

The handle turned easily and Miriam slipped into the long room, her lamp no more than a yellow glow in the dark for no candles were being wasted up here. But it wasn't that dark, after all. The curtainless windows that ran the whole length of one wall, that let in the north light during the day that Mr Avery had told her was vital for an artist, were now letting in brilliant silver beams as the moon appeared from behind a cloud and bathed the room.

Miriam could see quite easily that there were still a lot of canvases and easels waiting to be packed. The artist's palettes were stacked, clean and tidy, on a side table, along with the jars that held his multitude of brushes. She tiptoed across the room to where Mr Avery had a desk. Large canvases were stacked against the side, the painted side inwards for protection, some had already been fixed onto battens ready for transport, but there was no sign of the small sketch - all these paintings were large.

Then, to her surprise, she spotted a square package, wrapped in thick paper, lying on top of the desk. Holding up her lamp, she could see the label clearly - *Miss Malliot* - and knew instantly that here was the sketch. How kind of him to pack it for her: perhaps he wasn't as selfish as she had supposed.

Not bothering to unwrap it, she picked it up and turned swiftly for the door but as she did, one of her shoes slid and she stumbled and her leg hit the stacked canvases. The one in front, the biggest, trembled and fell back on the floor with a crash.

Miriam stood very still. Had anyone heard? She was doing no wrong, but it would be embarrassing if Fletcher found her here. But silence followed the crash and carefully putting down the oil lamp and her package, she picked up the canvas, ready to stack it against its neighbours. And saw the subject that Edmund Avery had drawn as a wave of sickness swept over her.

Nicholas had spent a boring fifteen minutes talking, at Elizabeth Darcy's request, to a retired Admiral who wanted to discuss the speed of the latest clippers on the China run. He was in a fever of impatience to return to Miriam, to apologise, to sort out their difficulties. Oh, he knew there were problems, some people would say unsurmountable ones, but his feelings could not be denied. Then, just as he had made his escape, a footman approached him.

"Mr Sullivan, Sir."

"Yes, James, isn't it?"

"Why yes, Sir." The young man with his shock of bright ginger hair looked delighted to have his name remembered. "This letter arrived express just now. It has been redirected from London. Mr Darcy said I should bring it to you straight away."

Nicholas took the envelope, recognising the heavy red seal on the back and knew, with a mixture of pleasure and despair, exactly what message it would contain. A quick scan of the letter inside confirmed his thoughts and he crushed it into his pocket as he headed back to the anteroom, but it was empty. A touch on his elbow - it was Bennetta, her dark curls just coming up to his shoulder.

"Are you looking for Miriam, Mr Sullivan?"

"Indeed, I am, Miss Bennetta. I need to speak to her immediately."

"So was I, just now. One of the footmen told me that he had seen her going up to Mr Avery's studio. I expect she has gone to fetch the sketch he made of her. She may well have been worried that he would forget to give it to her and take it with him down to London."

"I see. Well, I doubt she will be up there long."

Bennetta was busy retying one of the ribbons that had come loose on her sleeve. "I only hope she has taken a good lamp with her. It is very dark on those back stairs and we do not keep the candles lit when no one is about and sometimes the servants leave rubbish around. Mama is always complaining about it."

Nicholas frowned. "That sounds most unsafe. Perhaps I'll take a lamp and go to meet her. I'll bring her straight back to the ballroom."

The youngest Darcy daughter looked up at him, her eyes pools of innocence. "Oh, what a good idea. Gentlemen always have a plan for every eventuality."

Nicholas hurried through the dark corridors, eager to reach Miriam, determined to apologise for his juvenile behaviour, to explain why he had been so hurt, that her trust and regard were all he wanted and he had been devastated to hear she had thought so little of him.

He reached the top of the stairs that led to the studio and had just pushed open the door when there was a crash from inside. He raised the lantern he was carrying and its beam shot across the dark room that was lit only by a small lamp set on the floor. Miriam was standing, hands clasped to her cheeks, not moving.

Even as he took a step forward, the moon came out from behind a cloud and pale light crossed the room.

"Miriam! What has happened? My dear girl, you look quite ill. Are you sick? Have you fallen?"

There was no reply and as he moved towards her, she stepped back, thrusting her hands towards him as if to push him away. "Don't look! Oh please, don't look!" she groaned.

"What on earth - oh my Lord! What hell is this?"

He realised the light from his lamp was falling squarely on a large painting lying face up on the floor. There was a lot of crimson and gold, a chaise covered in what he supposed was to be white satin. A girl was lying stretched out, full length, wearing - well, to his horror she was wearing a few thin drapes that hardly hid her body at all.

But it wasn't the near naked body that he was looking at. The girl's head was thrown back to expose her long neck, she was gazing out of the portrait, her eyes full of longing, a cascade of bright red hair tangling down across her bare shoulders on to her breasts.

The face was, without doubt, that of Miriam Malliot.

CHAPTER 16

"But Mama, surely I can visit Miriam for ten minutes. She cannot be that ill. Why she was quite well last night at the ball." Bennetta yawned widely. It was early afternoon but she had only just appeared downstairs, still wearing her dressing-robe, her hair loose and unbrushed.

She sank down on a couch, wriggled her bare toes and yawned again. "Lord, I am still so tired and my feet are sore."

Her mother looked up from her writing desk. "Then you shouldn't have danced every dance, child. And Miriam caught a little chill and is having a restful day in her room. I don't want you bothering her."

"Sometimes, Mama, you talk to me as if I was six!"

"And sometimes that is just how you act! Why were you waltzing with Digby Frobisher last night? You were close to romping. Be glad your papa did not see you. Luckily he had...business elsewhere."

Bennetta pulled a face. "Oh it was just to annoy Anne. She was acting as if he was her own particular friend and I wanted to show her that he wasn't. That any of us Darcy girls would be of interest to him. I would have made him dance with Miriam if she had not left the ball early."

Elizabeth sighed. She had seen and understood all that had happened at the ball between Frobisher, Anne and Jane. She had seen the pain in the younger twin's face when Digby had danced with both her sisters and not herself. Did Jane consider herself in love with him? Oh surely not! That was a complication too far. And if she was, had she spoken to Anne about it? If so, then Anne's behaviour was very wrong and something would have to be said.

"Am I the only other person awake this morning?"

"Well it is afternoon to be accurate and the boys and your papa were up early and out, but there has been no sign of Anne or Jane just yet. Now do go and get dressed, Bennetta."

"Yes, Mama. Although it hardly seems worth it as I will be going to bed again in a few hours. Are Mr Avery and Mr Sullivan still not awake either?"

Elizabeth studied the letter she was writing intently and said, in a vague fashion, "Oh, I am afraid you missed Mr Avery - he departed before first light as he was keen to reach London and Mr Sullivan has been called back to his ship. He will be leaving very soon. I believe he has been promoted to captain and must ready the vessel for a long voyage to the South Seas."

"Goodness!" All tiredness dropped away from Bennetta as she listened to the news, wondering how Miriam would feel with both men departing from Pemberley without so much as a bow or a kiss on the hand.

She wandered to the window and watched the sunlight gilding all the new green leaves showing now in the great park. She envied Mr Avery and Mr Sullivan. How wonderful it must be to just pack up and go, whenever and wherever you wanted. She knew that as a woman, even if she was a Darcy, that would never be something she could aspire to do. She might have funds of her own, but she doubted if she would ever have the chance to use them as she would wish.

Sighing, she wandered back to her room, feeling the irritability that comes with the ending of a much planned project and, although her coming out ball to be held in London in the summer was to be the highlight of her year, the belief that nothing pleasant would ever happen again still remained!

Elizabeth sighed and returned to the letter she was writing to her sister Jane, telling her of all that had happened the night before. She knew it would cause her distress, but she could have no secrets from Jane who sometimes could see silver linings behind the blackest of clouds because she stubbornly refused to believe that anybody could have a nature that was all bad.

"So my dearest, I have never seen Fitzwilliam so angry before, not even when he talked of George Wickham and his dreadful betrayal of trust. When Mr Sullivan came into the ballroom and insisted that he speak to him privately, I had no idea what was occurring, although our sea captain was quite white beneath his tan.

"The ball happily continued - my dearest when you are well again, you and Charles must try "the waltz" - and then Fitzwilliam returned to say that he had ordered Avery out of the house immediately, that he had paid him for the portrait of the children but on no account was it to be hung in any of our galleries but put away in an attic. Apparently he and Mr Sullivan were about to take some very offensive painting outside and destroy it. Fitzwilliam would not even allow one of the footmen to undertake the task!

"None of our guests was any the wiser, thank the Lord, but after they had left, I learnt that Mr Sullivan had threatened to horsewhip Avery and that my poor husband had been hard pressed to keep them apart.

"And when I finally saw the cause of all the trouble - before it was destroyed - I could not blame him. I have no idea who the original model was, but my dear, she was in a state of complete undress and Avery had painted our Miriam's face onto this other poor unfortunate girl's body!

"For one very bad minute, I confess I considered if Miriam had been the model herself! Oh, excuse the ink blot, my emotions are affecting my fingers. Memories of Lydia's behaviour flooded into my mind and Miriam has had such an odd upbringing that I did wonder if perhaps she had not realised how shocking that would have been, but then I came to my senses. She may be wild and headstrong, but I am sure her moral compass is as reliable as that of our own dear girls.

"I gather that the item was to be hung in a gentleman's club in London, but Mr Darcy would not give me any more information. So infuriating! Would you not like to have just a peep inside one of those clubs! Now Jane, I can guess what you are thinking as you read these words...did Miriam know what he was doing...?

"Oh my dear, I do wish Mary would hurry up and return to England. I will be so relieved to pass the care of her daughter back to our sister. And now to other gossip...do you remember meeting the Frobishers' son, Digby at Catherine's wedding?"

The girl in question was upstairs in her bedroom, sitting on the window seat, gazing out at a beautiful spring morning and seeing nothing but disaster. Miriam was shivering, even though she had wrapped a blanket round her shoulders. Her head ached violently and she knew her eyes were swollen and red from crying. Sleep had been impossible; every time she tried, she had seen the expression on Nicholas' face as he stared at the dreadful, lewd portrait.

She recalled very little of what had happened next - she thought she had been close to fainting for the first time in her life. She remembered the despair she had experienced as Nicholas crossed the room, took the parcel from her hands and tore open the packing. There was her face again, but just her face. She was smiling and looked happy, but that dreadful hunger Avery had painted on the big canvas was missing. This was indeed just the sort of sketch any mother would have been proud to possess.

Nicholas hadn't spoken, just taken her arm and half led, half carried her out of the studio, downstairs to her room. "I shall have to fetch your uncle," he had said at last. "Don't worry, Miriam, we will deal with this atrocity."

And then he had left. His words had been spoken in an even tone, there had been no trace of disgust in them, but she could only imagine what he was really thinking. She could sense the tension in his body, as if he was consumed by disappointment, although he was too much the gentleman to show her his true feelings - his face was devoid of all expression.

He had professed his regard for her - she could still see in her mind the blaze of passion in his eyes. Perhaps she could even tell herself that he loved her. But then he had been hurt by Mrs Tremaine's words; he would have seen that as a betrayal of trust. Even if he had overcome that, to find that the object of his regard had apparently posed as a model - and such a one she could hardly bear to think about. Surely no man of honour and moral worth would look twice at such a girl. Any feelings he had had for her must have been swept away in the violence of such horror.

She knew Aunt Elizabeth had come to her room, had helped her undress, not sending for Grace.

"We will talk in the morning, my dear," she had said quietly. "I will not tell you to sleep because I am sure your mind is far too disturbed to do so, but do try and rest at least. Mr Darcy and Mr Sullivan will get to the bottom of this atrocity and all will be well, believe me. I think it would, however, be wise not to speak of this to anyone else, especially not the other girls."

Miriam had clasped her aunt's arm in sudden terror. "I will not have to see Mr Avery again, will I? I couldn't bear it, Aunt. I am so ashamed."

"You have nothing to be ashamed of, child, and I am quite certain you will never have to see Mr Avery again. Now, lie down and rest. I must go back to my guests for the remainder of the ball."

But of course those words were easy to say, but harder to follow. Miriam had lain awake all night, wondering how she could possibly face Nicholas or her uncle in the morning, knowing that they had seen the painting. She didn't really care what her uncle thought about her; she had always suspected he didn't care for her, thought her a disruptive influence in his well-ordered home, but Nicholas!

Was this what a broken heart felt like? This fiery pain inside that spread and spread, consuming her. To live in a world where she had lost his respect, let alone, possibly, his love. That was hard indeed.

Now that time was drawing near: she knew she couldn't stay in her room for ever. Bennetta and the others would wonder what was wrong; they would ask questions and should they ever find out what had happened, she could just imagine the disdain that would appear on Anne's face. But what if the first person she met downstairs was Mr Avery?

Suddenly, a flood of anger submerged her hopeless distress and the temper that went with her red hair began to rise. She would not stay here in her room as if she were a prisoner. She had done nothing wrong; why shouldn't she face Edmund Avery and demand to know why he had done such a dreadful thing?

Impatiently, in a fever now to confront the family, she rang the bell for Grace; it was important that she looked cool and elegant this morning, with her hair up in a fashionable style. She would wear her best lavender day dress and meet everyone with confidence.

A tap at the door and a small, thin girl in the pale green uniform of a Pemberley maid, wearing a frilly cap that seemed far too big, appeared and dropped a respectful bob, although the wobble as she rose gave her a comic appearance.

"Miss Malliot." Her voice quavered between high and low and she seemed very nervous. She wasn't pretty but Miriam could see at once that her eyes were bright with intelligence.

"Oh, who are you? I rang for Grace."

"I'm to be your new maid, Miss. My name's Sally Finch. I'll try and give satisfaction."

Miriam stared at the girl who could surely be no more than fourteen. "But where is Grace? Is she sick? I'm sure you will try your best, Sally, but I need my hair put up today. Can you undertake such a task?"

Sally, who had arrived at Pemberley as kitchen maid from the local orphanage three years before, stared at the rippling mane of wild red hair and tried to look confident.

Grace's sudden departure had left the servants' hall in some disarray. It was rumoured, although not in her presence, that Miss Reynolds was reluctant to employ another full time lady's maid just for Miss Malliot. It was well known that the poor relation from Africa would be leaving soon to live down south with her mother. So Sally had been told by Miss Reynolds that she should maid Miss Malliot.

She knew that the housekeeper did not like her; it had been obvious to Sally from the day of her arrival at Pemberley that Miss Reynolds did not care to have orphans foisted onto her household. Sally had once overheard her talking to the cook, saying that Mrs Darcy's kind heart would be her undoing one day; she would employ the child of some dreadful criminal and they would all be murdered in their beds.

Sally was quite convinced that she had been given this job in order to fail. If Miss Malliot complained about her, then she would be shown the door and who would employ her if Pemberley turned her out? So she had listened to the advice of "do your best" with mixed feelings. She had been forced to take a bath, although she had had one only two weeks ago. Miss Reynolds had inspected her fingernails, exclaimed over their bitten state but agreed that at least they were clean.

The housekeeper's opinion that she might not be good enough had stirred a stubborn streak in Sally. For all of her young life she had been told that very same thing, had been rejected and overlooked, told to work hard, keep silent and know her place.

She had watched and listened to Grace, admiring the older girl in some ways and in others believing she was a fool. Grace had a family in the local village; she had been brought up in safe home and given a job in the best house in Derbyshire. She had been walking out with Archie, the head groom, whom Sally thought really handsome.

Recently, though, Grace had spent hours telling the rest of the servants that she was destined for a different sort of life than being married and having a passel of babies before she was thirty.

She might well have wanted to spread her wings and fly away from Pemberley, but Sally, who had sadly never read the old Greek fable of Icarus and his wings of wax, because such books were not available at the orphanage, would still have understood that flying too close to the sun could cause you all sorts of trouble.

"I reckon I can put your hair up real pretty, Miss," she said now, reaching for a comb and hairpins. "I saw how you had it at the ball last night. Us maids were peeping round the stairwell when you was all dancing. You were partnering that Mr Sullivan in the new dance everyone wants to try. Lord, you should have seen us all in the kitchen, trying to keep in time to cook singing!"

Miriam tried not to let her expression change at the mention of Nicholas. "There is no need to make it too complicated, but I must look tidy. So Sally Finch, what has happened to Grace? I do hope she isn't too unwell."

Sally's flying fingers hesitated on a tiny braid she was making. She had no idea what she was allowed to speak about to Miss Malliot. The housekeeper had instructed her not to gossip, but the young lady had asked her a direct question and Sally knew it was against the Commandments to lie. Why, hadn't she been at the family service in church only last Sunday when that new Reverend had spoke such a long and difficult sermon all about lying? And his daughter had worn such a pretty blue bonnet!

"Grace has gone to London, Miss."

"London!"

"Yes, Miss. She left with Mr Avery at dawn. Well, before dawn, the sky was only just a little lighter over to the east. Mr Avery's fine carriage was readied and off they went. Grace didn't even say goodbye to us. Not even to Archie - he's the head groom in the stables Miss and Grace was walking out with him until...well. She never said goodbye, anyways. I heard he was proper upset to see her go."

Miriam sighed: so Grace had gone to London to be with Fletcher, the man she loved. At least someone had had a happy ending to their romance last night. And her prayers had been answered - Edmund Avery had left - she was in no doubt that his abrupt departure had been hastened by her uncle. A man who could use the image of an innocent young woman in such a way would not be allowed to stay at Pemberley, mixing with the Darcy family, no matter how brilliant an artist he was.

She watched in the mirror as Sally put the finishing touches to her hair; the maid had done a remarkably good job, even if she had used an extraordinary number of pins! "That looks very good, Sally. Thank you. Now, help me with my dress and I will write a note for you to deliver to Mr Sullivan."

"But Mr Sullivan has left too, Miss."

"Left Pemberley?" Miriam was thankful that her back was turned to the maid as the girl tied the sash on her dress and smoothed out the creases in the skirt. She was sure that the expression on her face would have portrayed her anguish only too clearly.

"Oh yes, Miss." Sally was only too pleased to be able to relate another piece of news. "Seems he got a letter about some old ship of his. He's to be a captain, which James and Archie think is very grand indeed, and is off to foreign parts. South America, so they say, which is a mortal long way away, and dangerous, being full of cannibals and such like. He has to sail across a great ocean and James says there are sea monsters that can swallow a ship whole! I'd like to see a monster. That I would."

Miriam fought back the tears. So she could not even ask to speak to him once more, to try and explain, to assure him she knew nothing of Edmund Avery's actions. He might not have believed her, but at least she would have tried, no matter how demeaning a conversation it would have been. But he had gone, off to the wide oceans, endless skies, foreign ports and people she would never see.

She had always known that this would happen, but she had, in her heart of hearts, believed that they would part as friends and that she would always carry with her the warmth of his affection into her dull future life.

Dismissing Sally, she made her way cautiously downstairs. It was past lunchtime, although she was sure Miss Reynolds would bring her a repast if she asked. There was no sign of Bennetta or her brothers and sisters. The great house seemed to lie slumbering in the Spring sunshine that streamed in through every window. Oh, how she longed for fresh air, to be outside away from all these walls with the portraits of men and women who stared down at her with accusing glances.

Determined not to encounter her aunt or uncle if she could avoid them, Miriam made her way through the passages and stairways towards the servants' part of the house to where a small door opened out into a sunny courtyard where the maids had hung the washing to dry in the warm breeze.

She had never considered before how difficult it must be in this part of the world to dry things quickly, how important it was for the beds to be stripped whenever the sun shone or the wind blew.

At home, in the hot sun, linen would dry in minutes; here it was a task that required the utmost caution and awareness of the changeable weather.

Modestly she averted her eyes from where the families' undergarments hung, but watched as lines of sheets billowed in the wind, reminding her instantly of the white sails that had filled with great snapping noises as the *Sea Sprite* ran for home across the dark green sea. Here there was to be no respite from her memories. It seemed her fate that everywhere she turned, something would remind her of Nicholas and a love she had been so close to receiving.

Miriam stood for minutes more, then pushed her memories of his smile, the warmth of his hand, the passion in his gaze, to the back of her mind. She could not avoid her aunt any longer: she must go indoors and discuss what had happened. As she turned to go, a man was coming out of the door.

Miriam gasped in surprise. Surely it couldn't be? But there was no mistaking that figure, the supercilious expression - it was Fletcher, Mr Avery's valet, not on the coach headed for London with his master but still here at Pemberley!

CHAPTER 17

"Why, good afternoon, Fletcher. I am surprised to see you here." Miriam was suddenly overwhelmed by the thought that he might well have seen the painting. But there was no sign of disrespect or over familiarity in his expression and surely such a knowledge would have shown on his face?

The tall young man stopped and nodded respectfully. If he had been confronted by one of the Darcy sisters, he would not have replied, but their cousin had always treated him kindly, as if he existed as a human being and he knew she would not find it impertinent if he spoke.

"Good afternoon, Miss Malliot. I am on a quest to find my laundry which I hope to discover is dry. I need to pack before I leave."

She frowned. "You did not travel to London with Mr Avery?"

There was a long pause, then, "I have left Mr Avery's service, Miss."

Miriam was puzzled. Surely such a prize position was not to be discarded lightly. "I thought you were happily settled, Fletcher. Surely, with Grace going to London - "

The valet's look of disapproval grew even stronger! "I am afraid that - " and then he stopped, realising whom he was talking to about such personal matters.

"I wish you both nothing but good," Miriam said earnestly. "I am sure you will have a happy life together."

Fletcher looked confused. "Both of us? I fear you are under a misapprehension, Miss Malliot. I have no relationship with Grace Frost. Indeed, not. She has left Pemberley under the protection of Mr Avery."

There was a silence, broken only by the snapping and billowing of the sheets on the washing lines. Miriam was so astonished that she hardly knew what to say. Grace and Edmund Avery? That couldn't be so. Surely the girl hadn't put herself into such a position with a man whose morals were questionable at the very least.

"She has gone to be a maid in his household, perhaps? Or work in the kitchen? I know she longed to see London and so would take a lesser position than here."

Fletcher fixed his gaze on the wall behind her head. "I believe Grace Frost thinks that Mr Avery will marry her, Miss."

"Marry her!" Suddenly Miriam saw how she had, in her innocence of such affairs, completely misread all the signs that she had seen. It had never been Fletcher who had been the subject of Grace's affections; all this time she had wanted Edmund Avery. That explained her annoyance at Miriam being summoned to the studio by him so often, her pleasure when he cancelled an appointment.

With that knowledge came another revelation. That woman's body in the painting, the naked body on which Avery had transposed a copy of Miriam's head and face - that must have been Grace's. Oh, how terrible! Unthinkable. If she was right in her surmise, the girl was lost, completely lost.

"Certain events have taken place that I found I could not countenance," Fletcher said pompously. "I have always been aware that life with a famous artist is different to that I would experience in the households of other gentlemen. But things have transpired here at Pemberley that made me so bold as to approach Mr Darcy and ask him if he was in need of another valet here."

"But you said you are packing? So you are not staying here?"

Fletcher smiled and for a second or two lost his supercilious expression and seemed like a good natured young man.

"I am to go to Clifton Park, to serve Mr Charles Bingley. His current valet is, I am told, an elderly gentleman and I am to study under him. If I am found suitable, I believe the plan is for me to take over that position in due course."

He nodded his head and turned away to walk further into the lines of washing. Confused and angry, Miriam made her way indoors, back to the family side of the house, through the doors that shut off one world from the other.

Her mind was still upset, her concentration wrecked at the thought of silly, pretty Grace throwing aside all claims to respectability, to marriage to someone like Archie who would give her security, or even if marriage was not to be, then to still have a place to live and work in relative comfort and safety.

She was desperate to talk to someone about what had happened. Before she had been reluctant to speak to her aunt, ashamed and worried that Elizabeth Darcy might think she had known what Edmund Avery was doing with that dreadful picture. But her own feelings were of little importance now. Surely there must be some way of rescuing Grace, of retrieving her from Avery's company and returning her to Pemberley?

As she passed through the door that led from the servants side to the main hall of the house, her aunt was coming down the wide, curving stairway and saw her.

"Miriam! My dear, there you are. I have been looking for you everywhere." She took her arm and escorted her back up the stairway to the yellow drawing-room. "How are you?" she asked as they seated themselves. A footman brought in a tray of hot chocolate and she waved him away and poured it out herself.

"Quite recovered, Aunt, thank you. I am ashamed of myself for being so missish and silly last night. I admit it was a shock to see my face on that...well, on that other girl's body, but I know I am quite innocent of any outlandish misbehaviour and hope my family will all believe that, too."

"There is no need for anyone else to even hear about what transpired. Your cousins were oblivious to the scandal and apart from Mr Sullivan, none of the guests were any the wiser. Your uncle will certainly not talk of the matter again, he considers it closed. And Mr Sullivan has been summoned to London to take command of his ship. I am sure he has far more important matters on his mind than what happened last night."

'Yes, I am sure he does,' Miriam thought sadly. 'Oh, if only I could be sure that he doesn't think I am in any way responsible. It is beyond belief that he should sail away to the far side of the world with his opinion and respect of me shattered.'

But her cares must be put aside for now: there was someone with a greater need of help. "Aunt Elizabeth, there is one other matter concerning me greatly. It regards my maid, Grace Frost."

Elizabeth raised her hand to stop Miriam speaking. "I can let you go no further, my dear. Grace has left our employ."

"But if someone went after her? Insisted that she return to the safety of Pemberley? Oh Aunt, if we don't then what will become of her? She is no older than I am. How can we let her life be ruined without trying to intervene?"

Her aunt's expression was solemn. "I am afraid she is beyond help, Miriam. Miss Reynolds, who is in charge of the servants, spoke to her before she left and assured me that the girl was quite determined to go with Avery. Stupid and headstrong and foolish, and I fear already ruined, but set on making her way in a world she knows nothing about."

"But..."

"And I fear that even if we could persuade her to leave him, she could not return to Pemberley. The best we could do is find her another position, some place, perhaps, where her history would not be a matter of concern - if such a place existed! But sadly she apparently seems convinced that her future is secure with Mr Avery, so there is nothing more we can do. Now, let us turn to happier matters - look, my dear, this is why I was coming to find you. At last a letter has arrived this morning from Mary."

"From Mama!" Miriam reached out for the creased and torn sheet of paper. "Goodness, it looks as if it has suffered in its journey here."

"Indeed - but the news is good. Mary writes to say she has two people interested in buying the school, so she is packing and soon will be taking a berth on a ship bound for England. She must be on her way by now - indeed, we may hear from her at any moment to say which ship she boarded."

"Oh!"

"There is no letter for you at the moment, but Mary may not even have received yours telling her that you are living at Pemberley. Her missive to you has probably gone to the Bingley house in London."

"But we have no home yet! Mama will be expecting to move into a house straight away."

Elizabeth concentrated on pouring a little more chocolate into their cups. She felt sorry for the girl. She could well imagine that her independent spirit would soon be crushed by the boredom of being company for Mary and probably helping out Kitty and her husband with all the various church affairs that any parish had in abundance.

But there was no alternative. A house must be found near Longbourn; Mr Darcy was opposed to Mary living near to Pemberley. He had never felt any affection for her sister. Charles Bingley was less vehement in his opinions, but Jane - even though her nature was such that she tried to see the best in everyone - had said she felt exhausted at the idea of Mary being close enough to visit on a daily basis with offers of help, guidance and religious quotations.

"Well, it has been decided that in a few days time, Mr Darcy and I will travel down to London with you. It should take us two days. We can call briefly at Longbourn, so you can meet your grandmother - who is rightly annoyed that she has yet to see you - and your Aunt Kitty and gather information about local properties for rent, then continue to our house in Grosvenor Square. There is no room to stay with the Collins' family. Longbourn is not a big residence, although Jane and I still have very happy memories of growing up there."

Miriam was silent. She gazed around the beautiful drawing-room, one of her favourite places in the house. When she had arrived from Africa, she had thought Pemberley too big, too cold, too unfriendly, but now it was her protection from the world.

It wasn't the luxury that she would miss, although she was certain her life with her mother would be far more mundane. But here were all her recent memories of Nicholas, good and bad. She could picture him in so many places. Yes, she would be reluctant to leave, but leave she must, she could feel the prison bars of her future life beginning to close around her.

"I will need to pack everything," she said quietly. "I shall be a visitor when I next see Pemberley again."

"Well, let us hope that will be a regular event," Elizabeth said brightly. "You must try and come back very soon to see Cassandra's baby. This infant is making everyone wait for its entrance! I do declare poor Richard is a wreck of a man. Becoming a father does not seem an enjoyable experience for him, even though he is a doctor. But then, Mr Darcy always said he suffered more than I did during the birth of our children, mentally if not physically!"

Smoothing down her skirts, Miriam stood up. "I will go and gather together my possessions in order to pack them. I am sure my new maid will help."

Elizabeth frowned then said, "I would suggest you leave Sally Finch here, my dear. She is so young and really quite unsuitable as a lady's maid. She was taken in from the orphanage to be a scullery maid and hopefully progress to kitchen maid. I have no idea why Miss Reynolds sent her to you. There are plenty of other girls in the household who will undertake the duties well. I am quite happy to pay their wages for a year, until your mama's affairs are settled."

Miriam felt a flash of irritation. It was clear that Sally was just as much a misfit in the Darcy household as she was herself.

"That is kind of you, Aunt, but if it is not a great inconvenience, I would prefer to keep Sally. I have taken a liking to her and she is very neat and anxious to please. But I do thank you for paying her wages for a year. I know Mama will be delighted to learn of your generosity."

"Quite." Elizabeth bit her lip. She was quite certain that Mary would expect a lot more from her family than the wages of one very small maid! "Well, if you are happy with Sally, then we will say no more about it. I am sure it will make no difference to Miss Reynolds, and to be honest, I have heard that the child has a sharp tongue that sometimes lands her in trouble. Perhaps removing her from Pemberley will be to everyone's advantage.

"Now, run along and tell Bennetta and the others your news. They will be sad to see you leave, but no doubt pleased your mama is arriving very soon and you will be comfortably settled. I am sure we will all be meeting up regularly in London in the months to come. We are already planning for Bennetta's coming out dance which will probably be held in July in London. You can consider yourself invited to that already."

It is a fact that one person's disappointment might well be a dream come true to another. Such was Miriam's proposed move from Pemberley. Sally Finch could hardly believe her luck. London! She was going to London! She had never dreamt that such a thing could happen to her. Orphan girls in Derbyshire with nothing but hard work and their wits to keep them from the poor house, never got a chance to travel, even to towns such as Manchester or Liverpool.

London was a fairy tale city, gold lined the pavements and even if it was only for a few weeks until the Malliots were established in a cottage in Hertfordshire, it would be an experience she would treasure for the rest of her life.

Although she felt her whole being cloaked in misery at losing Nicholas and having to leave Pemberley, Miriam couldn't help but smile a little at Sally's pleasure. How odd life was when what she considered a misfortune gave such pleasure elsewhere. She left the maid packing her trunk and cases in a fashion she was sure would not reach Miss Reynolds' high standards, and set out to seek Bennetta.

She found her on the terrace that ran outside of the garden room. Reclining on a chair, with her feet on a footstool, enjoying the late afternoon sunlight, she waved a hand lazily at Miriam.

"Mirry! I have just heard your news from Mama. I don't know whether to be pleased that you will soon be reunited with your mother or sad that you will be leaving Pemberley. How do you feel?"

"A little of both." Miriam sat on the low stone wall that bordered the terrace and stared out over the flower gardens that descended down a slope towards the orchards beyond where Spring flowers were busy spreading a carpet of yellow and white. She hoped that whatever house they found in Hertfordshire would be close to open space, somewhere she could escape to, somewhere she could feel the wind in her face.

"I will miss you, but as you know the twins and I will be in London a great deal in the months to come - especially for my coming out dance in July. That will be very exciting. I am sure your mama will spare you to visit us whenever we are there. Lord, I am so tired. Did you enjoy the ball? You went to bed so early, I suppose you are not weary at all."

Miriam just nodded; she was well aware that Bennetta and her sisters knew nothing of Edmund Avery's infamous behaviour and that her aunt did not want them informed as to why he had left Pemberley so abruptly. For a minute or two she sat, wondering wistfully how nice it must be to be guarded and shielded from the more sordid aspects of life.

"La, here is Mr Sullivan, come to make his farewells, no doubt."

"Nicholas!"

Miriam spun round, colour rushing to her face. How could it possibly be him - Sally had told her he had left Pemberley. Or perhaps she had meant he was about to leave? Whatever the reason, here was the one person who, apart from her uncle and the artist himself, had seen that dreadful portrait. A man whom she was sure had been about to declare his feelings until he had learnt that she had not trusted him - and how grateful he must now be that fate had stepped in before he could utter those vital words. Nicholas Sullivan, a man whom she loved but one whom she knew would soon be leaving her to her mundane existence while he set sail for foreign lands.

Nicholas walked slowly up the terrace steps, tall, broad-shouldered, his fair hair pulled back, clubbed with a strip of leather into a tight bunch, dressed for riding, his boots gleaming in the afternoon sunlight. "Miriam, Miss Bennetta."

Miriam slid off the wall and curtsied to him, keeping her face lowered, hoping upon hope that the blush in her cheeks would diffuse and vanish, scared to look into his eyes in case she saw disdain and condemnation there.

"Mr Sullivan. Please take a seat. I hear you are leaving us today?" Bennetta smiled up at him. "We shall all miss you, won't we, Mirry, but especially Henry. I do declare that if you had remained here at Pemberley much longer, he would have insisted on stowing away on your ship in order to see all the wonders you have talked about."

"Perhaps your parents should look to the navy for a career for Henry. He is quite old enough to sign on as a midshipman. A very hard life, but a very fulfilling one for a young gentleman."

"Well, I know Mama and Papa have considered the navy as part of Henry's future, what with Fitz inheriting Pemberley..."

Miriam could not concentrate on the conversation; she was only aware that the heavy blue of his sleeve was so close to her arm that she could have reached out and touched the broad, bronzed hand that rested on his knee. It was hard to realise that those powerful fingers could haul on a rope and play exquisite music equally well.

Finally summoning all her courage, she raised her head and caught his gaze. He was looking at her gravely, even as he spoke to Bennetta about the difficulties of Henry being a second son. At last he paused, then changing the subject said, "I hear that your mother is expected to arrive from Africa any day now, Miriam?"

"Yes, a letter reached my aunt and uncle, although I am yet to receive a direct missive myself. I travel to London in a few days' time to be close by when she reaches England. We are to take a house in Meryton to be near my grandmother and my other aunt, Mrs Kitty Collins."

"You will no doubt be pleased to have your life well-ordered and settled. It has been anything but of late!"

Miriam bit her lip at his dry tone, guessing what he was referring to, a wave of anguish passing over her. She was vaguely aware of Benetta's curious gaze and felt herself torn. If they had been alone she would have told Nicholas that she had played no part in the portrait but she had given her word to her aunt that no one should know except those involved. She could not start on any explanation with her cousin sitting there. Bennetta would want to know the whole story from start to finish.

"My time at Pemberley has not always been spent as I would wish," she said carefully, aware of the steady gaze from the grey eyes she loved so much.

"Oh Mirry, poor Mr Sullivan is well aware of that. Why, was it not him who was your saviour when you were trying to rescue that kitten from the river!"

"Indeed it was and I will always be grateful to him. For that and everything else he has done for me." She paused for a second, then went on with, she hoped, meaning in her voice, "I do hope he realises that, although I have made mistakes, believed people to think stupid thoughts when I should have trusted my own judgement, I have not always been at fault and have never acted with indiscretion."

Nicholas nodded; he knew only too well that she was referring both to Mrs Tremaine and Avery. "Sometimes blame for what happens to us in life has to be laid at the feet of other people."

Miriam felt the colour flood back into her cheeks but his words comforted her. He understood that the artist was at fault. He must realise she had not posed for the dreadful portrait but from his remote manner, she wondered if he thought she had known that her face had been used. That was too painful a situation to bear.

"You must be looking forward to seeing your mother once more."

"Yes, Sir, I am," she answered honestly. "She has gone through a great deal of grief and has been dealing with all kinds of problems on her own. I know she will be eager for us to settle down here in England and it is my duty as her only child to make her life as comfortable as I can."

"Oh Mirry, how dramatic! You sound as if you are being condemned to a life in prison. You can't possibly imagine that you will spend the rest of your life looking after Aunt Mary. You will meet so many people in Meryton. Why, I declare I think you will probably be married long before me or even Anne or Jane!"

Bennetta tossed back her dark curls and laughed, her sharp gaze flicking between the sailor and her cousin. "And if you find a nice suitable husband, why I'm sure he would have no problem with your mama living with you after your marriage."

Miriam shivered, although it was still warm on the terrace. How easy it was for her cousin to talk of marriage and a life she herself would never have to experience. A marriage of convenience, for that was what it would be, was not something Miss Bennetta Darcy of Pemberley would ever have to face. No, she would be allowed, within reason, to follow her heart. She would never have to face the prospect of a future without the only man she would ever love. Even the thought of marrying someone else when she loved Nicholas so much caused Miriam to feel sick and giddy.

"I shall never marry," she said quietly but with a steely determination that brokered no argument.

Nicholas stood up suddenly. He could bear the situation no longer. There she stood, the brave, stubborn girl that he loved so much and he knew she was destined for a life of, if not unhappiness, than of boring duty.

It was all he could do to keep his voice and tone under control, to show as little of the emotion he was suffering as possible. He had, at one time, hoped Miriam had feelings for him as strong as those he had for her, but obviously he was wrong. He was certain that she had not known of Avery's abominable behaviour, but that did not mean that she had not cared for the artist. If she had loved him, then his betrayal must have doubled the pain she felt.

"I must be on my way," he said and bent to kiss the hand Bennetta held out to him. "I wish you a safe journey, Miriam, and a successful reunion with your mother."

"Will we see you when you return from the East?" Bennetta asked. "I long for a length of scarlet silk, if any should come your way."

Nicholas nodded and smiled down at her. "Your wish is my command. Pray, if your sisters or brothers have any commissions for me, then I will be only too happy to serve. Perhaps you could make a list and I will call at your London house to collect it before I sail."

He turned to Miriam, his tall figure blocking the sun he was so close. She reached out a hand, almost imploringly and he took it and, unseen by Bennetta, turned it over and kissed the palm. Then he folded her fingers over his kiss, bowed again and strode away.

CHAPTER 18

Matlock House, the Darcys' London home, stood at one side of a quiet, elegant square; a flat faced, three storied, double fronted building. Only ten years old, its tall, graceful windows gazing out at the trees and bushes that flourished around the grass and flower beds that the gardeners worked tirelessly to keep looking beautiful.

It had been placed back from the roadway, a gravel sweep allowing carriages to deliver their passengers to where a flight of steps led up to the central front door, painted the dark green of the Darcy livery with a splendid ornamental fan window letting in light to the hall beyond. Railings shut off the two steep flights of stone steps that led on one side to the copious cellars and coal holes and on the other to the kitchens and sculleries.

Inside, Miriam had found as much to admire as she had at Pemberley; tall, elegantly furnished rooms with marble fireplaces and shining wood floors that showed all the discreet taste of their owners but still gave the appearance of a home rather than some cold, stately mansion.

The main living-rooms were situated on one side of the hall and on the other was the doorway to a small but lavish ballroom. At the rear of the hall, a sweeping curved stairway hid the door to the kitchens and lead up to the next floor where the main bedrooms were situated.

There was no fault to be found with her own room - it was the one apparently used by Bennetta when she was in town, but Miriam felt as if the walls were closing in on her and spent as much time as she could out in the square, sitting on a bench in the fresh air, accompanied by Sally Finch.

But even in the square she felt imprisoned - houses all around, no views, just a small patch of sky above her and the heavy odours of London, the chimney smoke, the horse dung that constantly littered the streets, the waft of the unwashed from the numerous beggars that gathered round public places, all caught in her nose and throat and made her feel sick and giddy.

How she longed for open spaces, for the brisk wind coming off the hills of Derbyshire, the acres of woodlands in which to walk. But how could she complain? She was living in luxury and everything that she needed was there for her use and convenience, until she could take possession of the small house that Mr Darcy had found for her mother to rent in the town of Meryton.

She was hard pressed to remember it now. The visit to Lambourn had been hectic and had only gone to support her notion that the Malliots would be the very poor relations of the family in the years to come.

"Oh, what a great tall creature you are!" her grandmother had exclaimed. Small and elderly, dressed in an old fashioned way with a great deal of lace and frills, Mrs Bennet had examined Miriam from red head to booted foot and obviously not been impressed with what she saw. The daughter of her difficult, middle daughter held no charms for her.

"I am pleased to meet you at last, I'm sure. I have no idea what Mary was thinking of in sending you to stay with the Darcys. You should have come straight here. We have plenty of room. You could have shared a room with Harriet's nursemaid."

Her Aunt Kitty had been far too involved with her dressmaker to do more than greet Elizabeth and Miriam. It was difficult for Miriam to believe that this large bosomed lady, smelling strongly of some very powerful scent, with a constant expression of dissatisfaction on her face, was sister to her Aunts Elizabeth and Jane.

She hardly mentioned Mary's imminent arrival at all, except for saying her help in the various charities that her husband, Mr Collins, ran would be useful. Most of her conversation was aimed at bringing in references to "my stepdaughter, Lady Courtney" over and over again.

Miriam had found herself echoing her Aunt Elizabeth's sigh of relief as their carriage finally drew away from Lambourn and headed back into Meryton. Mr Darcy had stayed in the town - he had no desire to meet his mother-in-law or Mr and Mrs Collins - talking to his lawyers and making sure that one or two important repairs would be done to the house before Mary and Miriam moved in.

The house had been much as Miriam had expected and feared - a respectable, plain building in a respectable, plain, busy street, not far from the market and the church. There was a small yard at the back but there was not so much as a glimpse of hills from the upstairs windows.

Her aunt had sounded enthusiastic; to her it was exactly what she had hoped to find for them; two decent size living-rooms, three bedrooms and a tiny room in the attic for a maid servant. She busied herself with lists of what was needed in the way of furniture because they still had not heard from Mary as to how much of their African home she had shipped back to England. She was quite sure that between the Darcys and the Bingleys they could furnish the house and make it comfortable for their sister.

"I think you will both be very happy here," she said. "Everything close by, shops, market, church and I am sure Mr Collins will send his carriage every weekend to carry you to Longbourn for dinner. Indeed, it is not that far to walk, only a mile - we often did so as girls and I know you love to wander, Miriam."

Miriam was too unhappy to take much notice of the house. It was as if a sheet of glass had descended between herself and the rest of the world. She looked and commented, answered questions and made decisions, but all the time she was thinking of Nicholas, of how much she missed him, of how much she would always miss him.

Ten days had passed since they had left Pemberley and there was still no word that Mary had reached England. Mr Darcy had made copious enquiries: no vessel was reported missing, thank goodness, but no one by the name of Malliot had disembarked from any ship arriving from an African port.

Miriam was well aware that her uncle was anxious to return to Derbyshire but her aunt was reluctant to leave her alone in Matlock House. It was decided that they would wait another week, and then, if there was still no news, Miriam would go to stay with her grandmother and Aunt Kitty until Mary arrived and the Darcys would return home.

Elizabeth was anxious to travel north. Word had finally, joyfully, arrived that Cassandra Courtney had been safely delivered of a daughter and she was keen to see the newest addition to the family circle.

"They have named her Victoria, in honour of the young Princess Alexandrina Victoria," Elizabeth announced with satisfaction as she read the letter over the luncheon table. "Victoria Susannah Elizabeth - it is very sweet of Cassandra to ask me to be a godmother."

"I am delighted all is well," Miriam said, trying to inject some enthusiasm into her voice, wondering when her frozen emotions would relent enough for her to experience genuine feelings again. "I see that there is still no letter from Mama."

Elizabeth frowned. "No, nothing at all. I really do think it is careless of Mary to leave you so precariously situated. I have no doubt that she is well aware we will care for you, but she should at least let someone in the family know on what vessel she sails."

Miriam had no defence of these words; she was beginning to be alarmed by her mother's silence but if any ship had foundered at sea, then it would be public knowledge by now. All she could imagine was that some problem had occurred with the sale of the school and her mama had been forced to delay her departure from Africa.

"There is, however, a letter to you from Bennetta. She enclosed it with her news of Victoria's arrival. Here, I am sure you will enjoy all her gossip from Pemberley."

She handed Miriam the folded sheets then continued, "Mr Darcy and I intend to visit the British Museum this afternoon. Mr Darcy is keen to study some items they have on show that have been collected in Japan. Do you wish to accompany us?"

Miriam shook her head. She had not the slightest interest in Japanese artefacts and knew for certain that Mr Darcy would much prefer to have his wife to himself, rather than the niece he disapproved of joining them.

"I think I will walk in the park, Aunt. I like looking at the children sailing boats on the lake."

"You must not go alone."

"Oh no, I shall take Sally Finch with me."

Miriam thought that the diminutive maid was hardly likely to be of great use as a protector, but at least it would keep her reputation intact. She also didn't mention to her aunt that one of the attractions of the park was Sally's utter enjoyment in watching the grand carriages drive up and down the road that encircled the inside of the vast green space. Her comments on the ladies' outfits were always amusing. Indeed, listening to her maid's sometimes outrageous remarks had been the only thing to bring a smile to Miriam's face since leaving Pemberley.

They found a shady spot under a tree and Sally spread out a rug she had carried from the house. Miriam leant back against the warm tree trunk and unfolded Bennetta's letter as Sally sat, gazing happily at the fashionable carriages that passed by, the troops in their bright uniforms exercising their horses, a military band with shining trumpets and noisy drums, water carts soaking the sandy road to keep down the clouds of dust, hawkers and traders shouting their wares and all the varied folk of London, from every station in life, walking in the sunshine through the park.

"My dear Mirry, I write in great haste as I am shortly to ride over to visit Cassandra and her dear little baby. Cassie is very well and the child thrives, apparently. Richard is very much relieved and I have caught him

smiling in an idiotic fashion when he looks at his daughter. I'm sure Papa never looked at me like that! I can only ever remember him frowning.

"Anyway, I am glad to get out of the house for a while; Anne and Jane have had an argument - I don't know what about although I am desperate to discover the problem. It is so odd - Jane is so quiet and I have never known her have cross words with Anne before. With Mama and Papa away, it makes for very unhappy mealtimes, as you can well imagine. But I am sure they will soon be friends again; it must be difficult being a twin, especially a twin to Anne. It is hard enough for me being her little sister!

Mama writes that you have found a house in Meryton and I will await your direction so we can correspond. I do hope you will have heard from Aunt Mary by the time you read this. In the meanwhile, hopefully you will see Captain Sullivan before he sails - can you please tell him that apart from my scarlet silk, the twins would like some white and gold embroidered gauze, Fitz wonders if a book in Chinese symbols would be possible and Henry wants a parrot. I'm sure the silk and the book are suitable but I think Mama would wish you to forget about the parrot!

Do give him my very best wishes for a safe journey to the East and home again. Heavens, I am told by Fitz that it might be over two years before we see him again! It is a shame he will miss my coming out party in August. Yes, the ball has been put back another month because Papa has to make a journey to Ireland to deal with a problem with our estates there that Great Uncle Gardiner looks after. Mama wants him to sell them and I have a feeling she will get her way.

That will at least mean that our beloved Great Uncle and Aunt Gardiner and their children will be coming back to live in England. I know Mama wants them to settle nearby. It will be lovely to have them close enough to visit regularly. I do not know them nearly as well as I would like, Ireland being so far away and the only time I might have seen them, I was in disgrace and forced to stay at home! Still, that is how Cassandra and I met so every dark story has a silver lining!

It must be difficult for Captain Sullivan to leave England and all his friends. One in particular, I am certain he will miss! I could tell when he said his goodbyes that he had strong feelings for you. You were both trying to pretend indifference, but I am an old hand at deciphering the expressions of those in love. I knew about Catherine and Sir Robert almost before they knew themselves!

You would make a handsome couple, Mirry, and for some reason I cannot quite define, even though he is only a merchant sailor, I feel he is more of a gentleman than Mr Avery. That is another secret I am determined to discover - why our handsome artist left Pemberley in the middle of the night with Grace Frost and why our family portrait is not to be hung in the picture gallery? I am sure I can guess about Grace - I am not the child Mama thinks I am - but banishing the artwork to the attics puzzles me.

Do write with all your news, cousin. Life is very boring without you here. Cassie is completely absorbed by the baby and has little time for gossip any more. I do not feel I shall ever marry and have children. They seem to dull one's mind.

as ever, Bennetta in a hurry.

Miriam folded the letter away into a pocket with a sigh. Had her feelings for Nicholas really been so apparent? Did everyone guess or was it just her sharp eyed cousin who had seen through what she had thought was a brave facade?

Carefully crossing the road between carriages, she wandered down to the edge of the lake, gazing out at the small sail boats that skimmed the surface, urged on by little boys whose one aim seemed to be to escape from their nursemaids' care and plunge into the water up to their knees.

She stared at a particularly large toy yacht, the white sails flapping in the light breeze, remembering, so clearly, standing on the deck of *Sea Sprite*, gazing up at the vast set of sails outlined brilliantly white against the blue of the tropical sun. And once again, her memory refused to give her peace but brought her the figure of Nicholas Sullivan, swarming up the rigging with as much ease as one of his sailors, to stare out from the crow's nest at some distant view.

She wondered what he was doing now - *Sea Sprite* must surely be ready for sea? What feeling had Bennetta spied on his face in those last few moments when they said goodbye? Miriam tightened her fingers over her palm, remembering the feel of his lips on her skin, the way he had closed her fist over the kiss as if insisting that she kept it forever.

Sighing, she turned away from the white sails - it didn't matter if Nicholas did love her; she had promised her papa on his death bed that she would always care for her mother and that was a sacred vow she could not break. But suppose, just suppose, she thought, some way could have been found - a companion for her mother, perhaps. Surely her aunts could have arranged that? But that was idle speculation; he had not spoken and it might well be two years before they met again, if indeed they ever did.

Miriam turned back to where Sally was standing, waiting for her on the far side of the road. She waved, stepped forward and just then a very fine carriage, painted in red and yellow, drew up alongside her, the wheels dangerously close, the dust spattering her dress.

Sally Finch was very young, only just turned sixteen, but she had grown up in a hard world and learnt early on that you had to be aware at all times that danger could threaten you. She knew instinctively that her mistress, for whatever reason, was in that strange state of mind when she would not be concentrating on exactly what was going on around her.

Sally recognised the carriage; she had seen it often enough in the stable yard at Pemberley. All the gossip from the other servants rose up in her mind and, without another thought, she dodged between the cantering horses and a squad of marching soldiers, ignoring the furious shouts of the sergeant in charge, anxious to get to Miriam's side. For that was Edmund Avery's carriage and she was quite sure that no good could possibly come of a meeting with that gentleman.

Stepping back in alarm, to Miriam's astonishment the window was let down and a familiar face appeared. It was Grace Frost! But not the girl Miriam had known; the once clear, creamy skin was now heavily powdered and rouged, her hair was swept up in a ridiculous riot of curls and ringlets that must have taken a good hour to achieve and under her heavy satin cloak, it was obvious that her dress was so low cut as to be almost indecent.

"Grace!"

"Miss Malliot. I thought I recognised you as we drove along just now. I asked for the carriage to be turned round so I could come back this way."

Miriam was at a loss as to what to say but eventually she managed, "I suppose it belongs to Mr Avery?"

"To Edmund. Oh yes, indeed. Everything he owns is of the finest. I have never seen such luxury, even at Pemberley. I am sure you never dreamed of seeing me riding through London as good a lady as anyone." She lay her hand ostentatiously on the window ledge, so that the rings on her fingers gleamed in the sunlight.

"I would be happier seeing you safely back in Pemberley! It is surely not too late to go home. Arrangements could be made."

Grace tossed her head, the feathers and beads on her hat fluttering. For a long second there in front of her opened up another path she could tread, another life she could lead. Then she noticed Sally standing just behind Miriam, her mouth open, gazing up at her in astonishment and disdain and her mind hardened.

Sally's life, that of a servant, was one she had rejected. She was just as good as Miss Miriam Malliot, the Darcys' poor relation - indeed, Edmund had chosen her from all the girls who modeled for him. Had told her that she had the body of a goddess, a body that inspired him to great work. And if she played her cards right - and she had already made plans that were well underway - she was certain she would end up as Mrs Avery! And that would be so funny. How she would laugh if they met up with the Darcys at some society party and they had to be civil to her, Grace Frost, their one time servant.

"Pemberley! Why would I want to return to Pemberley? To a life of servitude?"

"A life of respectability, surely. Or..." Miriam hesitated. Was she being too cynical, jumping to conclusions that were unfounded by fact.... "or perhaps you are already married to Mr Avery."

There was a long pause. Miriam was aware of horses passing, their hoof beats softened by the sandy track, a drum was beating in the distance as a squad of soldiers passed by, people were laughing and talking, an old lady was selling lavender and a girl with a large basket of strawberries in their small woven pots was calling out her wares. A group of beggar children jumped up and down as they watched an organ grinder's monkey perform his tricks to an appreciative audience and she was aware that Sally had crossed the road and was standing just behind her.

"Not yet, but then Edmund has been so busy since we came to London that there has been no time to discuss the future. But as you can see - " she waved her hand again to make the rings sparkle - "he dotes on me - silks, furs, this carriage whenever I need it - I am in no doubt of his affections."

She smiled, maliciously. "I do hope you did not have hopes in that direction yourself, Miss Malliot. I know you modeled for Edmund as did I, although I think I had far longer sessions than you and gave him far more of what he required!"

Miriam felt a chill run through her and shivered, even though the afternoon sun was warm. The girl's meaning was quite obvious, that her naked body had been used in the dreadful painting that had destroyed so many of her dreams.

"I am afraid that as talented as he is, I also think Edmund Avery a black-hearted scoundrel and I am glad my uncle insisted that he leave Pemberley immediately, without so much as a formal goodbye to anyone. I am saddened that you have thrown in with him, Grace, and beg you to reconsider."

But the girl just laughed and leaning forward called to the coachman to go. The carriage started with a jerk and swung out in front of a rider whose horse snorted angrily and reared up, pawing the air. Clever horsemanship brought the startled animal to a standstill and, through the cloud of dust raised by the carriage wheels, Miriam found herself gazing up into stormy grey eyes she knew only too well.

"Nicholas! I mean, Mr Sullivan."

"Miriam! That was Avery's carriage. I would know that red and yellow trim anywhere." He swung down out of the saddle and lead his mount off the road, back to the shelter of the tree and tethered him to a branch. "Surely he did not have the impudence to stop and accost you? Surely you did not speak to him?"

He stared at her in sudden anger and alarm. Anger because he couldn't bear the thought that she could be charmed once again by that villain and alarmed because beneath her yellow sun bonnet, her face was pale and strained. His beautiful girl looked as if she hadn't slept for days and he had the feeling that an identical expression could be found on his own face.

His mind was in torment. He knew he loved Miriam Malliot deeply, wanted her for his wife, to be at his side. But he could not speak out. He would be away from England for at least two years on a dangerous voyage; how could he possibly ask her to be his wife, to be engaged to someone who might never return?

Miriam insisted she would never marry, would spend her life caring for her mother, but circumstances changed. What if for some reason she was left alone in the world with very little money? Agreed, the Darcys were always there to help, but he knew how independent Miriam was. His girl - oh, how he wished she was - would hate to take money from them. Marriage, even without affection, might seem like the most suitable way out of a difficult situation. But if she was engaged to him, a man who was travelling on the other side of the world with no way of knowing what was happening back in England, her life would be impossible.

No, he could not ask for her hand. If duty bound her actions and her life, then it did the same to him.

Miriam felt a flicker of anger in response to his own. Did he really think she was so malleable that she would be seduced into continuing a relationship that had caused her nothing but pain and grief?

"Mr Avery was not in the carriage, Sir. As you can imagine, I would not have spoken even if he had been. No, it was Grace, the girl who...my maid, who..." She could go no further and turned away to stroke the horse's mane, blinking back tears, hoping Nicholas could not see just how upset the encounter had made her.

"Forgive me, I spoke without thinking, from anger towards Avery and all the harm he has done. Of course I am quite certain that he would be the last person with whom you would wish to converse."

"Grace Frost was Miss Malliot's maid. She ran off with that Mr Avery," Sally piped up, completely unafraid of the burly figure in front of her.

All the staff at Pemberley had liked Mr Sullivan: he had been courteous and generous, handing out several coins when he left. She had heard all the gossip that raged below stairs about a certain painting no one was supposed to know about, although Fletcher, the valet, had told them what had transpired! They had all been shocked; Miss Malliot might not be a Darcy, but she was family and as such had their loyalty.

There was very little that went on above stairs that the servants did not know about and it was quite obvious to Sally and the rest of the female staff that Mr Sullivan and Miss Malliot had feelings for each other.

She was determined that the sea captain should understand the situation because at the moment he was standing, looking at Miss Malliot as if he didn't know what day of the week it was.

"Proper shock it was to see her. All done up in jewels and feathers, she was. With her face painted like...like a hussy! Goodness knows what Archie would think - she was walking out with Archie, the head groom, before she left, you see."

Nicholas nodded, beginning to understand a lot that had been unclear to him before. So that was where Avery had found his original model. He had seduced one of the maids, ruined the girl, whether she was willing or not, and had now set her up in his establishment as his mistress. He could only imagine what a shock it must have been for Miriam, bringing back all the memories she was probably trying so hard to forget.

"It was unfortunate that the carriage came past just now," Miriam said at last, trying to pull herself together from the delight of seeing Nicholas again. "If I were to live in London, I might worry about encountering Mr Avery, but I will soon be safely in Hertfordshire and my life will be such that such an opportunity will never happen."

"I am quite sure that the Darcys will not invite him to any function or attend any party where he might be a guest," Nicholas said quietly, recalling the rage that had flashed across his host's face, quickly followed by an icy calm of manner that was, in itself, more frightening. Avery hadn't just abused his position as a guest at Pemberley, he had involved a family member in his nefarious schemes. He himself had wanted to horsewhip the blighter, but he had the strongest feeling that Mr Darcy could ruin Avery as an artist if he so wished.

"So, your plans are settled, Miriam? You have found a home for you and your mother?"

Miriam turned to face him, willing the tears away. She wanted to recall every second they spent together, remember every aspect of his face. Tears that blinded her eyes would prevent her from doing that.

"Yes, Sir. It is in the little town of Meryton. Once my mama arrives from Africa, we will move there immediately."

Nicholas frowned. "I thought she would surely have reached these shores by now."

"There has obviously been some delay. Perhaps her vessel has been becalmed or had to put into a distant port for repairs. There has been no report of a disaster, so although I am concerned, I am not worried."

"I leave tomorrow morning, on the tide. I was just on my way to Matlock House to obtain the list of goods your family might want from the East."

"You sail tomorrow?" Miriam's voice was no more than a whisper and in it was all the pain of losing him. Sally, who was busy putting little braids in the horse's mane and apparently not listening, raised her eyebrows out of the couple's sight.

"Yes, there have been delays obtaining a crew and various last minute repairs, but all is now in order on *Sea Sprite.* We head down the Thames from our moorings tomorrow when the wind and tide should be in our favour."

"And so we shall not see you in England for a very long time."

"It will be over a year, I fear, probably closer to two. I am to take the ship round the Cape and on to the Far East."

"A very long journey indeed. And hazardous, I am sure."

Nicholas nodded, but Miriam could tell from the gleam in his eyes that it was a journey he was looking forward to taking. She felt a swell of envy. How she would love to travel the seas, discover new places, strange foreign ports and people.

Then the envy was vanquished by a surge of sadness at the thought of not seeing or hearing from Nicholas for such a long time. If he had only spoken again of his feelings for her, surely if he truly loved her, he would ask her to wait for him? And she would have done just that - willingly.

Sally watched silently in the background as her mistress and Captain Sullivan stood, talking in jerky, polite sentences that failed to hide from her sharp eyes exactly what they were really thinking and feeling.

She wanted to shout at them to stop acting in this silly fashion, to say what you wanted to, regardless of the consequences. But she had noticed before that the quality never made things easy for themselves.

Now the Captain had taken a small notebook from his jacket pocket and was writing down the list of items the Darcy children had requested from the Far East. Now he was smiling at Sally and handing her two gold coins! Now he was holding out his hand and taking Miss Malliot's and as Sally watched, he kissed her fingers, held her hand against his cheek for a moment, then abruptly swung up onto his mount and without another word, turned, cantered away towards the park gates and with a final wave of his hat, was gone.

CHAPTER 19

A wet and windy dawn was breaking over London as Miriam hurried down the back stairway of Matlock House, muffled in her travelling cloak, sensible boots on her feet. She had spent a long night in despair. She had shed no tears, she thought perhaps she was beyond that release. The pain of lost love was so great that she felt her very soul was damaged.

Then an hour ago, she had made a decision. Nothing would help her to feel better, but she wanted to watch the *Sea Sprite* sail, even perhaps catch one last glimpse of Nicholas on deck, giving orders, setting his face to the south and all the adventures that awaited him. She would wave her handkerchief and perhaps he would spot her and know he was in her thoughts, as he always would be.

Miriam was well aware that if she had asked her aunt for permission to go to the docks, it would have been refused. That area of London was rife with crime; gangs of men, out of work and desperate, roamed the streets: indeed the newspapers reported that there had been riots in many towns across England but she didn't care about the danger.

She knew that what she was doing would be frowned upon and she would get an even worse reputation for unruly behaviour. But she wasn't scared; the docks of Cape Town had been her childhood playground and she was sure the ones along the Thames would be safe enough if she was sensible.

She had just unlocked the side door that lead to the basement steps when a gasp behind her made her jump and turn.

"Miss Miriam! What...where are you going?" Sally Finch, still in her nightdress, bare footed with her hair tangled over her eyes, was standing in the kitchen doorway, clutching a ewer of hot water.

"Sally! Hush! Do not speak so loudly. Is there anyone else in the kitchen?"

"Not yet, Miss. Bessie, the scullery maid's just getting up. I share her room. I wanted to get some water off the stove whilst it was hot. But Miss, it's powerful early. You can't go out by yourself at this hour. Where are you going? Wait till I get dressed and I'll come along with you."

Miriam shook her head. "No, I shall be quite all right. I am going to the docks to watch the *Sea Sprite* leave. I shall take a hansom cab from the rank at the end of the square and will be quite safe. The drivers are known to be honest men and all that I have to fear is a loss of reputation and for that I care not."

Sally stared at her, not knowing what to say. A young lady going to the docks by herself! Even in her wildest imaginings would she ever have thought of doing such a thing. "But what do I say if the mistress asks for you?"

Miriam hesitated; she did not want the girl to lie for her, that might result with her losing her position in the Darcy household.

"Tell my aunt that last night I requested not to be disturbed until lunch time. That I was very tired from all our recent travelling. I shall be back long before midday and all will be well. I know you don't understand, Sally, but I have to take this chance of seeing Captain Sullivan just one more time."

And with those words she pulled her hood over the mane of red hair that she had not bothered to plait, and slipped out of the side door, letting in a gust of rain and wind.

Sally closed the door after her and locked it again, knowing there would be a great fuss if it was found open. She hurried back upstairs with her hot water, puzzled and alarmed. Gentry were very odd folk - that was something the superintendent at the orphanage had often said and Sally was beginning to agree. Poor Miss Miriam - so in love with the Captain that she would risk venturing alone to such a rough part of town just to watch him vanish down river!

It made little sense to her, but she was already fiercely fond of the red-headed girl who had brought her to London against the Darcys wishes, and knew she would do anything in her power to help her. Although she had to admit that what that possibly could be evaded her at present.

Once dressed, she ate breakfast, sitting quietly at the end of the staff table, trying to keep out of the attention of the elderly housekeeper, whose eyes, although old, were just as sharp as those of Miss Reynolds up at Pemberley.

She slipped away to tidy Miss Miriam's bedroom, collected her washing and was heading for the laundry room, wondering how she was going to get the garments dry on such a rainy day, when she passed a footman carrying the morning mail on a silver tray, heading for the breakfast room.

"Nothing for me?" Sally grinned at him - John was a young man she liked, one of the few who didn't treat her with disdain for not being born in London.

"No, Sally. Your sweetheart must have forgotten the address! Or else he's found himself another pretty young maid to love." He laughed and ran his hand over the letters. "Master and Mistress will be pleased to see some from South Africa, though. Reckon they've been waiting for news from Madam's sister out there. Or so the talk goes."

Sally watched as he carried his silver tray in to the Darcys and loitered in the shadow of the stairway until he came out again. She wanted to know what was in those letters. If it was bad news, then she needed to be prepared because if anything dreadful had happened to Mrs Malliot, if her ship had been wrecked, then there would be no house in Meryton. Miriam would be forced to live with Mrs Collins and Mrs Bennett and Sally was quite sure she would be sent back to Pemberley, her glimpse of a different world over.

John had left the breakfast room door ajar and although Sally knew eavesdropping was a sin, she sent up a quick prayer for forgiveness and sidled up as close as she could to the opening.

"Married! How can she possibly be married?" Mr Darcy sounded astounded. "You must be reading the letter incorrectly, my dear."

"I can assure you I am not. Listen, "*... have written to tell Miriam that my situation here in Africa has altered for the better. I expect you, too, will be surprised to learn that I am now Mrs Ogden, wife of the Reverend Ogden who purchased the school. Two gentlemen were interested but the Reverend was most insistent. He is a good man and I am very blessed that the dear Lord has provided for me.*"

"That's all very well and I must admit I am more than pleased that we will not have Mary sitting round our dinner table preaching at us, but what about her daughter? What about Miriam?"

"Let me pour you another cup of coffee and I will read more. There is a lot about the school, the Reverend Ogden's plans to extend it - a new harpsichord to be purchased - oh here we are

"*....I trust Miriam will be pleased at my news. She knows the Reverend Ogden and I am sure thinks highly of him. My letter to her is enclosed with yours. I think the best thing would be for her to live with our mother at Longbourn. I am sure she will be of great use to her in her growing old age and to Kitty with her small child. Of course, dear Jane might like her to be company to her daughters. I will leave that to the family to organise.*

" I am afraid I will not be able to make her an allowance, but she has the money that dear papa left her and I am sure you and Jane will be able to keep her in pins and stockings. Charity begins at home, of course." And then there is a long quote from the Bible."

"The poor child." Mr Darcy sounded even more solemn than usual. "All her plans will need to be changed and not, I fear, for the better."

Sally heard Mrs Darcy sigh. "I fear so. Although Mama will be happy to have her company at Longbourn, I know Kitty will be delighted to have more help and she can always come to us at Pemberley for a few weeks every year. I will take her letter up to her and let her read it in private."

The scrape of a chair sent Sally flying back up the stairs, still clutching Miriam's laundry. She reached the bedroom door and then turned as if she had just left the room as Mrs Darcy appeared.

"Madam." Sally dropped a respectful curtsey.

"Is Miss Malliot dressed, Sally?"

"She is still asleep, Madam. She asked me most particular last night to let her rest because she was so tired."

"Oh!" Elizabeth Darcy hesitated, fingering the letter in her hand, then deciding that the bad news could always wait a few hours more. Miriam would be better able to face her uncertain future after a good sleep. She bent and pushed the letter gently under the door.

"We will not wake her, then, but perhaps around noon you should try and rouse her. It is important that she read that letter from her mother."

"Yes, Madam." Sally curtsied again, but Mrs Darcy was already returning downstairs, in a rustle of silk.

When she had gone, Sally slipped into the bedroom, picked up the letter and stared grimly out at the rainy day. She could always wait and hope that Miss Miriam returned before noon, but what if she didn't? Would she get the blame for not telling Mrs Darcy?

Even more important was what she had just overheard. Mrs Malliot was now Mrs Ogden! Married to another Reverend, just fancy! You didn't think of those Reverends being that keen on marriage. Well, Mrs Ogden would not be returning to England and so Miss Miriam was free to choose her own path in life. She would no longer need to worry about taking care of her mama. Why, she could get engaged to Captain Sullivan now! Surely she would take the risk, even if it meant waiting two years for him to return to England.

But by the time Miss Miriam returned to Matlock House and read her mama's letter, the Captain would be long gone, down river and away into the ocean. She had to know what had happened before then, but if Sally left the house without permission, she would lose her place and probably be turned away without so much as a reference.

Hurrying up to her attic room, she pulled on her coat, bonnet and boots and burrowed under her thin mattress to find the coins that the Captain had given her when he left them in the park. She had never hired any sort of vehicle in her life but she was sure that the sight of gold would give her a good chance of getting someone to take her to the docks as fast as possible.

Miriam had had no idea of the size of the port of London. She had thought it would look like the one she knew in her childhood in Cape Town. But this part of London was vast. The docks stretched for miles along both sides of the Thames, lines of wooden warehouses, old houses, some derelict with broken windows, leant towards each other, darkening the narrow streets below.

Then, the city's lifeline. The mighty River Thames, and a riot of jetties, piers, coils of huge tarred ropes, piles of rusting chains, masts, sails and noise, even very early in the morning, men of every nationality were loading and unloading goods, the rumble of wooden cart wheels on cobbles sounded like constant thunder and the air was full of the smell of spices and rotten fruit. The rain fell, slowly but constantly, making it dangerous underfoot.

She had had trouble finding a hansom cab with a driver who looked trustworthy and was prepared to transport a young lady on her own, especially one who didn't know the exact dock she needed. The elderly man with his elderly horse were the only ones who didn't alarm her and although their progress was slow, hardly above a fast walk, at least the hansom had a waterproof cover. And for once the gods of luck and love were on Miriam's side: a shouted question by her driver to a passerby told where the *Sea Sprite* was to be found.

"If you're wanting to take passage on her, you'd best be quick, Miss," the driver shouted down to Miriam. "Wind's getting up. Reckon she missed the last tide, but she'll want to be on her way within the hour."

"Oh, I am not a passenger, Sir," Miriam said, wishing with all her heart that she was. "I just want to wish them a safe journey and quick return."

"Well, here's the jetty, Miss. And there's the *Sprite*." He pulled the horse to a halt with a slither and clatter of hooves on the wet cobbles. "Shall I be waiting for you, then?"

Miriam descended, paying him more than the fare he asked for because he had been kind. She shook her head. "No, I do not wish you to lose business. I am sure I will find another cab easily enough."

The driver touched his hat and clicked his tongue to his horse. This young lady was a puzzle and no mistake. He glanced back when he reached the corner but the girl had vanished into the rainy morning. A couple of minutes later, he had to pull his old horse swiftly to the side of the road with a muttered curse as another hansom cab came hurtling towards them, pulled at top speed, urged on by its driver's shouts and cracking whip.

In the soft rain, Miriam pulled her hood closer round her face and found shelter in the doorway of a warehouse, staring up at the ship she knew so well. It looked so big, gleaming with fresh paintwork and gilt, but she knew that once out on the ocean, *Sea Sprite* would seem very tiny indeed.

The sails were unfurled, only one gangway was in place and from the hustle and bustle on deck she was sure that at any moment a sailor would shout to one of the dockers to unloop the great tarred ropes that held the ship against the shore and the *Sprite* would be free to turn into the fast flowing Thames and head for the sea.

The jetty was crowded with men, sailors and dockers. Trunks and packages were still being carried on board - the ship was taking passengers out to Africa, that was obvious. They would already be on board, exploring their tiny cabins, scared and hopeful of a safe voyage.

At first she couldn't see Nicholas, then the crowd of sailors parted and there he was, soaked through from the rain, in shirt sleeves and breeches, his hair clubbed back from his face, pointing up at something in the rigging that he needed altering.

Her whole being yearned to run to him, to tell him how much she loved him - she even took a step forward towards the gangplank - but then stepped back into the shadows again. It was impossible - soon he would be crossing mighty oceans where all sorts of dangers lurked. To take with him memories of her unhappiness would be unfair. If you loved someone as much as she loved Nicholas, you would not let them carry that burden.

Miriam shivered as the wind coming off the river began to blow harder, driving the rain into her face and with the shock of the cold water came the arrival of common-sense. She was aware of odd glances and comments coming in her direction from some of the sailors and realised that she was being foolhardy in the extreme.

Once again her impulsive nature had resulted in putting her in a dangerous situation. It had been a silly, romantic idea, to wave goodbye to Nicholas as he left England: of course it was ridiculous;

he wouldn't see her and catching a cold and falling ill when her mother finally arrived was not a sensible plan.

"Miss Malliot! Miss Miriam! Oh, thank goodness I found you!"

Miriam gazed in astonishment as the small figure of Sally Finch bustled towards her. "Sally! I told you to stay at home. Whatever will my aunt say?"

Sally huddled into the doorway, ignoring the drips from above that bounced off her very wet bonnet. She delved inside her coat and pulled out a battered envelope.

"Here, Miss Miriam, take it, please. It arrived this morning, from Africa, from your ma. Quick, read it because everything is different now. She's married, your ma is, married to another Reverend. She isn't coming to England, Miss Miriam. She's staying in Africa!"

Stunned by the words, Miriam tore open the envelope, staring at the words that were blotting across the paper as the rain fell on the poor ink. But as blurred as they were becoming, she could see that it was true. Just as Sally had said, her mother had married the Reverend Ogden and would be staying out in Africa to help him run the school and give charitable aid to the neighbouring communities.

"Oh Mama - !" She realised tears not raindrops were stinging her eyes.

"Are you not pleased, Miss Miriam?"

"Yes, Sally, I am pleased for my mother. The Reverend Ogden is a good man and she enjoys her way of life out in Africa. I had feared that when she returned to England, we would both become the poor relations of the family, existing on the charity of my aunts and uncles. Mother would have hated that. This is far better for her, so yes, I am pleased, although it puts my future in doubt."

"But..." Sally fell silent. It was not her place to question her mistress. She glanced up at the ship, at the officers shouting commands to the sailors who were clambering into the rigging, hauling on ropes, stowing supplies in the hold, everyone frantic to catch the tide and be away from England once more.

Surely Miss Miriam must tell the Captain what had happened? Admittedly he was leaving, but she could now promise to wait for him with a clear conscience, knowing there was no one who would have a prior claim on her time.

Miriam sighed. She had seen Sally's look and guessed correctly exactly what was going through her mind.

"No, Sally, you don't understand. There is no way I can just go on board the *Sea Sprite* at this late hour and tell Mr Sullivan - what? That if he would care to make me an offer of marriage, I would accept him? I would not dare to presume that a gentleman wished to make me his wife before he spoke out himself."

Sally sniffed and rubbed her nose with the back of her hand, wishing she had a nose-wipe in her pocket. She didn't understand. Manners were important; that fact had been drummed into her at the orphanage and in the kitchens of Pemberley. But knowing when to speak, when to stay silent, not to eat peas with your knife or pass wind in front of your betters were all well and good, but not to tell someone you cared for them when it was quite obvious they cared for you? That was just bewildering.

"Well, Miss, I'm sure as you know best, but seems a crying shame to me to treat poor Captain Sullivan in such a manner. He could spend two years in mortal danger, all the time thinking you might be marrying someone else and not knowing that you aren't. Seems proper wrong and I'm sorry to speak out, I know it isn't my place."

Miriam stared up at the sailors working on the ship's deck, her hood falling back, the wind tossing her unbraided hair into a fiery halo. She could see Nicholas consulting a paper, a frown on his dear face. Then he lifted his head and gazed out at the dock, almost as if he was looking for someone and she knew, without a doubt, that he sensed her presence.

Even as she watched, he handed the paper to a sailor, crossed to the rail and raked the jetty with a gaze that could spot rocks and whirlpools at a thousand yards. She shrank back into the shadows. How brave it would be to step out and speak to him but even braver to let him leave without the worry of her being alone in the world.

Nicholas leant against the ship's railings and stared out at the busy, rain-soaked dockyard below him. *Sea Sprite* was nearly ready to cast off and set sail for Africa and the East. All the passengers were now safely on board, their luggage stowed below decks and the final pieces of cargo were now being hoisted into the holds.

He was so proud of his ship and knew he had a good, willing crew. They would sail round the coast, past Dover and Portsmouth, put into Plymouth to take on chickens, goats and sheep and then it would be out into the Channel, heading for the Bay of Biscay.

He should be the happiest man on earth, to captain *Sea Sprite* had been his dream for such a long time - he only hoped that once they were on the high seas, with all the problems that could bring, this dreadful feeling of loss would ease.

Suddenly a gust of wind sent everything flying on the jetty and a flash of brilliant red caught his attention. There, with her hair flying loose like a living flame, was the love of his life, the girl whom he thought of every hour of the day and night - Miriam.

It was raining harder now; Miriam pulled her hood back over her now soaking hair. She was cold and realised with a pang of shame that Sally was shivering violently, her cheap, thin coat no protection against the insistent drizzle.

"Come, Sally, we must go home. We will find a cab to take us." She took the girl's arm and hurried her along the jetty, through the crowd.

"But don't you wish to wave the ship goodbye?"

Miriam turned resolutely from the river. What good had she thought such a sentimental gesture might bring? Nothing would ease the pain in her heart: Nicholas was leaving; she must let him go.

"Yes, Miriam, don't you wish to wave me goodbye?"

With a gasp she spun round, her foot slipping in the mud, flinging her towards a burly figure who reached out and caught her, holding her for a long minute against his chest before he gently set her back on the ground. Then he clasped both her cold hands in his and rubbed them gently to warm them.

"Nicholas!"

"I saw you from the ship. We are just about to sail."

"I know. I...I didn't intend to bother you. I just thought I would like to watch you leave. You will be gone such a long time and..."

"...I am more than delighted that you came," Nicholas interrupted. "I have lain awake, night after night, cursing fate that continually pulls us apart. Miriam...I know you will not break your solemn vow to your father, and that two years is a very long time, but with all my heart, I beg you to wait for me. I love you so very much."

Just then the rain eased and a single sun beam shone down through the clouds, lighting Miriam's face as she lifted it towards his. He pushed back her hood and ran his hands through the soft wildness of her hair.

"I do not wish to wait," she whispered, turning her cheek against his rough hand.

His expression changed, the pain reappearing once more. "I must accept your decision, but..."

Miriam broke in - "I wish to be with you right away, Nicholas."

The Captain frowned, puzzled and Sally, unable to keep silent a second longer, said, "Miss Miriam's mother is staying South Africa, Sir. She has married again. The letter came today."

"Married?" Nicholas turned to her, his voice full of incredulity.

Miriam laughed, the bright sound healing all the pain he carried in his heart. "Yes, indeed, married to another Reverend gentleman, a Mr Ogden. I know him, he is a good man. She will be safe with him."

Nicholas clasped her hands in his, his grey eyes telling her everything that his lips could not. "Then that means...?"

There was a similar sparkle in her own eyes as she teasingly said, "I think my vow to my father no longer applies. If, from this day on, anyone should ask me to marry them, then I could say yes."

"I see." He smiled down at her, the expression on his face bringing the hot colour flooding into her cheeks. "I am not a man to hesitate where action is needed! Miss Miriam Malliot, my dearest, beautiful girl, will you do me the very great honour of becoming my wife?"

"Yes, Sir, most happily."

Nicholas carried her hands to his lips and kissed them again and again. "I wish your mother and her new husband great joy, for surely they have given us our heart's desire."

There was a shout from the ship and he swung round, senses suddenly alert. "Tide's changing, Miriam. I must set sail. Listen - will you come with me? Voyage with me across the seas? There are lady passengers on board, you will be well chaperoned. I feel sure you would be happier to have your mother's approval, but why wait for letters to travel between Continents. We can marry in Africa, under a hot sun, with your mother in attendance."

Miriam flung back her head and laughed. To leave England so suddenly, with a man! What he was suggesting was ridiculous, unheard of, scandalous, but it appealed to her spirit of adventure. Nicholas was her soul mate and she would follow him to the end of the earth if he asked.

"Yes, I will come with you! It will cause an enormous scandal in the family, but I don't care. I love you and will not waste another moment of the time we can spend together."

Sally stood, still shivering, shocked, wondering what exactly she was going to say to Mrs Darcy when she returned to Matlock House and how her mistress was going to cope on board ship without so much as a clean pair of drawers to her name!

"I wish you joy, Miss Miriam," she said softly, her teeth chattering. "I will think of you often, out on the wild ocean."

"Sally Finch, do you really think my lady can travel on board the *Sea Sprite* without a maid?" Nicholas said with a grin.

"What? Sir, I do not understand."

"Quick, I will write on the back of mother's letter, a note to my aunt. Go home, pack your trunk and mine and ask my uncle to arrange fast transport to - ?" Miriam glanced up at Nicholas.

"Plymouth, sweetheart. We dock there for final supplies. Here's a guinea for the cab, Sally. Now hurry. I am taking my lady on board our home." And he picked up Miriam in his arms and carried her effortlessly up the gangway, her hair hanging down over his shoulder, fluttering red and wildly in the gathering breeze.

Sally stood for a second, watching, hardly believing what had just happened. Then she took to her heels and ran for a hansom cab. Her mistress had got her heart's desire and she, Sally Finch, brought up in an orphanage, recently a scullery maid, was travelling to Africa!

CHAPTER 20

Later that night, Elizabeth Darcy sat at her writing desk in Matlock House, her pen spluttering across the paper in her hurry to get all her thoughts down in some sort of order.

"*.....and so, dear Jane, can you imagine the scene? That chit of a maid, rushing into the house with a scrawled note from Miriam, insisting that her trunk be packed, that she was already on board ship with Nicholas Sullivan and that they were to be married out in Africa!*

"I have seldom seen Fitzwilliam lost for words, but he was as overcome as I was myself. Sally, the maid, insisted that there were sensible female passengers on the Sea Sprite and that she herself would chaperone Miriam very carefully all the way to Africa.

"And so it is done. The trunks were packed, Fitzwilliam ordered the carriage to be readied and Sally Finch left London in some state. Although I disapprove greatly, I must admit there is a very small part of me that rejoices that Miriam is free from the confines of life here in England. It was like keeping a wild bird in a cage - something I do not approve of, as you

know. Nicholas Sullivan has set her free - or rather our Mary has, by taking another husband!

"I have written to Mama in case Mary's letter to her has been delayed. She will be delighted to know another one of her daughters has married again. And Lydia will be furious that she is not the only Bennet girl to claim two husbands!

"Keep well, dear Jane, we are leaving for Pemberley tonight so I will see you very soon. We cannot wait to get home and tell the rest of the family all about Miriam's dramatic departure. Bennetta will miss her a little, although Fitzwilliam and I are glad that she will not be influenced any more by her wild cousin's unsuitable views about life. Bennetta has enough of those already!"

A few days later, from her cabin on board *Sea Sprite,* docked in Plymouth, Miriam was rushing to finish her letters. Sally was waiting impatiently to take the mail ashore for this was the last chance of sending post for many weeks.

Notes had been sent to Aunt Elizabeth, Bennetta and Jane, thanking them for all their many kindnesses, assuring them that bolts of silks of all colours would be dispatched as soon as possible.

She hadn't bothered sending word to Miss Darcy. Anne would neither want nor expect to hear from her; she was probably only too glad not to have to see her across the dinner table. But she had written short notes to young Fitzwilliam and Henry, promising that if she found a suitable book for one and a parrot for the other, both would be sent home on the first available ship!

She drew a new sheet of paper towards her and wrote to Beth Bingley.

"...so I am to marry Nicholas as soon as we reach Africa. I cannot believe how fate has intervened to alter my life so miraculously. I love him so very much and believe his feelings for me are just as strong. I think of you often, taking care of dear Aunt Jane, just as I would have cared for my mama if it had proved necessary. My dreams have come true and I pray, Beth, that yours will too."

Finally, because of the spark of mischief that annoyed everyone - except Nicholas - so much, she wrote another, very brief note.

"My dear Mrs Tremaine, please do not be alarmed when you hear of my forthcoming marriage to Captain Nicholas Sullivan. He will keep me safe on our voyage round the globe. If I should meet up with any white slave traders, I will let you know.

Sincerely, Miriam Malliot."

Later that night, a great summer moon swam up into the sky, its beam showing a vessel under light sails, heading down the Channel before the wind. On deck, right in the prow of the boat, above the figure-head of the sea sprite that had given the ship its name, two people, wrapped in each other's arms, stood, gazing out towards an invisible horizon.

The sailors on watch averted their gazes, grinning at each other because they respected their Captain and were growing to like his intended bride with each passing day.

"Many hundreds of miles to go, sweetheart, before we reach Africa. Many, many days."

Miriam leant against him, glorying in the feel of his arms holding her close, his kisses on her neck and hair. Love, she was learning, was a wall that protected you, that offered you its strength without taking away your own. "All of them good spent in your company."

"And you have no regrets? No worries about the dangers of the life I am offering you? No settled home, no house, and if we are blessed with children - "

"My home is with you for as long as is possible. If we have children, then while they are small they will travel with us. We will educate them as to the ways of the sea until they grow older and then I shall send them to my cousin Bennetta - whom I trust will be married with a family of her own by then. They will learn about another way of life, but I am quite certain that they will return to us and the sea."

"Their destiny?"

Miriam turned her face for his kiss. "Indeed. My destiny was you and I am yours."

And they fell silent, watching the moonbeams on the waves, as the *Sea Sprite* carried them away to their new life together.

COMING SOON:

THE COUSINS OF PEMBERLEY,BOOK 4: JANE

The Darcys have always worried about their daughter Jane. Gentle and delicate, she has been cosseted and protected from the world.

But all the Darcy wealth and power cannot save Jane from heartbreak and betrayal. Can she find a courage no one believes she has?

Can she break free from the golden cage that imprisons her?